MEN DIED EVERY DAY IN BATTLE

But watching them die through the wonders of supertechnology was somewhat spooky, Brognola felt. Dead was dead, but this was something else entirely—real time, real flesh-and-blood dying as little more than a lit speck, an eerie video game.

There was still plenty of red-orange jumping all over the screens and lots of bad guys in play. Visual relay was shaky at best as the Phoenix Force warriors advanced, swung this way and that, ducked fire, blazed away in long raking bursts, left to right or vice versa.

Brognola watched as the tactical team relayed warnings and positions of bogeys. Encizo and Manning were monitored by Wethers, Kurtzman taking Hawkins and James, with Tokaido watching McCarter, the lone fighter out.

It was quite the grim and, yes, Brognola admitted to himself, ghoulish show.

DON PENDLETON'S

STONY

AMERICA'S ULTRA-COVERT INTELLIGENCE AGENCY

MAN®

SILENT
ARSENAL

A GOLD EAGLE BOOK FROM

WORLDWIDE®

TORONTO • NEW YORK • LONDON
AMSTERDAM • PARIS • SYDNEY • HAMBURG
STOCKHOLM • ATHENS • TOKYO • MILAN
MADRID • WARSAW • BUDAPEST • AUCKLAND

First edition February 2005

ISBN 0-373-61959-6

SILENT ARSENAL

Special thanks and acknowledgment to
Dan Schmidt for his contribution to this work.

Printed in U.S.A.

SILENT
ARSENAL

PROLOGUE

Myanmar

Colonel Ho Phan Lingpau feared the jungle, was borderline terrified of the dense pre-Jurassic rain forest encompassing the compound like a vined and walled fortress. These days there was plenty to fear, he thought, as he pondered murmured rumors he'd overheard among the rank and file. There was menace out there in the jungle. And beyond, ragtag bands of armed rebel savages.

He'd heard the terrible stories recently of man-eating crocodiles crawling up the banks of the Ayeyarwady River to chomp down on the leg of some unsuspecting villager, dragging him or her into the black waters, their bodies thrashing in the behemoth's death roll the final sighting of the victim. Then there were rumors of tigers on the prowl, the beasts leaping from nowhere out of the brush, claiming human meals in a frenzy of disemboweling claws that left little to the imagination. And there were reported elephant stampedes throughout the Kachin and Shan states. Three days prior, he recalled as he shuddered over the images left dangling in his mind by the report, a herd of the beasts had gone berserk, crushing half of his thirty-pony caravan, trampling four of his soldiers to bloody pulp as they'd hauled refined product to the paddle wheeler on the river.

At first he had believed these wild tales to be mere fabricated excuses from the comrades of AWOL soldiers who held as much loathing and fear of the jungle as he did—only they had dredged up the nerve to defect his unit at the risk of a firing squad if caught traipsing back for the comfort and safety of Yangon. However, only after witnessing a rhino charging then knocking one of his transport trucks onto its side before the animal was shot down in a hail of bullets had he begun to allow silent credence to an ominous notion.

The jungle was alive with an animal evil. Wildlife had seemingly gone berserk, the creatures of the forest having evidently evolved to some vicious counterattack mode on humans, nature tired from fear of being the hunted. Mother Nature, he believed, was in revolt against man. No nature lover, no tree hugger—since he was the chief architect for the slash-and-burn of countless acres in the region to make room for more poppy fields—he entertained a fleeting wonder. How would he feel if he was destined for slaughter, his hide providing a coat or rug for some rich man's mistress, perhaps his penis used, much like the tiger's, as an aphrodisiac, maybe his head mounted on the wall for the hunter's admiration? As if the grinding fear of animal attack wasn't enough, there were the various and sundry rebel groups lurking the Kachin, all of them trigger-happy when it came to blowing away any uniform marched out there by Yangon. By day, the jungle frayed his nerves badly enough, rebel phantoms hidden in the lush vegetation, framing a uniform pasted to flesh drenched in sweat from steaming heat through the crosshairs of a high-powered scope. At night, with all the caws and chittering and howling in the dark, he found himself unable to sleep, unless his HQ was ringed by sentries and he drifted off with a brain floating on brandy.

As a top-ranking officer of the State Law and Order Restoration Council—SLORC—he knew there was no room, however, for any voicing of the slightest anxiety, much less complaint about one's duty for the ruling military junta of Myanmar. Still, he was city-born and raised in Yangon, accustomed to the best food, clothing, housing that a man of his stature deserved. This stint, he thought, swatting at a mosquito the size of a mango, was little more than some supervisory outing better suited for a subordinate, some gung-ho underling eager to prove himself to the other twenty-one members of the SLORC. If he thought about his present assignment long enough, he knew protracted bitterness and resentment might distract him from meeting next week's deadline.

Still, despite the encroaching deadline and possible reprimand from Yangon if the shipment fell short, he remained holed up for the most part in his bamboo-and-thatch-hut quarters, brooding in isolation instead of being out there in the refinery, barking orders or pacing among the peasants in the poppy fields, cracking the bullwhip over the backs of the workers if they didn't meet the day's quota: two burlap sacks of milky juice per head. And if he failed to ship out the requisite ten metric tons of heroin, divvied up between their wholesale distributors in Laos and Thailand, his gut warned him Yangon would make this foreboding stretch of impenetrable jungle in the Kachin State his indefinite HQ.

Or worse.

Lingpau eased back in his leopard-skin recliner, one of several creature comforts he had managed to smuggle out of the city in his personal French Aérospatiale helicopter. There was a fully stocked wet bar in one corner, with enough brandy and whiskey to get him through six months of this drudgery. He had three giant-screen TVs, and his attention was torn between the satellite piped-in news from al-Jazeera and CNN and the latest porn flick he'd just slipped into the VCR.

Perhaps life among the savages wasn't that bad,

after all. Naturally, with rank, certain perks and privileges were expected, even necessary since an unhappy commander could become apathetic, simply killing time, shirking duty if his own needs weren't met. And he was in charge, no mistake, lord and master of this jungle domain, surrounded by tough, seasoned soldiers who could claim plenty of rebel blood on their hands. What was to fear?

Lingpau was pouring another brandy when he heard the sudden outburst of voices raised in panic outside his hut. He pivoted, heart lurching, brandy sloshing on his medallioned blouse. Then he froze, staring at the bright shimmer of light dancing over the bamboo shutters, certain they were under attack by rebels. The shouting of men, the pounding of feet beyond his quarters leaped in decibels, his mind swarming with fear-laden questions as he picked up his Chinese AK. How many attackers? Did he have enough soldiers, firepower to repulse even the largest army the Karens or Kachins could field?

As he burst into the living room, Lingpau found three of his soldiers piling onto the upraised porch beyond the front door, skidding to a halt as their stares fixed on their commander. The mere notion they could be under a full-scale assault by a guerrilla force sent another shiver down his spine. The Kachin State, he knew, was home to some of the most vicious and largest rebel armies in Myanmar. With a hundred-plus-strong army, with antiaircraft batteries, scads of rocket launchers, with tanks and helicopter gunships, he couldn't imagine any rebel band, no matter how large or well-armed the force, would be brazen, or foolish enough, to attack a SLORC compound. But what rational mind could possibly fathom the desperate motives of a people on the verge of extinction? In his experience, the question of living or dying meant next to nothing to desperate men—and women—who knew they were just this side of the walking dead.

But there were stories, however, some of which he knew were based on truth. It boggled his mind, galled his ego, stung his soldier's pride, just the same, that he might be under attack by the rebel leader the Karens called the Warrior Princess. If they were being attacked by guerrillas, though, where was the gunfire, the crunch of explosions that, he had been warned, signaled a rebel onslaught? What was this weird halo of light shining beyond the shadows of his men on the porch?

They were pointing skyward, their babble rife with fear and confusion.

"Stop yammering!" Lingpau shouted at the trio, searching the grounds for armed invaders but finding only his soldiers scurrying about the poppy fields with the night workforce, other gaggles of troops frozen near the transport trucks parked in front of the massive tent refinery.

"Rebels? Are we under attack?" Lingpau saw them shake their heads, mouths open, his sentries clearly left speechless over whatever they'd seen. "Then what? Answer me!"

"The sky, Colonel, it is falling!"

"The heavens are on fire!"

"It is going to crash right on top of us!"

Teeth gnashed, cursing the fool bleating something about a craft plunging in flames from outer space, Lingpau hit the ground, whirling, shouting orders, calling out the names of his captain and lieutenant. His voice sounding shrill in his ears, eyes darting everywhere, he ordered the perimeter sealed, the workforce detained in their tents, full alert and double the guard around the refinery. He was forced to repeat the orders, uncertain of his own voice, limbs hardening like drying concrete as he realized he was looking skyward.

"What…"

Lingpau's first conclusion was that the descending fireball was the result of a rocket attack. Only the massive size of the unidentified object, the white sheen that seemed to spew tentacles of luminous blue fire for miles in all directions and, finally, the trajectory of its fall, told him it was something other than a missile. But what? he wondered, squinting against the harsh glare illuminating the heavens, hurtling night into day, the mushroom-capped jungle canopy rippling against the blinding light as if the inanimate threatened to come alive.

Yes, he had seen meteor showers, shooting stars, and what little he knew about comets no giant rock from outer space could slow its own descent, appear to hover, change directions. There were other stories he had heard, though, fantastic tales from the jungle he had dismissed without a second thought, told around campfires, no doubt, by bored peasants with too much time to waste and too much imagination perhaps inflamed by opium. Tales told of alien spacecraft that flew at impossible speeds over the countryside, blinding lights that fell over a man and saw him vanish into the sky. Was it possible? Could it be?

He watched for what felt like an hour, waiting, dreading the moment when the giant flaming orb would squash the entire compound, nothing but a smoking crater choked with pulped corpses, crushed poppy and strewed product testament to the calamity here. Then it seemed to float away, or suspend itself in midair, or retreat—he wasn't sure. The halo above its slow-motion free fall appeared to spread mist next, rolling it out like a carpet. He saw it was destined to crash far to the north, figured five or seven miles away, and felt a moment's relief. The shouting of men was muted by the rolling thunder of the distant explosion as the white fireball plunged from sight. There were numerous Karen and Kachin villages in that direction. Whatever had plummeted to the jungle, whatever it was, he knew it required an investigation, a follow-up report to his superiors in Yangon. If this was some new weapon being tested by the rebels, perhaps some high-tech rocket the American CIA or DEA supporters had

given the insurgents, and he failed to inform Yangon
of its existence…

He shuddered at the thought of the grim consequences he could suffer for any dereliction of duty.

Lingpau was barking out the next round of orders,
rounding up his lieutenant and ordering three full squads
to board the Russian HIP-E helicopters and the Aérospatiale when he spotted a pair of eyes shining back at
him from the edge of the jungle. Lifting his assault rifle,
barrel sweeping up before his eyes, he was prepared to
empty the entire clip into the brush. But the big cat was
gone.

Lingpau scoured the impenetrable blackness, willing his legs to carry him to his helicopter. It was a fleeting albeit dangerous thought, yearning to return to
Yangon, even if that meant abandoning his duty. Whatever had just dropped from the sky, he was certain yet
one more evil was about to claim the jungle.

KHISA AN-KHASUNG neither wanted nor felt she deserved the Nobel peace prize. It was true, though, she
had become something of a legend throughout
Burma—Myanmar—if not most of Southeast Asia,
viewed as heroine by the poor and the oppressed, de-
nounced by SLORC and Laotian and Thai warlords
and narcotics traffickers as a radical and criminal to be
shot on sight. She took honor that she was seen by
friend and foe alike as something of a stalking lioness,
prowling the jungle, even hunting down the hyenas in

human skin who would devour her pride. Defending the weak and the innocent had called on her to do more than just remain a rabble-rousing activist in Yangon or Mandalay, or to chase whatever accolades bestowed her as a lauded poet and writer of short stories, all of which, naturally, were published in the West. Had she chosen this path in life, she wondered, or had the path chosen her?

Whichever, there was the blood of many slain enemies on her hands, and a trip to Stockholm to be honored for a virtue she had never contributed to was hypocrisy in her eyes. It was pretty much the grandiose chatter of foreign journalists, anyway, Europeans, even Americans, all of them as transparent as glass to her. They came to her country—often specifically seeking her out in search of a story or a hero—men of questionable principles and motives, leaving with no more understanding of the horrors and the cruelty of life under military rule than when they'd arrived. The only honor she sought was for her land to be free of terror and tyranny.

And these days there was more avenging than defending.

Ever since the Barking Dogs of the SLORC had expanded their heroin operation north from the Shan State, she had seen the rain forest nearly burned and chopped down to perhaps a few thousand remaining acres of hardwood and mangrove. But there was no comparison, she knew, between their slash-and-burn of the jungle to the toll in human suffering the Barking Dogs had inflicted on the peoples of the Kachin. Where they weren't brutalized or outright murdered by the Barking Dogs, they were seized by soldiers for slave labor in the poppy fields.

When villages were raided, where they were not razed by fire and the inhabitants weren't all executed on the spot, she knew young daughters were taken from their families to be used as sex slaves by the Barking Dogs. When deemed soiled goods, they were then sold by the SLORC to rich cronies in neighboring countries, their families—murdered, worked to death in the poppy fields or dispersed to die in the jungle—never to see them again.

It was another form of genocide, she supposed, killing the men, abducting young women, extinguishing all hope the bloodline of the minority groups would continue. She knew all about the indignities, the humiliation the SLORC could inflict on a captive female. And she bore the scars of torture and rape on her own soul, her thoughts right then threatening to wander back to the four years she'd languished in a Yangon prison…

No. Her enemies were in the present, and perhaps the salvation of the Kachin State rested square on her shoulders.

Swathed in thick vines and brush, her fighting force of sixty-two spread evenly to either side along the jungle edge, she scanned the compound through infrared field glasses. With the help and support of both DEA and CIA contract agents in the Kachin, the Karen National Liberation Army of the Karen National Union was better armed and equipped than their predecessors—including her father and three brothers—who had been captured and executed during a SLORC raid when she was—about eight years old. So long ago—another lifetime, it seemed—it often took strenuous thinking to even recall her own age of twenty-four.

Too young, she thought, to feel so old.

There was, she knew, no turning back.

Even though they wielded rocket launchers, the hard truth, she knew, was that they were still outnumbered and outgunned by the Barking Dogs. They could attack this compound, her strategy already laid out to her freedom fighters. They could encircle the refinery, toss around a few white-phosphorous grenades, burn up the poison, cut down a few dozen or so Barking Dogs with their assault rifles and machine guns, but there was another hard truth beyond what would amount to little more than a suicide strike. No matter how many SLORC thugs they killed, Yangon would swarm the jungle with two, even three times the numbers she found before her. The painful thought that perhaps death was just another word for freedom and peace flickered through her mind, but she quickly cast aside any pessimistic notions that would render her less than a leader.

She knew they needed outside help if they were to

drive the Barking Dogs from the Kachin. With her contacts to the CIA and DEA, a plan as to how she could achieve such a victory had nearly solidified the next path.

She was lowering the night glasses, wondering how or if they should launch an attack on the soldiers and the refinery, when the sky flashed above the jungle. She winced at the brightness, her fighters edging closer to open ground where the jungle gave way to the closest poppy field to gain a better view of the sky. They were muttering, pointing, searching for the source of light in the heavens. She ordered silence, told them to fall back. She believed another rebel group in the area had preempted her own strike, then she saw the utter stillness of soldiers and workers alike as they gazed at whatever the source of light in the sky.

Assault rifle in hand, she waited for an attack that never came, then surveyed the entire compound for the next few minutes, taking in the commotion, the air of panic mounting among the workers and soldiers. Arms were flapping now, soldiers darting around the compound, shoving the field hands into tents, doubling the sentries around the refinery. She couldn't see the source of light, but the soldiers were aiming fingers and weapons to the north. She heard the rumble of a distant explosion, then found a contingent of thirty or so soldiers boarding the gunships. Despite her order, she caught the whispering among her fighters, sensed the mounting fear around her in the dark. Gauging the impact point of the blast, the vector of the gunships, she knew the explosion had erupted to the north. That, she also knew, was where a large population of her own people had yet to be molested by the Barking Dogs.

Khisa An-Khasung rose, AKS sweeping, her thoughts locked on to the mystery of the light and the explosion. She melted into the dark and told her fighters to follow.

GENERAL MAW NUYAUNG had stalled the task as long as he dared. He had his own superiors to contend with, and they had become impatient over the past two and a half days for answers, even while he debated with his comrades how the catastrophe should be most efficiently handled. He had handed off a number of excuses why he shouldn't personally undertake such a grisly chore best relegated to lower-ranking officers and medical experts already on the scene. But the supreme hierarchy of the SLORC had seen through his flimsy sales pitch, sent him packing with veiled threats on his way out the door about failure to fulfill his duty. Since the Kachin refinery had been built at his insistence—despite reservations about growing rebel armies and the distance to both Laotian and Thai borders from his colleagues in the SLORC—the generals with more stars, fatter bank accounts and political muscle had singled him out to investigate the mysterious explosion over the Kachin.

It was directive number two that found his bowels

rumbling, heart racing, the sweat beads popping up on his bald dome and trickling down his craggy face from under the cap.

Determined but anxious to get this ghastly business over, he stared out the cabin window as the paddies swept several hundred feet below the custom-built VIP helicopter. The flight plan had already been mapped out before leaving Yangon, his pilots sticking to the arranged course, sailing east for the sluggish brown waters of the Ayeyarwady. They had just cut a wide berth around the quarantined area surrounding the refinery, en route now to the Buddhist temple, then a quick fly-by of the Kachin and Karen villages being sanitized by arriving fresh battalions. A final search of the paddies and he felt relief stir at the sight of farmers and water buffalo still standing, man and animal toiling under the sun. Perhaps, he thought, the horror had been contained. If not he—all of the SLORC—was threatened with a crisis of proportions not even known in the worst of nightmares.

In fact, the calamity was already threatening to reach nationwide critical mass.

According to the weather report, a modest breeze of six to eight miles per hour had been blowing northeast since the explosion. But whatever the biological agent—presumably released before and during the blast—the wind had shifted due south, toward Yangon, and was gathering strength. If common citizens began dropping in the streets in a city teeming with four million…

General Nuyaung decided he was in no rush to hit the ground.

Exactly what had happened almost three nights ago remained a puzzle, but a mystery rife with horrifying implications for the entire country, he knew. Beyond the outbreak of plague, there was the matter of internal security, now threatened by foreign intelligence agents looking to capitalize on the supposed good will of a concerned global community.

Already there had been leaks about the disaster to the western media, CIA or DEA in-country operatives, most likely, pushing panic buttons around the globe, seeking only to infiltrate agents into what they branded a closed society, wishing to subvert and overthrow the ruling powers, disrupt or eradicate the production and flow of eighty percent of the world's heroin. The hue and cry from the shadows was working.

Already the United Nations, Red Cross and even the American Centers for Disease Control were offering aid and assistance. He wasn't fooled by the charade of proposed charity. Nuyaung—as did the other members of the SLORC—feared their troubles had only just begun.

Nuyaung wondered what nightmare he would find when he landed at the refinery, even though the intelligence report, complete with photos of victims and initial medical analysis, was perched on his lap. The unidentified object had been painted on their radar screens in Yangon, he remembered, as he had been called in to the Supreme Command and Control Center as soon as it had been picked up, forty-something thousand feet directly above the Kachin State. It had dropped like a streaking comet out of the sky, plunging to earth at more than seven hundred miles per hour before any fighter jets could be scrambled to destroy it. Then, incredibly, the object had slowed its own descent and cut to a mere impossible hover before sailing north.

At first they'd believed they were under attack, frantic speculation even that perhaps the DEA was striking the poppy fields with some supertech thermite bomb meant to incinerate the countryside of what had become the lifeblood of the SLORC. Their technical experts had measured the object at two hundred feet across, sixty feet top to bottom. Beyond the dimensions of the object there was little more than roundtable guessing over what it was. Initial reports stated a white cloud had been observed erupting from the unidentified object, spreading over one square mile before dispersing. That much, he knew, had been verified, the first dead and afflicted struck down in the immediate area of what Yangon tagged Ground Zero. It was the living, dying in other quarantined areas, contaminated by a plague yet to be identified, that concerned Nuyaung the most.

He glimpsed the rolling green hills, their peaks swaddled in white mist, then perused the report once again as the chopper began to vector over the jungle canopy. Including villagers, his workforce and soldiers, the body count, as of six hours ago, now exceeded three hundred. Within several hours of the explosion the first symptoms marked the onslaught of the mystery illness. He recalled the dying words from his last radio contact with Colonel Lingpau.

"General…help us. We are all dying…fever. I am burning up…it feels…as if even my eyes…are on fire. Even my sweat…it is like blood. I am told it is blood…"

Fever. Convulsions. Black urine. Sweat filled with blood infected by plague. Was it an airborne contagion? he wondered. Could he be infected if some blundering fool accidentally brushed up against him? Could it spread through water, food? Was his merchandise contaminated?

The more he thought about it, General Nuyaung suspected someone had launched germ warfare against his country. But who? Why? Relations with neighboring China, Laos, Thailand, India and Bangladesh were anything but strained. The surrounding countries, naturally, guarded their borders, and those in charge of any nation always frowned and attempted to turn back or eliminate refugee hordes. There were, he knew, the occasional border skirmishes, usually involving contraband, but nothing so volatile as to warrant their neighbors unleashing a plague that could wipe out the entire population of Myanmar. And if the attacker was a neighboring country, they risked cross-border contamination. Then who?

It was an hour of madness, he knew, either way, but extreme measures were being initiated to, hopefully, contain the outbreak. There was still hope—if the situation was at least under control in the quarantined sectors, or all potential human contaminants eliminated, infected corpses removed then burned in some inaccessible stretch of jungle—he could save the product and meet his self-imposed deadline. Peasant workers and soldiers alike were easy enough to replace. His greatest fear, beyond personal risk of infection, was that perhaps the vast acreage of poppy and the refinery itself were contaminated.

Nuyaung flipped the file on the seat beside him. He tried to will away the images of the contorted death masks of victims and their faces riddled with red sores and bumps oozing pus, but they were branded in his mind. Perhaps, he considered, it was a grave mistake, after all, to expand heroin production outside the Shan State. But worldwide demand was up, particularly now that various Islamic organizations were gobbling up massive quantities of product, using the funds to finance the future of jihad, no doubt in clamoring search for weapons of mass destruction.

Having lost himself racking his thoughts for solutions to a variety of problems, he suddenly found his chopper hovering over the courtyard. The latest arrivals, some five hundred soldiers, were divided as evenly as possible throughout the stricken zones. Nuyaung stared into the inferno below, then saw a squad of

SLORC soldiers dragging two robed monks past the three statues of the warrior guardians set near the three lions and three-headed elephant in front of the temple. The monks were still alive, one of them attempting to break free of the latex-gloved hands clamped around his shoulders. Nuyaung knew the filter masks the troops wore would be no protection against the plague if it was an airborne contagion, assumed the stench of burning flesh down there would bring his men to their knees if their faces weren't covered. HAZMAT suits— the few that could be scrounged from various military and medical facilities—were reserved for the team of doctors. Depending on what he heard, he would pull rank, claim a HAZMAT suit for himself.

Nuyaung turned away as the monks were tossed into the fire. He glimpsed the towering plumes of black smoke, north and east, decided he could wait on reports about the sanitizing of contaminated peasant villages. He punched the intercom button, told his pilot, "Take me to the refinery. I will tell you where to land when we arrive."

"THIS IS NOT the right time, Khisa. They are too many."

She felt the fire burn behind her eyes, willed herself to hold back the tears, holding on to rage and hatred.

Ashre Nwa was right, she knew, but wondered, just the same, how much longer she could bear to watch the slaughter of innocent people she had sworn to protect, or avenge, before raw emotion compelled her to strike. If an attack was potential suicide before, the odds against even a pyrrhic victory were now clearly insurmountable.

Whatever happened as a result of the explosion had seen the quick arrival of more Barking Dogs, more helicopter gunships than she could count. A shock attack, unless she was committed to suicide and the senseless massacre of her fighters, was beyond hope. Five tanks had been airlifted into the surrounding area just after dawn, followed by still more soldiers, armored personnel carriers, antiaircraft batteries—an impregnable barrier.

Then there were men in space suits and the plastic tents hastily erected outside the perimeters of the villages, cylinders and steel tubes and vats, computers and other equipment she couldn't possibly identify....

They were makeshift laboratories, she knew, the men in space suits drawing blood from both villagers and soldiers alike who had fallen ill. What had happened here? If this was some testing ground for a biological weapon engineered in Yangon, surely the SLORC wouldn't use their own soldiers as guinea pigs. And if she and her fighters remained in the area, would they, too, become stricken by whatever sickness appeared to claim the lives of victims within a matter of hours?

For more than two days now she had remained with her fighters, high up in the hills, hidden in the forest, an umbrella of mist of suspended clouds shielding them from the flock of helicopter gunships patrolling the skies. With mounting rage, she had watched the Barking Dogs gun down every man, woman and child of the three largest villages in the vicinity of where, she assumed, the blast had detonated. They dragged them out of their bamboo huts. They dumped bodies—some of which, she observed, were still moving—into pits dug out by heavy machinery flown in by still more giant transport helicopters. They poured gasoline over both the living and the dead, ignited mass graves with flamethrowers before soldiers moved on, torching every last hut, every living thing. The screams of victims burning alive still echoed in her head. The call of the murdered, she told herself, crying out for justice from the grave.

Demanding vengeance.

She looked away from the burning pit, the meandering space suits, the soldiers with flamethrowers burning down what few huts still stood, and searched the faces of her fighters. Beyond anger, she saw they were frightened, wondering, most likely, what horror had been unleashed on the Kachin.

"We will return to camp. We are going to need outside help," she told them. "I know what has to be done."

She turned away, shaking with fury, leading her fighters down the hill toward the river. Whatever was happening, they all knew there was far more to fear now than just the Barking Dogs.

"REPORT. AND DO NOT tell me you have no answers."

General Nuyaung was still waving back Dr. Ang-khu, working nervous surveillance around the space suit, taking in the commotion of soldiers hard at it, disposing of corpses. The filter mask staved off the fumes of burning flesh, but now that he was on the ground, smack in the middle of a contaminated zone, Nuyaung felt the fear rising. Bodies were still being hauled by soldiers from tents, dumped into a mass grave, men in space suits wandering in and out of the plastic tents, heavy machinery unearthing more mass graves. He spotted the bloody carcass of a tiger, a figure with leaking guts stretched out near the large bamboo hut. He saw Angkhu follow his stare, the doctor's voice muffled by his helmet.

"Colonel Lingpau."

"Speak up!"

"He was attacked," Angkhu said, "this morning. It is most unusual, distressing to inform you this, but I would urge caution, especially at night. Three other tigers have been seen—"

"I do not care about that. A tiger can be shot! And why hasn't Colonel Lingpau's body been burned?"

"Major Kyin. He was uncertain whether you would desire…such a disposal of a fellow officer."

Nuyaung bellowed at the closest group of soldiers to throw the colonel's body and the tiger carcass into the fire.

"What are we faced with?" he shouted at Angkhu.

"I…we… Initial tests are inconclusive."

"Inconclusive!"

"It is a filo or a thread virus. But it is unlike any virus we have ever seen. Its DNA appears a combination of smallpox, malaria, perhaps another genetically mutated virus—we are not certain. But whatever it is, it multiplies at an extreme rapid rate in a host. First symptoms of outbreak occur within two hours."

"Is it airborne? Can you become infected by mere contact with a carrier?"

"For our purposes, I believe we would be better served if we could study this back in Yangon—"

"No one leaves here until I have answers. What about the refinery?"

"If you are asking if the refinery is contaminated, the answer is no. Viruses do not simply go away, they merely hide. A virus needs a live host."

"Watch your tongue! I am not completely ignorant of the situation, Doctor. I sense you are holding something back. What is your expert opinion? How bad is it?"

"The virus, in my expert opinion, is a hybrid cross, created in a laboratory. It—"

Nuyaung gritted his teeth, waiting, the look in Angku's eyes warning him he would not like the answer. "Speak!"

"I am afraid this particular virus, General, is one hundred percent fatal."

NAHIRA MUHDU no longer prayed for deliverance from evil. God, she believed, knew the horror she was leaving behind, aware, too, of her needs. If she—and her only surviving family—were to survive the journey, reach safety inside the border of Kenya, then it was God's will. She was too tired, so parched from thirst the tears had ceased flowing, too weak from hunger, even, to pray.

It had been…what? she wondered, feeling the blood squish in sandals worn down to ragged strands of leather, each yard earned over rock-stubbled broken ground shooting pain through every nerve ending. Three weeks? A month since she had set out on foot with the other villagers from Bhion and the vast surrounding southern plain?

They had been driven out by marauding rebel troops at war with the government of Addis Ababa, and the entire country appeared under assault by rebels and soldiers alike, men who were more like wild beasts than anything human. Killing. Burning. Looting. Raping. The horrors of a new war with Eritrea had spread from the north where Eritrean soldiers were invading the Tigray region. She had heard her country was losing the latest war with Eritrea, mauled Ethiopian troops falling back to the plains of the south, renegade soldiers taking what they wanted from defenseless villages so they could live to fight—or murder—another day.

Famine, drought and civil war were nothing new to
Ethiopia, she knew, but the past six months had become a living hell, her country gone mad with violence
and brutality, villages in flames from the Tigray to the
Darod, reports of mass graves littering the countryside.
Drought, then starvation and, finally, the invasion by
Eritrea had unleashed anarchy, an evil, it seemed to her,
that was much like an avalanche gathering momentum
the longer it kept rolling.

And the evil of other men had found her. Remaining in her homeland was certain death. Small comfort,
but she wasn't alone in misery.

Her anger and grief had withered some the first
week out of the village, exhaustion and hunger damp-
ening raw emotion, but the memory of her husband,
shot dead by the killers of the Free Ethiopian Order of
Islam, was still fresh, as if it happened only minutes
ago. What they hadn't burned, they plundered, seizing
every last grain of wheat, every handful of sorghum
they could find. The horror of the past, the dreaded un-
certainty of tomorrow, and she wondered if peace
would simply come with her own death.

And they had been falling dead in greater numbers
the past week.

Only yesterday had she buried in a shallow grave,
dug by rock with the help of fellow refugees, two of
her three sons, ages four and six. The weeping was
over, only the ghosts from a life taken haunting her
every step. So weary now, her fingers aching, the flesh

raw and crusted with dried blood where she had clawed out the hard earth, there was nothing to do anymore but to keep moving, to keep hoping. There was a life to consider beyond her own, the tiny, emaciated frame of Izwhal, swathed in filthy rags, she determined, her final reason to live. She couldn't recall the last time either of them had eaten.

Which was why the refugee camp of Barehda lit a flicker of hope inside her punished body, rubbery legs finding energy at the sight of the food lines near the massive transport plane. Her only thought that food might sustain life until God opened another door.

The net veil was some protection against the buzzing hordes of flies, but she gagged as the fumes from the initial wave of rotting and diseased flesh and bodily waste clawed her senses. She followed the others toward the plane, appalled and pained at the sight of their stick figures, bodies sheared of muscle by malnutrition, dark, sagging flesh like leather, aware she looked every bit a walking corpse herself.

They skirted the outer northern perimeter of the camp, weaving past camels, goats and mules, their hides likewise worn to the bone. She heard the faint sobs of children, saw mothers cradling tiny bodies in spindly arms, skeletal fingers pushing some sort of grainy oatmeal into their mouths. But the infants, and even the older children, appeared almost too weak to chew. God, she had heard, might create drought, but man made the famine. What had been created here as the result of man's inhumanity, she thought, had to be an abomination in the eyes of God.

She looked at the smattering of plastic tents, spotted shells of dark figures stretched out inside the flimsy covering, but most of the refugees were forced to bake under the sun, the suffocating heat, she knew, only compounding their suffering. She fell farther behind the others, shrouded in dust, her heart sick at the sight of so much misery, aware she and her son would most likely die here.

The refugees were eating all around her, a hopeful sign, she thought, the older males—teenagers mostly—shoveling the gruel into their mouths, slurping some white liquid from small plastic containers. There were a number of men, even small children, with missing arms and legs, cruel and sudden amputations as the result of countless land mines buried across both Ethiopia and Somalia.

She scoured the sea of displaced and starving, head spinning from the stink and the sight of so many living dead. She felt the cry of anguish burn in her chest, the thought that this would soon be the open burial ground for so many too much to bear when she saw tin containers suddenly falling to the ground. Refugees began clutching their stomachs, men, women and children convulsing, vomit spewing from mouths like burst faucets, bodies slumping over. Paralyzed by horror, she watched, listened to the cries fade, infants spilling from the arms of mothers who tumbled, thrashing on

the ground. It was no mystery, she knew, disease was
a major killer throughout Somalia, but something else
was happening across the camp. The ravages of whatever the affliction were too sudden, too violent, to be
any illness she had ever seen.

She found herself alone, the others now falling into
the food line far ahead, unaware of what was happening,
caring only about whatever food was being dispensed.
She watched those she had made the trek with, fear
mounting, something warning her to flee this place.
There were armed men, wearing filter masks and white
gloves, she saw, some of them barking orders to the refugees to hurry, other gunmen handing out the tin containers from the ramp of the silver transport plane. Why
were they protecting themselves from breathing the air?
No Red Cross or United Nations relief workers she'd
ever seen came to the camps, heavily armed, donning
protection as if they feared close contact with the local
populations. That was no UN plane, either. She strained
to make out the emblem on the fuselage: a white star inside a black ring, a fist that looked armored inside the
star. They were westerners, that much she could tell. Another group of white men, she could see, stood on a ridge
where the plain gave way to a jagged escarpment, far to
the east, well beyond the camp. There were the dreaded
technicals, she noted; Toyota pickups with mounted machine guns, too many armed Somalis to count, their eyes
watching the camp over scarves or from behind black
hoods. Why were they laughing among themselves?

It struck her as a bad dream, food being distributed by armed men laughing at the sight of so much suffering and death. It all felt so hideously wrong…it was evil, she decided

She flinched, gasped when she felt a hand tug at her shoulder.

"You just arrived?"

He spoke Amharic, the language of her country. There was fear in his stare. She answered, "Yes…I…"

"Did you eat the food?"

She shook her head.

"Come," he said. "They have all been poisoned."

"But what of the others?" she said, nodding toward the refugees around the plane. "I must warn—"

"No. If you do that, the Somalis and the white men will most likely kill you and your child. We must make our way to the farthest edge of the camp. Night will fall soon, then we will make our way out of here and run to the Kenyan border. I have family there. You will be safe. But we must make our way now."

Could she trust this stranger? she wondered. Why, if what he said was true, poison all of them? It made no sense. But in a lawless land like Somalia, where only violence and mayhem ruled, why wouldn't mass murder of refugees, viewed as a blight and a burden, be acceptable?

She watched in growing horror, knew she couldn't stay here, counted perhaps another ten refugees toppling to the ground, then let the stranger take her arm and lead her and her son deeper into the camp. She avoided looking anyone in the eye, felt like a coward for fleeing, leaving them to die without warning. But perhaps, she decided, it was God's will she and her son survive. Afraid more than ever, Nahira Muhdu found the strength to silently implore God to deliver them from this evil.

YASSIF ABADAL WAS thinking God did, indeed, work in mysterious ways, bestowed wondrous gifts to those who remained faithful and loyal and patient. Sometimes God even used the Devil, he thought, to do his work.

As chieftain of his Nurwadah clan, controlling the deep southwest edge of Somalia, he had his sights set on far loftier goals than simply dominating an area populated mostly by nomads and bandits. Mogadishu was the ultimate prize. But he needed a mighty sword's clear edge, some overwhelming power that would see him crush rivals, bring the entire country under his rule.

The white men, he believed, had brought him, it appeared, all the power of the sword he could have ever hoped or prayed for.

The refugees were spilling all over the camp in droves, their feeble cries flung from his ears as his warriors chuckled and made jokes among themselves. Snugging the bandanna higher up his nose, he watched as the white men quickly handed out the tin containers and the milky-looking drink to the newest Ethiopian horde. They were so concerned with only filling their bellies, they seemed unaware their fellow countrymen were right then dying in their midst.

Toting one of the new G-3 assault rifles, he looked at the white men fanned down the ridge beside him. It was, indeed, the strangest of alliances, he thought, looking at their blond heads, blue eyes that were as cold as chips of ice, catching the arrogance and contempt in their voices for these refugees as they barked in their native guttural tongue.

He had never seen a German in the flesh, but his predecessor had somehow gotten his hands on an old black-and-white film of World War II. It had galled him, back then, how their late leader had so admired white racist barbarians who would have enslaved the indigenous peoples of North Africa if they hadn't been driven off the continent by the British and Americans. But when the role as leader was passed on to him, Abadal came to see the stunning power of their blitzkrieg and other military tactics, understood the brutal discipline and the steely professional commitment to war that even he now preached to his clan.

If these Germans could propel him into the future glory of complete victory over every rival clan, and if he was destined to sit in the presidential palace in Mogadishu with their help, he had no problem walking into tomorrow with the devil by his side. Nor did it matter how many rivals, refugees or common Somalians died in the bloody path to the crown.

They had flown in a group of emissaries for the first round of negotiation a month prior. It was an unauthorized landing in a country so hostile to the west, Abadal had been, at first, anxious, even unnerved by their brazenness, their lack of fear, but perhaps whatever intimidation they felt was only masked with contempt. The ice was broken, however, when the Germans came bearing gifts of cash and weapons, including heavy machine guns, handheld multibarreled rocket launchers, flamethrowers. The high-tech gear—cell phones with scrambled lines, the ground and air radar, night-vision goggles and other state-of-the-art wonders only dreamed of in Somalia—had required some lengthy instruction. But Abadal and his top lieutenants had gotten the gist, enduring gruff explanations by the Germans until they felt proficient enough to at least get the high-tech goods up and running.

For their generosity, these Germans had a proposal, and they had chosen him to be ruler of all Somalia. Why him? he'd asked. They had grunted, shrugged and answered, "Why not?" Did he wish to remain a nomad in the desert with a few old AKs, some rusty technicals and indulging wishful thinking about greatness? Of course not, he'd countered. What did they want in return? They had claimed nothing more than a possible base of operations when the other clans were wiped out and he controlled the destiny of his country. They had a weapon, the first group had claimed, one that was as potentially devastating as any weapon of mass destruction.

Now that he had seen the almost instant and clear catastrophic effects of this invisible killer, Abadal had questions, most of which were based on concern for his own safety. He found their leader; the tall, muscled one named Heinz with the bullet head and black leather jacket, and walked up to him.

"Ah, my Somali friend. What do you think?" he said, admiring the view as shriveled figures in rags thrashed throughout the camp. "As good as promised, I hope?"

"Tell me something. This virus in the food, can it be spread to others who have not eaten it? Can it be caught through the air? By touch?"

"First of all, this was an experiment. Our way of showing you the future that, uh," he said, voice thick with his native tongue, "we are prepared to place solely in your hands. Second, it is a biologically engineered parasite, not a virus, taken from the female Anopheles mosquito."

"I am seeing an outbreak of malaria?"

Heinz shook his head, chuckled. "Yes and no. The details are very complex, scientific jargon you would neither understand, nor do you need to concern yourself with. And if you are worried about contamination, you will only become infected two ways. If you eat what is basically pig slop made from simple microyeast or you come into direct contact with bodily fluids."

"Blood?"

"That would be a bodily fluid."

The German was talking to him like a child now. Abadal scowled. "But you said you can deliver an airborne plague, that you have the vaccine."

"That is true."

"When?"

"Shortly. I will consult with my superiors. But, I must tell you, there may be a few more conditions before we are prepared to hand this country over to you. A plague that is spread deliberately…well, it is something that requires serious planning, contingencies to be thought out, and so forth. There is also the question of loyalty, compensation, reward and the like."

And there it was, Abadal thought, suspecting all along it was too good to be true. "So there is more in it for you than using my country as simply a base for whatever your intentions."

Abadal heard the quiet laugh again as Heinz told him, "A man of vision such as yourself surely must understand personal greatness and glory comes with a price."

"And what will mine be?"

"We will be in contact with you. In the meantime, I suggest you thoroughly sanitize the area as we discussed."

Abadal clenched his teeth, angry that the German,

this arrogant foreigner who had come to his land as if he owned it, would just walk away, dismissing him, a flunky. "You realize I could either decline your offer…or take what I want from you."

Abadal watched as the German kept walking, smiled at the death being spread below, then laughed out loud. "Yes, perhaps you could do just that, my Somali friend, but there would yet be another price to pay."

THE HORROR BEGAN just after nightfall.

She was struggling to keep up with the man who told her his name was Mawhli. Beyond his name, she knew nothing about him, but if promised flight to Kenya…

At the moment safe passage into the unknown future was her only option.

Nahira Muhdu stumbled, Mawhli turning at the sound of her cry. He caught her before she was flung into a headlong tumble down the steep incline for the wadi, a fall that might have ended any hope of escape with broken bones or her son crushed in her arms.

There was screaming behind her, brief hideous wails that chilled her to the bone. She gasped when she saw the tongues of fire, glowing waves shooting from hoses extended in the hands of shadows moving away from the technicals, a ring of death that encircled the camp.

"There is nothing you can do for them, Nahira."

"Why?"

"Only God knows that."

"Then he knows he cannot allow such evil men to go unpunished."

"I believe that, also. Come, we must hurry!"

She hesitated, sick to her stomach, the stench of burning flesh carried to her nose on the wind, the heat from the fires touching her face. The breath of Satan. She turned, began following Mawhli into the wadi, melting into the darkness. She prayed for the life of her son, for safe passage into Kenya, then asked God for something she would have never believed herself capable of doing.

Nahira Muhdu asked God to deliver retribution against the warlord and his murdering beasts.

CHAPTER ONE

"Sixteen years old, and Boise is the closest she's been to a big city. Hops a Greyhound and I find out about this two months ago—no clue, no threats, no kiss-my-ass. Not even Mrs. Evans number three—Ilsa of the SS I tell ya—with all her keen female intuition, saw this bomb dropping. And here I was, thinking I was father of the year. The cop the press maggots used to call Dirty Harry on Steroids, lower than the lowest now. I can't even hold my family together. Three-time loser, huh. Maybe that's what you're thinking?"

"That's not what I was thinking, Jim. And I'm not the enemy."

"Right, yeah, you're a buddy, ex-cop, once my partner."

The man he knew from the old L.A.P.D. days was on an angry roll, fueled by whiskey and the torment of the day, steaming more mad at the world with every snarl and speck of flying froth. Carl "Ironman" Lyons figured the best thing to do was to let him vent, expend all the fury before he started firing off his own questions.

"Fuck me raw. I keep asking myself why? It's like some sick tape I keep running through my head, all these horrible images of everything that could happen to her. Wandering the street, maybe on drugs, some pimp… Goddammit, Carl. All I wanted was for her to have a decent life—you know, clean air, big sky, small town. No drugs, no crime, no gangs, a little slice of peace and sanity to grow up in, not drowning with all the other human turds in that toilet we knew, Los Angeles. We know the city can eat up someone her age. And with her looks… You see a picture of her, you're looking at an angel, a goddamn princess. Now I track her here, one of my worst fears comes true. I find out she's been dancing in a strip joint, for God's sake."

Lyons didn't believe in coincidence or fate, didn't cater to psychic babble or all those crystal-ball hotlines that mapped out someone's destiny, cradle to grave, fame and fortune and bliss on earth written in the palm of the hand. A former detective of the Los Angeles Police Department and currently a commando working out of Stony Man Farm—an ultra-covert intelligence agency nestled in the Blue Ridge Mountains—he believed in action, truth and just the facts. But, he had to admit, bumping into another cop he had partnered with for more than a year in a police department clear on the other side of the country—a man he hadn't seen, heard from nor thought about in well over a decade— was on the hinky side of coincidence.

But there Jim Evans had been, seconds away from either getting bounced on his ear out of the bar or breaking the joint up with collateral damage to door- men and patrons, a guest stint in a D.C. jail with the kind of unsavory characters he loathed, had busted up and feared his daughter falling into league—or bed— with. Bizarre fluke or some guiding cosmic hand, Lyons couldn't help but wonder, just the same, about the events leading up to the chance encounter.

After three days decompressing from the latest mis- sion, Lyons had rounded up the other two-thirds of Able Team for a quick getaway until duty called again. Restless, feeling confined at Stony Man Farm in the Shenandoah Valley in Virginia, Lyons, the leader of Able Team, had piled the three of them into the over- size War Wagon—which wasn't supposed to leave the Farm's premises for a mere joyride—then driven them to the Key Bridge Marriott where he'd paid for a pent- house suite for a week. Still restless, tired of watching Hermann "Gadgets" Schwarz and Rosario Blancanales enthralling themselves with the same movies on cable or playing computer games until he was sure they were bug-eyed, he had set out by himself for a few belts and beers, a tour of downtown D.C. strip joints on the play- card, fantasies of getting lucky urging him on. Cheap thrills had a way of bringing trouble to Lyons, and this time out had proved no different. It had been touch-and-go back at the titty bar, wrestling Evans free of the bouncers, packing the ex-L.A. detective, drunk and belligerent, into his Lexus rental, trying to get both the story and the facts straight.

Lyons, sensing Evans about to launch himself on the verbal rampage again, was not sure he was willing to sit through another diatribe. Judging from whiskey fumes strong enough to gag a buzzard, one cloud of cigarette smoke after another blown out in long, angry exhales, he didn't see the man calming down anytime soon. Add the snail's pace the Stony Man warrior was forced to keep the rental creeping through George-town and Lyons found his own aggravation level ris-ing.

He looked over at Evans, found a wrinkled, leather-faced, heavier version of the cop he'd once known. With his black Stetson, sheepskin coat and cowboy boots, Evans in his Wild West garb was damn near a circus act in a coat-and-tie Beemer and Evian town that looked down its nose at anyone who didn't fit the yuppie and PC parameters. Then again, Lyons, with his knee-length black leather trench coat, aloha shirt alive and flaming with palm trees, flamingos and scantily clad island girls, with white slacks and alligator shoes… Well, he knew he didn't have much room to judge the fashion show. In fact, he recalled one of the musclebound punks with an ear-piece back at the bar tagging him "Don Ho" and ordering him to get his buddy, Wyatt, back home to the ranch.

Kids these days, he groused to himself, no respect for their elders.

Evans, he recalled, hadn't been a particularly good cop, nor a bad one, at least not the renegade he was purported by the press to be when Lyons had worked with him. There were rumors of brutality, charges of racism, L.A. media making a big stink over a couple of questionable shootings before the man had transferred to Lyons's division. They had gone through some doors together, solved some tough cases, but Lyons had never found himself ready to cozy up to the man, on or off the job.

He had never been able to put a finger on his feelings toward the man, supposed he was just plain mean-spirited, with or without a badge, the whole world crap, not a decent human being anywhere, a borderline bully out to control, dominate or punish. He wasn't the kind of man Lyons would sit down with and drink a few beers, but Evans had jumped in front of a bullet for him, getting seriously wounded in the process, commendations eventually pinned on both of them.

What was this moment supposed to mean? he wondered. Was Fate, after all, calling in a marker? Was some cosmic force urging him to extend a helping hand, if not for Evans, but for the innocent life of a young girl? Whatever the emotional quandary, it was a rare day on the planet, he figured, when just about any man's intentions and motives were altruistic.

So far, Lyons had the gist of why Evans had come

to town. Up to a point he supposed he could understand the man's pain and anger over a runaway child. Hadn't he once been married? It was true, he had a son, Tommy, but he hadn't spoken to either the ex or his boy—now fully grown—in quite a while. What was he feeling now? What was he thinking? Did he regret the path in life he'd chosen, sloughing off whatever responsibilities as a father he should have seen through? If so, why? Because it was a big bad savage world out there, after all, and his skills as a warrior were more needed for the greater good of humankind, instead of raising a family? Was he on the verge right then of doing some voyeuristic dance through another man's broken family life? Was he thinking he could and should help Evans find his daughter, despite his true feelings for the guy?

Lyons jostled through a bottleneck of vehicles playing bumper cars, lurched ahead as a light turned red and a few horns blared their ire at him.

"Did you report her missing?" Lyons asked when Evans fell silent.

"No."

"Why not?"

"Hell, I was embarrassed. I didn't want anyone to know, or think I'd failed as a father. Judy, even though she's not Deirdre's real mother, somehow found plenty of ways to want to blame me, but that's another stinger to pull out of my hide at some point. Didn't come right out and say it, but she had her way of telling me she's my problem, I deal with it. How do you like that?"

Another marriage made in hell, Lyons thought. "Seems you picked up the trail pretty quick."

"She left with an older girl, a Susan Barker. I heard she'd been hanging around with her. Susie's something of the town good-time girl, nice way of saying she's just a whore. I own a bar—maybe I told you that—and I hear things. One rumor led to another. I had a talk with this girl's sometime boyfriend."

"And a little chat with the boyfriend pointed you east to this fair city?"

"Let's just say I got a few answers the old-fashioned way. And, my daughter absconded with a couple of my credit cards. Easy enough to track them both to a motel here—the bills started coming in—but Susie's sometime squeeze filled in a few blanks about their little jaunt to D.C. Seemed Susie filled Deirdre's head with a lot of nonsense about how they could make it big here, she had friends in the area, some kind of big shots in the entertainment business. I already had my head crammed with visions of pure assholes she'd come here and get scammed by, or worse. Only I get the impression it was something more than just…stripping for a bunch of assholes who oughta be home with their wives and kids. Just today I found Susie holed up in some crack motel up New York Avenue, staked it out, followed Susie to work, where you found me. She goes by the name of Candy. Get this. Walk in, like a regular asshole, I see my daughter's picture on the wall in this dump, goes by Dee-Dee. The bastards— no better than pimps—had her all dolled up in some cowgirl outfit."

"Did you, uh, run into your daughter back there?"

Evans scowled. "No. I was told she was off tonight."

"I got the impression you were making a hard pitch."

"Yeah, like telling the manager he's got a sixteen-year-old girl taking her clothes off in his place, and if he didn't want the cops shutting him down or my fist doing a rectal probe, he'd better tell me where my daughter was. That's where you entered the picture."

Lyons cleared his throat, already knew the reaction he'd get when he dropped the bomb. "I have to ask, Jim. Are you leaving anything out?"

"Such as?" Evans growled.

"Kids run away from home for a reason."

"Why don't you just come out and ask it, Carl, instead of tap-dancing on my nuts."

"Okay. Was there any abuse?"

Lyons found his former partner staring at him, steady, no sign of anger or resentment.

"No. None whatsoever of any kind. But I understand you asking. I may be a mean SOB on the streets, but I take care of my kids, never raised a hand to them or touched them in any way. End of story."

Lyons fell silent, wondering how far he should go with this. Then Evans asked, "If you don't mind me asking, what are those two cannons you're packing? Couldn't help but notice. I figure you're into something needs punch like that."

The question didn't catch Lyons off guard, but he felt uncomfortable with the sudden glint in Evans's eyes—the Stony Man warrior sure his former partner was entertaining ideas about going vigilante if he discovered any more dark secrets about his darling Dee-Dee. They were twin .45s, butts-out, stainless-steel, the double bulging package obvious beneath his coat, Lyons knew. But he had the bogus Justice Department ID just in case the issue of concealed weapons was pushed by any law on the prowl. The twins had been made by John "Cowboy" Kissinger, the Farm's resident weaponsmith. With fifteen Rhino or body-armor-piercing rounds in each clip, Lyons had let Kissinger talk him into trying out hardware other than the .357 Magnum Colt Python he usually carried. Lyons told Evans what they were, but left out the details.

Evans chuckled. "We might have lost touch over the years, but I figured you put in your twenty, retired, maybe got yourself a boat, move up north like a lot of L.A. cops do when they leave the job, maybe write crime novels."

"I did. Retire, that is. But sitting still on a sailboat or in front of a keyboard isn't my speed."

"So what are you doing to keep busy these days?"

"I do freelance security work."

Evans nodded, looked at his cigarette, savvy enough

to know not to push the subject. He paused, working on his smoke, then said, "Know what I'm thinking right now, Carl? I'm thinking I played a bad hand back at that toilet bowl, blew any chance maybe getting Susie to talk, find my daughter. My gut tells me she's into something way over her head, and you could see I was in no mood or shape for any subtle approach."

"So I saw."

"I don't mean to sound like some judgmental prick, but you actually enjoy going to those kinds of places? What is it? Some kind of Peeping Tom jolt, look but don't touch, the lonely guy's masturbatory fantasy in living color?"

"I guess it beats sitting around watching sitcoms every night."

"Suppose there was a time I did, too." Evans grunted, Lyons thinking he could almost read the man's thoughts regarding another chance encounter if he hadn't been there ready to tear the place apart. Whatever he was chewing over, the anger faded from his eyes. "You, uh, you doing anything special the next couple of days?"

"You're thinking you'd like me to pick up where you left off tonight."

"That's what I'm asking. Maybe you can make some inroads, talk to Susie, at least steer me in the right direction if you learn something. Right now, with a load on, and being too close to it, I'm no good to anybody."

"I agree, but when I start something, I like to finish it my way, my terms."

Lyons wished the night had turned out the way he'd originally envisioned, Evans's world, safe and tucked in back in Idaho, but here he was, boxed in the spotlight. He debated the matter, wanted to tell the man he was on his own, but a combo of chivalry, guilt and a vague sense of being a good guy got the better of him.

"If I do," he told Evans. "I can't make any promises you'll get whatever the end result you want. And, if I do, I have a couple of conditions, no questions, no tirades, no strings. You don't like what I find, go off half cocked, you're on your own. Don't even call me for bail money."

"Whatever they are, I'll live with the terms. And I'll pay you whatever you think is right for your time and trouble."

"This isn't the 'Rockford Files.' I don't need your money. Consider this returning a favor for when you took a bullet for me."

"Fair enough. So, you'll help?"

"Give me a second," Lyons said, juggling cell phone and the wheel as he turned them onto Key Bridge, a Volvo cutting him off with horn blasting and the middle-finger salute shot his way.

Seven, eight trills, Lyons gnashing his teeth over the delay. Then he heard Schwarz come on, his teammate forced to nearly shout over a background score for a shoot-'em-up he knew they'd been watching every time it came on Cinemax and HBO.

"This better be good, Carl."

"I knew it! I can hear your five Elvis impersonators shooting up the Riviera Casino clear across goddamn Key Bridge. How many times you two clowns need to watch *3000 Miles to Graceland*? Figure by now you must know every word of dialogue by heart. It's becoming kind of obsessive-compulsive, don't you think?"

"I'm partial to the Kurt Russell part. I see you as that psychopath, Murphy, especially when you go down in a hail of SWAT bullets at the end, bleeding out to 'I Did It My Way.'"

"You're going to see my foot up your ass if you don't turn off the TV and look alive! I'm bringing up company."

"I bet you've been out trolling the nudie bars. I sure hope you don't come through the door with just one chippy, me and Pol—"

"It's a cop I know from the L.A.P.D. We're going to work—tonight—and I'll buy you clowns the DVD for Christmas. You can watch *3000 Miles to Graceland* all you want but only on your time."

"You promise?"

Lyons punched off, found Evans treating him to a curious look. "Despite what you just heard, they are professionals."

HAL BROGNOLA WAS no fan of spook games, intrigue or mystery. Just the same, he was moving in a shadow world this night, prepared to meet a faceless, nameless emissary shipped out by the President of the United States to get the particulars on a brewing but unnamed crisis.

Beyond his public role as a high-ranking federal agent in the United States Department of Justice, he did, however, lead a double life as director of the Sensitive Operations Group, based at Stony Man Farm. Brognola was also the liaison to the President of the United States, the chief executive's go-to man in the Farm's world of high-stakes covert operations.

The Man sanctioned nearly all of the Farm's missions, the dirtiest of wet work against enemies to national security, either of the foreign or homegrown variety. There was direct contact, usually by phone, between Brognola and the President before the starting flag was waved, the utmost protocol of secrecy maintained where it regarded Stony Man Farm and the Justice man's netherworld role behind the public face.

So he had some reservations about the rendezvous, the normal channels bucked, unknown entities operating as cutouts. The Man had sounded terse, even abrupt, earlier when he'd called him at his Justice Department office on the secured line to begin casting shadows over what Brognola suspected would become a long night melding into even longer and tense days ahead. But if the President—who had everything to lose if the Farm was exposed—trusted the setup, who was he, Brognola figured, to question his judgment?

The crisis was either so serious and the President too busy...

Brognola shut down his reservations, got a grip on what was actually normal professional anxiety and paranoia. In his business, reality was rarely as it appeared.

He proceeded across the Mall, vectoring for the Red Castle of the Smithsonian, flanked and dwarfed by the distant dome of the Capitol and the Washington Monument. It was a short walk from the Justice Department building in the Federal Triangle, and a check of his watch showed he was on time. At this late hour, the museums along Jefferson Drive were shut down to the public. No traffic, vehicular or human, in the area, but there had been a series of armed robberies around the Mall lately, which had thinned the herd of after-work walkers and joggers to virtual extinction. Briefcase in hand, Brognola was mindful of the weight of the Glock .45 shouldered beneath his suitcoat, figured there were enough rounds to split the difference between muggers or spooks with malice of heart.

He was unwrapping a cigar when he spotted the trio of black vehicles rolling his way. They parked curbside in front of the Smithsonian. Government plates, black-tinted windows all around, two unmarked sedans sandwiched a limousine. Doors opened and four suits with earpieces got out, scanned the street, the Mall, before one of them beckoned for Brognola to climb into the limo. The sunglasses were a little much, he supposed, figured the shades for intimidating intent.

The big Fed crossed Jefferson, squeezed through the doorway, claimed an empty section of cushy seat beside a minibar. The door closed and Brognola found another pair of sunglasses across the well. He had a full head of coiffed black hair, cashmere coat, but beyond that the guy was nondescript. Another civil servant. Yet there was something in his silence, the way Brognola found himself measured, wishing he could see the emissary's eyes...

Sunglasses to wingtips, the guy was spook, Brognola concluded.

"Time is short on this one, Mr. Brognola," Sunglasses said, producing a thick letter-size envelope stamped with Classified-Eyes only and the presidential seal, handing it to the big Fed. "The fate of the free world and a not-so-inconsequential matter of the possible extinction of the human race may have just fallen into your hands."

"LOVE THE 'Miami Vice' look, but don't you think the sunglasses are overdoing it?"

Lyons pushed the Blues Brothers shades snug up his nose. "What can I say? Your presence is blinding."

Cop instincts flaring up, he could see her gears mesh, Susie-Candy wondering how to handle him, but already knowing what problem had walked into her life. All of three seconds looking at her, Lyons heard the bullshit radar in his head blipping off the screen, blond bogey at twelve o'clock.

She finally took a seat in the booth across from Lyons, blowing smoke his way, glancing around, then crossing a leg, the strap-on pump going back and forth like a piston. The damsel-in-distress look wasn't about to aid his cause, but Lyons didn't plan on staying any longer than it took to get the answers he wanted.

She sipped from a glass of watered-down champagne that Lyons had promised and paid twenty bucks for after slipping a fifty into her garter when she was on stage, shaking it for her coat-and-tie hyenas. A friendly chat, he'd told her, was all he wanted, nursing a beer while she took her sweet time getting over to him, working her platoon of admirers for a few dollars more. Now that she was his for the moment, Lyons felt the resentment and hostility from wannabes— more than likely on the lam from husband and father duties—boring into the side of his head. He wondered how much of her time he could commandeer before she either turned snippy during Q and A or the security kid with the mouth came over to tell Don Ho his money was no good here. He knew he was being watched, every fiber of instinct screaming the softer, kinder approach was probably just a dream.

Lyons gave it a few seconds before he cut to the chase, treated Candy to a smile that would have come from the heart under other circumstances. The frilly one-piece Roaring Twenties get-up did little to hide a package Lyons surmised lightened many a fat wallet, but the painted face was already showing wear and tear around the eyes from all-night shenanigans. He figured a few more years of life in the fast lane and she'd look every bit the jaded, used-up whore she was acting. Well, he was no one to judge character flaws, and so far he was unmolested by the security quartet. Still, something felt wrong, a lurking menace in the air, and he wondered who was about to do the fishing. A check of his six, and the guy he figured for either the manager or the owner still had the evil eye aimed his way, ready to march out the troops.

"Who's the guy over there with the bad perm, looking all mean and surly?"

"The owner."

The way she answered, sure she was in control, Lyons knew he was on the clock. He produced the photo Evans had given him, laid it on the table. It was a shot of the daughter in the saddle of her horse back at the ranch. She appeared relaxed, content enough in the photo, a beauty like Evans claimed, but there was something forced in the expression that told Lyons she wasn't the happiest camper in Idaho. Chalk it up to youthful disillusionment maybe, but Lyons had seen something more than suppressed rebellion. The truth was, he knew if he discovered Evans had lied about any abuse, he was prepared to walk away. These days, he thought, there was an epidemic of children being savaged, scarred for life by adults, if they weren't outright murdered. In all good conscience he knew he wouldn't be a party to returning Evans's daughter to a torture chamber of psychological and physical abuse if that happened to be the case.

"Tell me where I can find Dee-Dee."

She laughed, nervous eyes darting around, body language a stone wall of defiance.

"You think this is funny, Susie? She's sixteen, that by itself means I could get this place shut down, then you'd be out of a job, on the street, probably hooking, unless you're working the johnson on someone's husband, or pimping for some scumbag takes your money for crack."

"Kiss my ass."

"I'll take a rain check."

Lyons read the sudden fear in her eyes, but sensed it wasn't about being unemployed as she made another roving search of the crowd.

"Look at me, Susie."

She did, the cigarette trembling in her hand. "Maybe she doesn't want to be found."

"Maybe. If that's true, why?"

She blew smoke in his face. "You're a cop, like her old man. I can tell, all cops have this look…"

"Was a cop. I'm not interested in your psychoanalysis of a job I'm sure you've ever only been on the wrong side of."

"Touché. So, you a friend of his? A private detective? What?"

"I'm just some guy he used to know and he asked a favor."

She grunted, choosing her words. "Loneliness."

"What?"

Lyons watched as she paused, thought about something, the tough-street act almost fading away. "Look, she's a sweet kid, I like her, I'm her only real friend. All she needed was a friend, you know."

"Who doesn't."

"You want some answers, Miami, listen." Another look past Lyons, then she went on. "Dee-Dee was always kind of sad. She spent most of her time alone, but it was more than me feeling sorry for her. She has what I call a special heart, an innocence she deserves to keep, something I lost a long time ago."

"Oh, I'm sure she'll stay special working here."

"It's all an act, Miami. It isn't some free-for-all whoring you might think, like hand jobs under the table."

"Girl has to make a living, that it?"

"Dee-Dee deserves a lot more out of life than small-town Nowhere, U.S.A., and she knew it. How's that for psychoanalysis?"

"And so you come along and offer her the Promised Land."

She ignored the remark, went on, "She wrote poems, pretty good ones, and told me how her father didn't like that. He actually tore them up one day in front of her, told her he wasn't going to stand by and watch her dream her life away. Might as well called her a nobody. I'd say that's reason to want to leave home— wouldn't you?—someone reaches in and rips your soul out. She never wanted to leave Los Angeles in the first place."

Lyons resisted the tug at his heartstrings, but knew he failed.

"Yeah, there's a lot you don't know."

"Telling me she ran away with you, her mentor, because she missed the big-city lights?"

"If you're asking did her old man sleep with her, the answer is no. But he's a drunk, and he can be mean, and he's a control freak. As far as I know, he never hit her, either."

"I still have cop's eyes, Susie. And I'm looking at someone holding back. Keep blowing smoke in my face, but everything about you tells me she's in trouble. So cut the concerned-mother-hen act and tell me what you know. Now."

"Listen to me," she said, her voice lowering to a whisper, Lyons straining to make out her voice as it was drowned by the thunder of rock and roll. She pulled back, Lyons swearing he saw her eyes misting. "I—I made a mistake...you don't want to know..."

"Wrong. I want to know now more than I did when I came in."

"I can't."

Lyons could almost reach out and touch the wall of fear, her hand shaking as she ground out the smoke, uncrossed her legs. It was a bad move, as Lyons envisioned the cavalry en route, but he reached over, grabbed her arm.

"I'm not leaving until you answer my question."

"You're already gone, sport."

She was breaking away as Lyons heard the voice he'd already put the face to tell her, "Get dressed, and take off. Your VIPs are here."

"I wasn't finished."

"You're finished, sport, but first me and you are going to have a conversation. Now," he said, Lyons watching as the Perm settled into the booth, "we can handle this one of two ways..."

CHAPTER TWO

"I see I have your undivided attention."

Brognola was glancing up from the first series of high-resolution satellite imagery when the cocky grin vanished off sunglasses. The remark, he supposed, was in reference to how intently the big Fed studied photos. Whoever the shadow emissary—CIA, NSA, DIA—Brognola found himself impatient to get on with the brief. He sensed, though, some undercurrent of resentment building the more Sunglasses dawdled, sitting here, inscrutably silent, the watchful Sphinx likewise desiring for a mere civil servant of the Justice Department to know how important he was, a spook holding the key to some divine riddle. A crisis was being dumped in his lap, requiring the immediate resources of the Farm, and Brognola didn't have time or patience for spook nonsense, nor was he about to explain why he was the man of the hour and Sunglasses was designated the White House gofer. If that's what he even was, and Brognola didn't much care.

"I see HAZMAT suits," Brognola said. "A jungle compound, Asian soldiers. I've got what I'm thinking look like poppy fields, fires all over the place, high-resolution photos of corpses, and which, I presume, are being incinerated, presumably killed by some biological or chemical agent. Clearly a contaminated, quarantined area."

"Clearly. And you presume correct."

"Do you think you can tell me what I'm looking at in ten words or less and skip the *X-Files* routine?"

"You are looking at the Kachin State in Burma."

"Myanmar."

"Burma, Thailand and Laos, of Golden Triangle infamy, produce over eighty percent of the world's opium."

"I'm aware of that. You're here to talk about the scourge of dope?"

"Production of heroin in Burma alone has quadrupled the past five years, demand—so both the DEA and our intelligence community reports—rising exponentially as various terror organizations use funds from narcotics trafficking to expand their global jihad. Part of the dilemma from our standpoint is the State Law and Order Restoration Council—SLORC—has taken over heroin production from the rebels, making Burma an even more closed society than it previously was. Makes it tough to get operatives on the ground, infiltrate rebel groups sympathetic to the cause of freedom and justice."

Whose freedom, whose justice? Brognola wondered, feeling his cynical meter shooting up the longer he sat in the presence of Sunglasses. If this was headed where he suspected—dumping his Stony Man warriors inside Myanmar for some protracted jungle war against SLORC-sponsored drug armies—he would send Sunglasses back to the Man, tail tucked between the crack of his silk slacks.

The spook had to have read his look, said, "I say something wrong?"

"I'm assuming you're not here to enlist my services in the war against drugs?"

The spook cleared his throat, carried on in a voice that bordered condescending. "There are roughly thirty-five known major rebel groups, most of them fighting for independent chunks of real estate or to take back control of the poppy fields. The SLORC isn't about to let that happen. It appears some form of high-tech genocide is being unleashed on the indigenous Burmese, but we know it wasn't perpetrated by the SLORC.

"All drug roads may lead to Thailand and Laos, but the real gold at the end of the rainbow may lead to China, the lion that no longer needs to sleep. You have a major gas pipeline under construction in Burma, which may stretch all the way through Thailand to Vietnam, plans for an overseas pipeline reaching clear to Indonesia, the Chinese might even want to get into the act. The SLORC needs money for this task. They need more and bigger guns. Drug money is a fast and easy way to spread the corruption of their military junta around Southeast Asia. If certain situations can be corrected in Burma, the west has a great interest in helping to engineer this international pipeline.

"The SLORC and its drugs and this latest incident are the hurdles. Now, the Chinese have the weapons and the technology for delivering mass death, if the SLORC chooses to lie down with them. The fear is Yangon has either gone high-tech and is seeking, or has acquired weapons of mass destruction. There is a major principal, already known to our intelligence community, who has been looking to trade the technology for WMD but who are also interested in more money generated by narcotics trafficking. Shadows inside shadows, wolves coming to the table in sheep's clothing, so to speak."

So much for ten words or less, Brognola thought, perusing the horror show in his hands.

"What crashed in the Kachin was robotic space-craft," Sunglasses went on.

"A satellite?"

"The robotic spacecraft was in low earth orbit and was picked up and tracked by the NRO as it reentered Earth's atmosphere. Deliberate deorbiting, the Kachin, it appears, was chosen as a laboratory, victims the test subjects. The flight path was controlled by computers on Earth, we greatly suspect, but sufficient heat was picked up to tell us it was also using boosters but in reverse thrust. It actually slowed to a near hover, unleashed its payload, by aerosol first then remote-controlled detonation, spreading the whole mess over several square miles. Depending on the weather, contamination could have reached as far as Yangon. From there, cross-border contamination, we don't know."

"Who?"

"I'm getting to that."

Brognola scowled. "What's the agent?"

"That is the sixty-four-thousand-dollar question. Some sort of bioengineered virus is the educated guess, and which appears nearly one hundred percent fatal. It would appear to make a Level Four virus—the worst—like catching the flu in comparison to this Bio-Agent X. We have CIA, DEA in the Golden Triangle, contract agents—mostly rebels—but Yangon is keeping a tight lid on this particular boiling pot. We can't get any of our operatives close enough to the hot zone. Word of this disaster has leaked out to the UN, Red Cross, and so on, all manner of aid and assistance being offered to the SLORC from the world community."

"I take it that's not going to happen, not if Yangon thinks there's a coming foreign invasion to burn down their poppy fields."

"Channels of communication are open, but it will be a tough sale. It gets worse." Another pause for dramatic effect, then Sunglasses continued. "We parked a spy spacecraft over the area in question. It was attacked at 1000 EST by a roving military spacecraft trailing in the same high-altitude geosynchronous—east to west—orbit. An anti- or hunter-killer robotic spacecraft completely destroyed it. The measured blast radius picked up by our command and control data handling systems at the NRO, NSA and CIA was big enough to vaporize several city blocks. Whether its platform is also loaded with nuclear capability…we don't know.

"The political powers here in town are anxious to keep this from going public, since a number of key players were allowed to walk around with their agenda right under our noses. These, uh, key players, have been 'marked,' shall we say, in keeping with the new conventional wisdom that enemies to national security are fair game for hunting.

"Keep flipping. There's another situation—one, it is believed, that is related to the Kachin incident and the shoot-down of our spy spacecraft."

Brognola thumbed through the pile until he came to the high-resolution imagery of more corpses being tossed into fires. There was a shot of a silver transport plane with an emblem of what looked like a mailed fist on the fuselage, shots of men, white and black, and all of them armed, standing on a ridge overlooking a large camp on a barren plain. It was another scene of mass death and corpse incineration.

"You're looking at a Somali warlord and his cut-throats," Sunglasses said. "The corpses being burned are Ethiopian refugees fleeing a major civil war in their own country. We received initial reports with some degree of skepticism, but the CIA confirmed this incident with the flyover of a Predator drone. They were following up after an Ethiopian man and woman—the only survivors—managed to cross into Kenya to tell the story. This Somali warlord received a shipment, it is believed, of biotech food from the westerners you see. Only this food was deliberately poisoned. The symptoms of the outbreak are nearly identical to the Burmese guinea pigs."

"A killer virus spawned in...what, microyeast?"

"You have many of the pertinent details, the access codes for the CD-ROMs written down, some good leads. No one has all the answers, but I gathered from my briefing by the President you might know how to proceed."

"You never answered my original question of who?"

"Germans."

Brognola blinked.

"Yes, our good friends and allies. It is a cabal called EuroDef, run by German businessmen and military contractors who have contacts here in the United States. The workforce, technicians and scientists come from a number of different countries, including Russian and American microbiologists, virologists, scientists and so on, looking to sell their wisdom to the highest bidder."

"Am I hearing conspiracy?"

"One so dark and potentially embarrassing…well, I get the impression this will be handled in an unofficial capacity."

It was a lot to digest, but Brognola knew what the President was asking. The green light was flashed for Stony Man to cut loose its dogs of covert war.

The big Fed judged the spook's long silence for dismissal. "If that's all…"

"For now. Good luck, Mr. Brognola."

Without another word or look back, Brognola was out the door.

THE ONLY IMMEDIATE questions in his mind were how much pain he would be forced to inflict by way of multiple contusions, abrasions and broken bones, and how much collateral damage he would wreak before he walked out with the answer he wanted. Lyons mulled the possibilities, racked his brain for a peaceful solution.

As covert operatives, the Farm had a way of frowning on extracurricular melees that tended to bring police attention to Brognola's doorstep. Sure, the big Fed could always cut through red tape, and he could be on his merry black ops way, any charges vanishing into cyber limbo, even as he was aware he would be forced to endure sufficient and justified rebuke from Brognola. Okay, then consider the predicament with mature judgment and acute detail to responsibility.

Schwarz and Blancanales were in the War Wagon, staking out the door and the street. A quick call on his tac radio and Lyons could marshal up a little help from his friends, maybe they would play some conciliatory role as negotiators, usher him quiet and nice into the night, with all forgiven. He could have bobbed his head to the threatening noise the Perm was making, meek as a lamb, shuffled off, sorry if he'd caused any disturbance, bowing and scraping all the way out the door. He wondered if he was growing soft or getting too old to go on the muscle to thrash a guy who clearly deserved a can of whup-ass rammed into his throat or some other orifice.

Nah. Only in a perfect world, he decided, where there was peace and love and goodwill toward all men, and the young and the innocent weren't preyed upon by adult savages. The mature, responsible Carl Lyons, then, would have to wait for another day.

"You listening to me, sport?"

Lyons had his head cocked toward a booth where a quartet of new arrivals were in a serious discussion with two of the Perm's SS. Three looked like muscle, big and broad, clearly packing cannons beneath their sport jackets, while number four, decked out in a cashmere coat, wearing sunglasses, the goatee and ax face…

Wait a second, Lyons thought. He was sure he'd

seen van Gogh somewhere before. Where? Take off the facial hair, the shades…

He would have sworn he'd seen him on TV, one of those cable talking-head shows where everyone was such an expert they could have told all the little people the mysteries of the universe. No doubt in his mind they were the VIPs, as Lyons saw Susie materialize in a mink coat, before she was led away, van Gogh wrapping a hand around the furry arm.

The Perm, snapping his fingers now, snippy. "Hey, sport. I'm the one you need to be worried about. I asked you a question."

Lyons faced the Perm. "I heard you. All this 'you know people,' telling me you've got clout in this town. Outfit muscle, I'm guessing."

"I'm telling you, sport, you can leave here standing or I can have you wheeled out, dump your body in the Potomac and nobody would ever know. One look at you, I don't think you'd rate much attention."

"What if I told you I was a special agent with the Justice Department?"

"The kind of people I know own Feds, have half the politicians in their pocket, whistling to their tune. If I don't squash you like the insect you are, I know people who can get your badge yanked and pinned to your ass."

"You're a big man, is that it?"

"Bigger than you really want to find out, sport."

Lyons chuckled, nodded and grinned. "I've got it

now. I know who you remind me of." The Perm froze, Lyons glancing over his shoulder, found the bulldogs still on their leash. "'The Gong Show,' that's it. You look like that guy, the host, the one with the frizzy hairdo, shirt always unbuttoned to his navel, you know, showing off a chest I've seen with more muscle and meat on a starving Kurd refugee. Loved that show. I especially got a kick out of Gene-Gene the Dancing Machine. Remember that guy? Hey, maybe it's really you, that silly guy, you know, career change… What the hell was his name? Can you still mimic those Gene-Gene moves?"

The moment was sealed now and Lyons knew what had to be done. It was way beyond hope, mature or responsible.

"That's it…"

The Perm was rising when Lyons grabbed him by the earlobe, squeezing, twisting, lifting him to his feet. Funny what pain did to get the other guy's attention. The Perm's squeal was cutting through the rock music when Lyons clamped a hand over his throat.

And the SS was coming.

There was a general paralysis among the patrons, Lyons saw, catching a couple of scantily clad females mirrored in the wall glass as they scurried for cover. Lyons had the pair of goons marked in the mirror, as he spun the "Gong Show" clone around, gauging range to target number one. The foot shot out. Lyons rewarded by a whoof and eyeballs rolling back in the head as he scored a home run to testicles. Number two faltered, watching as his comrade folded at his feet. The .45 was out next, whipping sideways, slamming off number two's scalp. So much 250 pounds of bulging pecs and biceps, but Lyons liked the way he hit the floor, out cold, the odds cut by half. The dancer on stage screamed and grabbed up her clothes. Lyons adjusted his aim as goons three and four bulled their way through the crowd.

"Freeze!" Lyons shouted, the sight of the .45 thrust at their faces freezing SS Three and Four in their tracks. "Eat the deck, facedown!"

"Mr. Greer, do you want us to call the cops?"

"I am the cops, asshole. Last chance!"

"Do what he says...no cops," Greer sputtered.

When they stretched out, Lyons flung the Perm to the edge of the stage, the .45's muzzle pressed between his eyes. "One time. Where is Dee-Dee?" Lyons saw the Perm had trouble finding a tongue he was on the verge of swallowing, released some pressure. "What was that?"

"You don't know...who you're fucking with, Miami."

Lyons cocked the hammer to another shrill cry from somewhere near the stage.

"Room..."

Lyons bent closer, caught the number of the hotel suite. Time to exit stage left, but Lyons spotted a few wannabe heroes in the crowd, eyes angry, jaws working, shadows shuffling in the mirrors. He pulled the Perm to his feet, sweeping around the .45, barking at a suit to sit. He was halfway to the front door when he came to a table of three guys who looked set to throw up a barricade of muscle, twitching around in their seats, mouthing words Lyons couldn't make out.

"Here," Lyons told them, flinging the Perm over the table. A tumble through bottles and ashtrays, and the Perm flopped down, pinning them to their seats. "You three look like you could use a lap dance."

HERMANN SCHWARZ was getting antsy. He was sitting at the bank of monitors in the War Wagon, surveying M Street and the door to the bar, the picture piped in through a minicam, no larger than a pinhead, fixed to an antenna. A twist of the dial and he could monitor the entire street for several blocks, the high-tech eye doubling as an instant camera, able to take night snapshots, infrared lens capable of coming on with the flick of a switch.

"I don't like it, Pol. Our fearless leader's been in there too long. You know Carl, some places tend to bring out the beast in him, and that's saying something."

Blancanales had the wheel, his head rolling side to side as he surveyed the street. "He can give new meaning to bull in a china shop, I'll grant you that."

The whole setup was screwy, but they had already killed enough time hashing it over until they both knew it began to sound like a bunch of bellyaching. Still, that didn't mean they had to like it.

A former cop partner of Ironman's, Schwarz thought, dropping out of the sky, smelling and looking like he needed detox more than walking around in public, hunting down his runaway daughter. This Evans guy back in their suite, drinking their booze, watching *3000 Miles to Graceland,* when that should have been them. They were on R and R, sure enough, but Schwarz was waiting for the phone with secured line to start ringing off the hook any second, Brognola or the Farm's mission controller, Barbara Price, wondering why they had absconded with the supertech War Wagon to go tooling around downtown D.C. What would he tell them, provided, of course, he could even bleat out a word during the ass-chewing?

"Gadgets, I think there might be a problem. Start shooting pics."

After all of two seconds, watching as bodies began streaming out the door, suits harried and hustling off into the night, Schwarz read the body language, loud and clear. They were fleeing from a human wrecking ball.

"Pol, how come I get the weird feeling Carl made contact and the words 'please and thank you' weren't part of his vocabulary?"

"Gadgets, Pol!"

Tac radio in hand, Schwarz punched on, in sync with Pol's, "Yeah!"

"Get your fingers out of your asses and your heads out of Graceland. Four assholes and a chippy in a mink coat should be out front by now!"

Schwarz spied the party in question as they swung away from the front door, began marching down the sidewalk toward a waiting limo. Schwarz began snapping pictures even as Lyons barked for him to do just that. "I'm on it!"

"I'm especially interested in the guy who looks like van Gogh. You see him?"

"I've got him," Schwarz answered.

"What's the situation?" Blancanales needed to know.

Schwarz heard the name of the hotel and the suite number.

"You know where it is?"

"It's in Crystal City," Blancanales answered.

"I'll follow in my car, but you get there first, you wait," Lyons growled. "We just went tactical, so get yourselves strapped in to some serious hardware. On the ride, Gadgets, you can stay busy giving me a computer sketch of van Gogh sans the goatee and shades. You copy?"

"Roger."

Schwarz took one final shot of the limo's plates as the vehicle lurched ahead, gathered speed and shot past them. Blancanales was cranking on the engine, dropping it into gear when Schwarz spotted Lyons bulling his way out onto the sidewalk. "Hey, Carl. You

want me to take a shot of you for our scrapbook?"
Schwarz cut off their leader's voice just as he launched
into a tirade.

Blancanales was throwing the rig into a hard turn
to give pursuit when Schwarz said, "Hey, Pol, I just
thought of something."

"What?"

"When we write our memoirs I think I'll call it,
3000 Miles to the Farm. What do you think?"

"We're both going to be 3000 miles to nowhere if
we don't do what Carl wants."

Just then the red line beeped. Schwarz stared at it
as though it were a viper coiled to bite, said, "I think
no truer words were ever spoken."

"Are you going to answer that?"

Schwarz slowly punched on, attempted his best
winning, innocent voice. "Yes?"

"You three want to explain yourselves?"

It wasn't real hard to read the tone. Schwarz knew
Barbara Price wasn't asking how they were feeling.

"THEY WHAT? They're doing what?"

After so many years in the same office at the Justice Department and climbing the ranks, certain perks
now came with the job. Brognola's spacious office
was soundproof, bugproof, with recently installed bul-
let-and-bomb-reinforced windows. There was a small
conference table, a couch for sleeping, a personal
workstation, a giant TV built into the wall. All things

considered, they were the creature comforts necessary for a man who spent most of his professional hours on his feet and on the edge.

With perks, however, came more responsibility and worries. Translate added worry to the human factor.

He wasn't thirty seconds on the satellite link to the Farm, catching the sitrep from Price, when he was chomping on half a pack of Rolaids. He heard how Gadgets, with his infinite knowledge of high-tech, had most likely accessed the code panel in the barn where the War Wagon was housed. He heard about the task for a friend Lyons had undertaken, how the leader of Able Team needed a few more hours, they might be on to something big. Working at light speed to relay the data handed off by Sunglasses, Brognola feared a long night ahead for all of them.

"This isn't the first time they've pulled some bull-headed nonsense like this," Brognola noted. "Goddammit! Those three could test the patience of the Virgin Mary. I tell you what. If I end up having to bail them out of some police problem, they can bet their black bank accounts their next vacation will be in North Korea."

"That might be worth some serious consideration."

"I need them front and center in the War Room when I land at the Farm—no more than three hours from now. If that vehicle doesn't return in the same condition they took it, they will rue the day they pulled this stunt. I mean, there will be wailing and gnashing of teeth, and it won't be from either of us."

"I'll pass that on."

"Are you getting this?"

"It's coming through. We'll get right on it. Can you give me a quick rundown on what we're looking at, Hal?"

"The way it was told to me, we might be looking at the beginning of Armageddon."

"That's quick enough."

CHAPTER THREE

Their tail of the limo to Crystal City was a jagged blur of white light and angry noise for Rosario Blancanales. Even with radar jammer and GPS monitor guiding the way, it was a miracle of sorts, he thought, no cops had roared up their bumper. The limo's driver set the pace, however, flying along, whipping past other vehicles, oblivious or indifferent to potential speed traps. It left Blancanales to wonder if they'd been made, where they were really going, what, if anything, they had to hide. Somehow the Stony Man warrior maintained a quarter-mile distance to their target.

It was a juggling act, no mistake, manning the wheel, shooting through town on I-395, rocketing next down Route 1, needle pushing eighty, slipping on the custom-webbed rigging to carry the mini-Uzi, wondering which asp would bite first. There was Lyons on the tac radio, snarling out the game plan, which was about as simple and crazy as it came; crash the suite's door, bull-rush inside, no fix on numbers, but if it was armed, it went down.

Then there was Barbara Price, the Farm's mission controller, someone they didn't want on their ass if this night went to hell. Her calm but cold voice still chimed its potential death knell in his head as she laid down the law in no uncertain terms—back to the Farm in three hours sharp, not even bug splatter on the windshield, do not get nabbed by police. She left the threat of consequences—regarding their AWOL status and return of the War Wagon in mint condition—open to the imagination. This, as bizarre coincidence had it, as he shot them past Arlington National Cemetery.

Small comfort now, but he was finally bringing the super-tech rig to a halt on a side street facing the hotel. Even with body armor, Blancanales knew a wreck at 80 mph would have reduced millions of dollars' worth of space-age gizmos to smoking junk. Then there would have been cops...

Oh, but the mood Lyons was in, Blancanales figured the night was only about to get better, depending on the point of view. Lyons had seen, heard, something back at the strip joint to wire him up as bad as Blancanales could recall seeing. Whatever held the berserker in him on a tight leash, Blancanales trusted their leader's instincts when it came to smelling out the enemy, even a phantom that had shown no visible signs of menace to them or to society at large. But he bought

Lyons's version of events that led them to this moment of truth, their leader certain they were wading into battle with more than just kidnappers of a teenage runaway. What, Lyons couldn't say, but Blancanales was prepared for the worst, braced for any nasty surprise.

After a check of the load on his Beretta 92-F with its clip of fulminated mercury 9 mm Parabellum rounds, then stowing the pistol in shoulder leather, he followed Schwarz's lead, dumping one frag, one flashstun and one incendiary grenade in his coat pocket. He was out the door, palming the miniremote, which beeped once to lock and electrify the van one hundred percent tamperproof, when he spotted the big shadow of Lyons rolling out of an alley.

"Fall in," Lyons said, taking the lead, Blancanales a step behind on the right flank, Schwarz picking up the left wing. "What's the story?"

"Your four AIQs—Assholes In Question—and the CIM—Chippy In Mink—were roughly two minutes ahead of us," Schwarz said.

"I want van Gogh alive and squealing. You have that picture I wanted, Gadgets?"

"In my pocket. You may be right. Something about the guy… I swear I've seen him before."

"He's on the radar screen, so don't forget it."

They surged ahead in lockstep, rolling for the lobby doors.

Blancanales prided himself on role camouflage, blending in with whatever the natives and environment of the moment, but they were pushing their luck. A few steps before they swept into the lobby, their heads swiveling and taking in their six, Blancanales was sure someone would remember three men in leather trench coats, dark sunglasses and aloha shirts. The way Lyons was surging on, he only hoped the coat flap didn't fly open and some passersby spotted the massive SPAS-12 autoshotgun hanging from the special leather shoulder thong.

Two paces into the lobby and Blancanales was nearly bowled over by the bedlam. At first—perhaps it was the sunglasses obscuring his vision—he wasn't sure what he was seeing, but it was a wild kaleidoscope of living color that blazed all over the lobby, leaving him to believe he was stepping into some dream.

He could only hope their luck held, glancing toward the desk, where clerks were embroiled in a heated discussion with two elderly women whose hair was so blue it nearly hurt Blancanales's eyes. The effect seemed to render his surroundings even more surreal. Then what was happening began to sink in, as he checked the spacious lobby harder, blinking, surveying the bar.

"What the—"

Blancanales braked in midstride, nearly walking up Lyons's back as their leader froze.

They were in clown suits, painted up, floppy shoes, any number of crying or laughing faces blurring past in Blancanales's periphery. He spotted the badges pinned to their chests, saw balloons sailing all over, drunken laughter swelling the air, pulsing against his eardrums. Lyons threw a look over his shoulder, then resumed the pace, double-time. A clown convention, of all damn things, Blancanales thought, more worried now than ever that some sloshed Bozo would break their stride for a chat, or worse.

Blancanales felt the tension rise from his teammates as they made the bank of elevators, unmolested. Lyons stabbed the button, gave the corridor another look. Nothing but a few clowns. The doors parted, Blancanales trailing Lyons and Schwarz inside when he heard the giggling. Heart lurching, he was almost afraid to turn to look, certain the elevator was about to be packed with clowns, drunken Bozos looking to get feely-touchy.

Instead, he found two women, a brunette and blonde in evening attire. No clown paint—normal people—he could breathe again. The women hesitated, the laughter dying as Blancanales saw them flash a look between them, wondering. They moved into the car, turned their backs, punching the button for the fourth floor several times, nervous, as if they were trapped with three homicidal maniacs. Which, Blancanales thought, wasn't that far from the truth.

Blancanales looked at his teammates. He was grateful Schwarz had on his prebattle mask, no grin that signaled he was ready to crack wise with the stranded damsels.

They were rising, Blancanales tight with anxiety, but he fought off the thousand and one different scenarios of what could go wrong. Either way, they were here, going in hard, no choice but to follow through with Ironman's bulldoze strategy. A slaughter circus, he suspected, was poised to grab center stage.

Oh, well, he decided. Bring on the clowns.

"AND I AM ONLY hearing about this now, why, Herr Greer?"

Again Karl Skuber listened to the man bleat out the feeble explanation, felt his grip tighten around the cell phone as hot blood rushed into his brain, and he heard his knuckles pop. He began pacing around the bedroom, brushing the camera, snaked out a hand and caught it before it tipped off its tripod. He scowled, squeezed the bridge of his nose, but heard the air whistle out of his nostrils, thoughts racing for damage control. He moved into the bedroom doorway, knew the whore and the VIP had just arrived, caught both of them demanding one of his men fetch them a drink from beyond the end of the hall. The snorting from one or both of them or the other two whores already there, as they huffed up cocaine, broke through the racket of shooting from the action movie his crew was watching.

Skuber shook his head. He loathed the degenerate behavior of these Americans, but they were vital to the cause, indirect as their roles were to the end game. To keep them happy and compliant by feeding their perverse appetites was hardly his intention. The weak would serve, also, he thought. It was simply a question of exploiting whatever the weakness to his advantage.

"Hey, you there, sport?"

"I am listening, as difficult as it is."

"You think you've got problems? I've got cops crawling all over my place. They're so far up my butt they can see what I had for lunch, sport," he heard Greer whine. "They want answers, you understand. Half my girls heard or know what the hell is going on and why. This maniac claimed he was with the Justice Department, and I'm thinking her old man already put in the call to the cops. If that's true, I'm set to swirl down the toilet. I see the future. I see my liquor license—might as well put a match to it. If they lock the doors, then what do I do? I've got a business to run, a life of my own. You're not paying me enough to spend ten to twenty in some cage wondering who's going to pork me and when. I've got to come up with some explanation why this maniac—"

"Silence!" He waited a moment until he was sure the whining had ceased. "You are saying you told this alleged agent of the Justice Department where we were?"

"What was I going to do, sport? The maniac was ready to blast my head off, he tore up my joint, two of my guys were just wheeled out of here on their way to the emergency room."

"Shut up! Listen carefully. We will be in touch. And, I warn you, if you do not efficiently cover for us, I will personally see to it your worries come to an abrupt end."

"What is this, sport? My nuts are in a wringer here, and you're threatening me? Hey, you forgetting, I'm the man. I sent you the best junk in town, the best young ass on the planet, and you're ready to march out some hit squad?"

"I do no threaten. Again, I urge you to strongly consider your immediate future."

Skuber punched the voice off as it broke into another whine, then held his ground in the doorway for a moment, considering his options. He thought he was prepared for the potential crisis of dealing with American lawmen, but now he wasn't so sure. If Greer— whom he considered little more than a pimp—was being truthful, then trouble was on the way. All along he had believed NEB.com—New Earth Bliss.com— was a gross mistake, one that would come back to haunt him. He was a commando, formerly of the GSG-9, not some porn director. But he was faithful to the organization, believed in the future they were working to create, willing, now as then, when he had sold them his skills to help pave the road into tomorrow. To further the global agenda, he understood the need for more money, no matter where it came from, no matter how tawdry he found his duty.

"...please, don't...I want to go home...I want..."

Skuber looked at the source of his immediate problem. He saw Brahm snap the tourniquet off her arm, the needle coming out, the girl floating away on the heroin moments later, silent. Some of the whores performed willingly in front of the cameras, he knew, if the proper amount of money and drugs were offered as incentive. Some of them even allowed themselves to be sold to rich men overseas, unwilling or unable to return to whatever their shabby lives, greed eventually controlling their final decision. Without the drug in her system this one was near impossible to control, bawling to leave, threats about calling the police if she was not released. As young as she was, unsullied for the most part, he suspected he would fetch three or four times the money for her than most of the drug-addled whores he peddled to sheikhs, Russian gangsters, European businessmen in search of sex slaves.

"I believe that will keep her quiet and still for a few hours," Brahm said, baring white teeth at the naked sack of limp flesh on the bed. "Shall we resume filming? Perhaps our special guest would like another try?"

"Clearly you have spent too much time in America with the animals, Hans. We may have a situation that not even our own people may be able to protect us from. The party is over."

LYONS WONDERED if he was crazy, brave or stupid, then concluded he was a little of each. He was laying his head on the chopping block for a guy he never much cared for, risking his life and the lives of his friends and teammates, ready to charge in blind, guns blazing, clueless as to what they might really find on the other side of the hunt.

Still, his gut told him to keep going, that he was right, and whatever waited at the end of the line was wrong. He could feel it, something in his heart pumping out an urgent message to a brain that had recorded to memory every dirty little hint and implied threat the Perm had uttered.

Then there was van Gogh. The more he thought about the guy, the harder the grind in his memory telling him he should know the face.

Lyons led his teammates off the elevator, searching the hallway, on the move. No roving guests, in or out of clown suit. So far, so good. He picked up the pace, reading the numbers, going down, figured the party was under way at the end of the corridor. He spotted the fire stairwell—their own emergency escape—at the end of the hall. Lyons took that as a sign maybe the gods of war were smiling on them this night.

He signaled for Schwarz and Blancanales to drop into flanking position beside the double doors.

One quick search of the hall, all clear, Schwarz and Blancanales drawing their mini-Uzis, cocked and locked, and Lyons lifted the autoshotgun.

SKUBER CHECKED the load on his .50 Magnum Desert Eagle, slapped the clip home, chambered a round and

stowed the cannon. A crew of seven, he thought, a pal-
try number of shooters if there was an army of Justice
Department agents en route to arrest them, or worse.

He was reassured, nonetheless, that his men were
of the same mind and commitment to the cause, the
best fighters money could buy. So he clung to the hope
that firepower, skill and determination were enough to
get them to their private jet in the Virginia countryside
in the event they were forced to shoot their way out of
the United States. Back to the Fatherland, then, until
this crisis could be sorted out, figure more money perhaps needed to grease the right hands so he could return, back to business as usual. As for Herr Greer, he
knew the man's self-centered concern about losing his
business or going to prison was ill-founded. Herr Greer
would soon find himself burning in the great gentlemen's club in hell.

But now…

Crisis had been dumped in his lap. It wasn't neces-
sarily his blame to shoulder, but it was his task to perform, tidy up loose ends, whatever it took, on
American soil. If it came down to some pitched battle
with American lawmen—and he hoped to avoid any
armed engagement—not even the document on each
of his men would provide a free pass. The way the
pimp had described his encounter with the so-called
maniac, Skuber was taking no chances that mere de-
portation back to Germany was guaranteed.

He found the three whores and the VIP on the

couch, busy indulging themselves over the pile of powder. In German he began barking orders at his men to pack up the computers, CD-ROMs, videos. "The police may be on the way. If anyone attempts to stop us as we leave, you are to resist them at all costs. We are moving to another location," he told the Americans, switching to English, the VIP wiping at his nose, confused. "Now!"

His men began hustling to carry out the orders, Skuber satisfied they could evacuate within minutes. It disturbed him they might still be forced to confront American lawmen in a firefight, but there would be too many questions if they were captured, too much evidence lying around the suite that could trace back to his superiors, perhaps cripple the organization.

He turned away from questions flung at his back by the Americans and marched for the bedroom, demanding Brahm hurry up and dress the girl.

The blast was a trumpet of doom in his ears, thundered from the direction of the foyer. It branded an instant vision of armed invaders in Skuber's mind and dashed any hope for a clean getaway.

WHOEVER THEY WERE, they shot first. That was enough for Carl Lyons, but the Able Team leader knew that hardly solved their problems. His noisy entrance had scrambled the troops, and they were pros, he found, reacting hard and fast, no doubt already put on high alert by the Perm. How many? He counted at least five goons in black turtlenecks and slacks, the uniform of the day, he guessed. A few of the hardmen were slower on the trigger, but the group was swinging a variety of subguns and big stainless-steel pistols their way, ripping loose with heavy metal thunder. The enemy was seeking cover, jigging this way and that, but the few seconds they lost, bumping into one another, getting untangled, kept them out in the open.

The other worrisome factor was noncombatants. Lyons glimpsed three women and van Gogh. No matter what, he had no desire to see the unarmed—even if they were the not-so-innocent—mowed down in the crossfire. They were wailing through the din of weapons fire, leaping to their feet, van Gogh shouting something Lyons couldn't make out.

Sure, they were in, Schwarz and Blancanales peeling off to cubbyholes beside the foyer, cutting loose with twin streams of 9 mm Parabellum rounds as the swarm of enemy fire pounded the wall and doorway behind them. But Lyons could see in two eye blinks the odds of getting out and eluding cops were long.

Too late now, and Lyons never second-guessed himself.

On the fly, he blasted away with two 12-gauge rounds, veering a zigzag vector for a fat pillar at the foot of the steps, bullets snapping past his scalp. From near the entertainment center, Lyons saw the goon in the shoulder-length black hair take his one-two evisceration to the midsection, the hardman's H&K MP-5 subgun sailing away into the red cloud of airborne slaughterhouse remains.

WHOEVER THE TRIO of invaders, Skuber knew they weren't any cops. Police didn't cave in doors without announcing themselves, as American law required. If they came to arrest or to tear the suite apart in a search, they would enter waving warrants. What little Skuber could see of the trio, he also couldn't picture American lawmen running around in aloha shirts or armed with submachine guns and massive automatic shotguns, shooting first, no questions. Or perhaps, he briefly considered, American law enforcement had changed tactics to keep pace with a society where the lowest criminal could carry an assault rifle.

As if it mattered who they were, he thought.

They were scything down his best and toughest right in front of his eyes, stoking both his fear and rage. Had the nameless trio crashed the door two seconds later, they wouldn't have caught his men out in the open, packed tight, a turkey shoot.

Skuber had mere seconds to turn back the tide. He saw the whores had the good selfish sense to throw themselves to the carpet, cover their heads. But the VIP was standing, frozen in terror, flailing his arms, shouting in hysterics. Two of his men, Skuber watched, were sidling hard and fast for the couch, triggering subguns. They had to have read his own thoughts about snatching human body armor, but they were blown off their feet before they grabbed the VIP. Their bodies diced to red ruins, they danced a spasmic jig, spraying lead toward the ceiling. The VIP was collapsing, but out of terror, perhaps fainting, since Skuber didn't see his white shirt erupt in red holes. His tumble was propelled through the glass coffee table by the flying corpse of Reinhert. One look a second later and Skuber found the VIP squirming out of the shards, on his hands and knees, heading his way.

Perfect.

The mammoth Desert Eagle in hand, Skuber barked at Brahm, "Throw the girl in front of you. When I move for our honored guest, you go out, also."

Brahm struggled to hold up the limp weight, an arm locked around her chest, H&K subgun thrust out and ready. "*Ja,* understood."

THE LOW RETAINING WALL in front of Lyons was taking hits, stone shrapnel and puffs of plaster hurled in the Able Team leader's face. Two more hardmen went down hard and bloody. Lyons fired off another 12-gauge blast, adding to the chorus of subgun fire from Schwarz and Blancanales as the converging streams nailed two goons on the fly for van Gogh. Lyons watched as van Gogh crashed through a coffee table, riddled bodies falling beside him, limbs twitching. The mystery man was scrabbling out of the glass next,

Lyons catching a blur of movement from around the corner. The buzz cut with the hand cannon did exactly what Lyons feared as he jacked van Gogh off the floor.

Van Gogh wasn't the only human shield, Lyons saw, but he was forced to focus on another threat, whirling around the pillar as a shooter tracked him with H&K subgun fire, a swarm of lead gouging out divots of stone. He was on the other side, coming out of his pirouette, the buzz cut shouting for them to throw their weapons down, when Lyons sawed another blacksuit in two, kicking him into a giant-screen TV. Shredded cloth drifted away from the smoking ruins of the set as Schwarz and Blancanales threw in a few 9 mm rounds for good measure.

Lyons hit the steps as the hardmen shuffled forward with their human body armor. Blancanales leaped over the banister, Schwarz falling in beside the Able Team leader, who was in no mood to get bogged down in a standoff. With all the racket of the gun battle, he was sure either hotel security or cops were en route. He couldn't be positive, but since no more gunmen reared up from any halls and doorways he figured they were looking at the last of the enemy.

Feet crunched glass as the goon with Evans's daughter took the lead. The way her head lolled, eyes fluttering open and closed, Lyons knew she was doped up. Somehow he doubted her condition was voluntary.

"We are walking out of here," Buzz Cut announced in a thick German accent.

Lyons opted for one of his .45s. "I don't think so."

"You do not think so?"

Without hesitation, Lyons triggered the .45, cored a bull's-eye, took off half the goon's skull, Deirdre tumbling back with the dead weight.

Buzz Cut's eyes widened as he looked at his dead comrade, then, jabbing the muzzle of the Desert Eagle in van Gogh's ear, rasped, "Do you know who this is?"

"No," Lyons said, stepping forward. Whoever van Gogh was, he looked silly, Lyons thought, quivering in terror, begging to be released, worried about number one, the pasted-on facial hair hanging off his jaw. "But I'm sure you're going to tell me."

"This is Marty Sheebl."

Bells and whistles went off in Lyons's head. The guy was all over the cable talk shows. Knowing, though, didn't make it any easier for Lyons to stomach why the man was here, whoring and using drugs, directly or indirectly responsible for the walking mummy that was Deirdre.

"Yes. The fine democratic senator from Illinois." Buzz Cut laughed. "Head of the Select Senate Committee on Defense and Intelligence."

Lyons lifted the .45, drew a bead on Buzz Cut's face, the goon not certain which of them to watch as Blancanales worked his way to his left flank. "Fuck 'im. I didn't vote for him."

And Lyons fired, taking off half of Buzz Cut's shoulder. A mix of grunts, curses and screams was washed away next as Lyons pounded out another .45 round, Schwarz and Blancanales triggering their Berettas, the fine senator from Illinois shrieking but dropping out of the line of fire. Buzz Cut was ventilated, crotch to sternum, the exploding rounds from Schwarz and Blancanales blasting apart the target's chest, hurling him into the wall. The body folded beneath a stream of running gore.

. "Sweep the place," Lyons ordered his teammates, moving up to the senator who was on his knees, hands clasped.

"Listen to me, I can explain…"

Lyons saw the white smear on the man's nose, ripped off the goatee and used it like a rag. "Here. You missed some, Senator." He wiped, squeezed, then slapped the disguise on the senator's chest. He moved for the girl, felt her neck and found a weak pulse. "Susie. Look at me!"

They whimpered, the women unhurt, as far as Lyons could tell, Susie-Candy looking up, brushing glass from her hair. Lyons saw Blancanales riffling through pockets, pulling out what looked like passports.

"What is she on?"

"Heroin," Susie said. "I—I'm sorry. I didn't know, I swear."

"Are you going to kill us?" another woman asked.

Lyons scowled. "Don't tempt me. Just keep your faces down."

Lyons was scooping the girl up in his arms when he heard Blancanales call out, "Hey. You'd better have a look at this."

Schwarz came out of an adjacent bedroom, toting a small duffel bag, showing it to Lyons. "We're clear. They had a sweet little comm room. I'm thinking mother lode here."

"If it's answers we're looking for about these guys," Blancanales said, handing Lyons the thin wallet, "I think we just stepped into a big fat pile."

"Karl Skuber," Lyons said, then cursed as he looked at the State Department seal. It didn't take much perusing to discover this bunch had full diplomatic immunity, even licensed and approved by SD to carry concealed weapons. "Take the rest of these," he told Blancanales, then dumped the ID in his coat pocket. "You're going with us, Senator. Do not bleat, squawk or whine on the way out of here, or I'll shoot you on general principle. And you're right, you've got a lot of explaining to do."

"HEY, YOU GUYS with the convention? You don't look like you're with us. What's with the girl?"

"Get the hell out of our way, clowns!"

Lyons shouldered through two drunken Bozos, marched out the lobby doors. Blancanales and Schwarz brought up the rear, manhandling the senator who was huffing and puffing, indignant, bleating for answers. Lyons heard the distant but closing sirens, hoped their luck held.

"Gadgets, cuff, stuff, gag and blindfold the good senator when we're in the van."

"You're kidnapping me? I am not some common criminal. How dare you—"

"Shut your face, asshole," Lyons snarled over his shoulder. "What you are is a poster child for political scumbags who, because they make the laws, think for some reason they're only meant for the little people who put them in office."

Just as they were piling into the van, Lyons saw the light show racing into the parking lot. Whether it was a simple lucky evac...

He didn't care. Right now they had a whopper of a mystery on their hands. The Farm, no doubt, would be screaming for their hides, sure to be a little more than annoyed they were about to dump one of the town's illustrious political giants in their laps.

"Get us to the nearest hospital, Pol." Lyons laid the girl on the floorboards as Blancanales pulled away from the curb, easing them past the long line of cruisers zipping for the hotel. Now for the toughest part of his night, he thought, taking the cell phone, Schwarz calling out the location of the hospital from the computerized directory tied into their GPS.

"Carl."

Lyons felt Schwarz's hand on his shoulder.

"We've done enough. You can't take her into the emergency room. It's a drug overdose, there'll be more cops, especially now with the mess we're putting behind."

Lyons punched in the numbers to their suite. "I'm not. Evans is."

CHAPTER FOUR

"You guys."

Since the news first reached Hal Brognola about their cowboy act and he'd ordered Able Team—via Price—back to the Farm, he knew he would eventually have to confront Lyons, Blancanales and Schwarz. While they had been on the loose, tearing up a strip joint, shooting up a Crystal City hotel for the past several hours, Brognola had engaged a mental Ping-Pong match. The debate was whether to blast them with the alpha and the omega of all ass-chewings, or let it slide with a shrug and a scowl.

Of course, they were in clear violation of Farm protocol again, and that much he was sure they knew. Absconding with the War Wagon was migraine enough for Brognola. But when he heard how the runaway human freight train finally wrecked at the end of the line—and who they were bringing back to the Farm—

he'd felt his blood pressure rocket off the monitor, certain the Big One was going to take him out.

Right then he could have issued any number of dire warnings, listed consequences for any such future shenanigans, dock them a black check or two. Even if he could terminate their employment, he wouldn't. The bottom line was, they were too damn good at what they did. Everyone gathered at the table—including Barbara Price and Aaron "The Bear" Kurtzman—knew it, and the silence from the mission controller and the cyber team leader spoke loud and angry volumes. Renegade antics and tackling jobs of their choosing, which put the Farm up to a window of clear public exposure, could not be tolerated. What to say, then? What to do?

Nothing. Sometimes, Brognola decided, a little latitude was called for when dealing with the best of the best.

Very little.

They were in the War Room, Brognola pacing, chewing on his stogie. They fidgeted, glanced at one another, cracked knuckles, waiting for the hammer to drop. And, if he hadn't seen it with his own eyes, he would have thought they looked, well, damn near sheepish.

"You guys," he repeated, nearly throwing in a rare F-word. "You're the reasons why there should be a ban on human cloning." He took the clicker, turned on the wall monitor, settled into his seat at the head of the table. As if relieved to focus their attention somewhere else, Able Team stared at the aerial shot of a large compound, Barbara Price handing intel packets to Lyons who passed one each to his teammates.

Brognola chewed on his cigar, then sipped from a cup of battery acid Kurtzman passed off as coffee. "They say everything in life is timing. I suppose that's true even if it's bad timing. Looks like the three of you got lucky, and it's a damn good thing you did. Seven dead German nationals with full diplomatic immunity. Whisking one of the top lawmakers of this country to the Farm, which, under different circumstances, would pass for kidnapping. That said, with your stunt tonight you stumbled into a viper's nest we may or may not have ever found on our own. Where the mess leads is anybody's guess. Okay. Enough said.

"You're looking at Nutricen-21, gentlemen. Basic layout on the wall, but how these air pics and interior shots were acquired, I can't say. The pertinent details, the players in question, are in your intel packets. You'll have time enough to scour those on your way to Arizona. Housed in southwestern Arizona in the Sonora Desert, they are on the cutting edge of classified attack satellite technology."

Brognola gave Able Team a quick rehash of the Myanmar and Somalia crisis. "This Nutricen was established, we believe, by the Department of Defense, two years ago. Only, the DOD stamp is buried beneath the Food and Drug Administration seal of approval.

Why, you ask? Well, the satellite technology is the private face. They're running a joint operation—DOD and FDA, I gather—to keep away the curious, any locals who might start spreading rumors they've got another Area 51 in the neighborhood. Supposedly this compound is a biotech facility. That's the public front, but one, or so the initial intelligence I received, would have me believe. Bear?"

Kurtzman, holding his own clicker, began shooting through a series of pics showing workers in lab coats, hovering near giant centrifuges and what appeared to be vats of a milky-white substance. There were also shots of sentries armed with H&K MP-5 subguns, most of them standing guard in front of massive closed steel doors.

"They're producing high-performance strains of microorganisms, such as yeast for brewing and baking, mutagens or genetic mutations in food. We don't know for a fact the source of the plague that struck the refugee camp in Somalia originated here. It isn't a giant leap to go from microorganisms—bacteria, fungi, algae—as yeast extract to genetically engineering a virus in yeast, breeding it with a microorganism as artificial food nutrient. Once eaten, you're infected.

"From what little we know about this virus, it appears one hundred percent fatal. According to intelligence gathered and sent to us from the White House, we're looking at a black project, most likely, we suspect, a legitimate operation that has gone renegade."

"A lot of this is speculation," Price told Able Team. "But after a few items we learned from the senator, we believe a group of shadow players—spell spooks—is running the show. In these politically turbulent times, it would become a national scandal if it was discovered a classified military base approved by the President and funded by Congress and the Senate was creating a new but far more insidious weapon of mass destruction. As you know, we aren't supposed to be conducting offensive bioweapons research as per our agreement with several nations, including Russia."

"When's a treaty ever stopped a weapons program?" Schwarz said. "Just ask the North Koreans."

Lyons cleared his throat as Price flashed Schwarz a look. "This is all interesting, but how do a bunch of German nationals with carte blanche from the State Department to carry concealed weapons fit in?"

"Not only that," Schwarz added, "but there was enough cocaine and porn videos there to make me wonder who in the hell would allow these guys to walk around with diplo immunity."

"We're not sure," Brognola said. "I'm going to have a long chat with the President. I'm going to order a full-scale investigation from my Justice Department people into State. Someone over there has a lot of explaining to do. Those documents you took may be forgeries, but I won't know until I do some digging.

"As for this owner of the, uh, gentleman's club, Carl," Brognola said, glancing at the Able Team leader,

"I have a team of agents putting him under around-the-clock surveillance. There's a good chance he can lead us to bigger fish. And if there's more frying to be done in D.C., I may or may not cut you loose on Mr. Greer. How far, wide and deep he's connected to what we've uncovered remains to be seen."

"The CDs you took from their suite," Bear said, "showed us these German nationals have set up a worldwide Web site called New Earth Bliss dotcom. Prostitution, Internet porn, even international slavery, get online, you can buy whatever your fantasy, even purchase the girl of your dreams for as long as you want her. I realize in the heat of the moment, Gadgets, you didn't exactly have the time to round up the mainframes, but we have enough to know the persons of interest are dirty. But we believe this whole Internet white-slavery operation is only one means to an end—money—to continue whatever the agenda of an organization called EuroDef."

"European Defense," Price said. "A cabal, comprised of rich European businessmen, mostly Germans, with a security force of former GSG-9 commandos, among various and sundry characters of questionable reputation. They have the backing of the German Ministry of Defense. And they have contracts with American aerospace companies, namely Nutricen, who, as far as we are concerned, are apparently rising fast to knock off the competition, Northrop-Grumman, Boeing, Lockheed and so on. EDEF is, it would appear on the surface, a sister company to Nu-tricen-21.

"As for the good senator, he stated he was being extorted by those same Germans you shot. The usual sins for a politician, getting filmed out of bed with a woman other than his wife. Throw in drug use, the fact he was having relations with girls underage. Ugly, to understate the matter. He implied these Germans were part of EDEF security, sent specifically to America to make sure they received contracts and funding to continue their own satellite program."

"Problem is, he's a political big shot, head of the Senate Committee on National Defense," Brognola said. "He seems more concerned about scandal and losing his job and maybe getting slapped with divorce papers than the fact he's a traitor."

"How are you going to handle him?" Blancanales asked.

"I'll get to that soon enough," Brognola said. "For now, I think we've pulled enough of the senator's teeth, but we have enough to dirt to go ahead and take a run at Nutricen. Now, there were blank checks being cut to Nutricen, handed off by the senator to a cutout he believes takes frequent trips to Arizona."

"Another German national?" Lyons said.

"Yeah," Brognola said. "Trouble is, all we have only leads to more nagging questions."

"And our job?" Lyons asked.

Brognola gnawed on his cigar. "To find out what

Nutricen is really all about. If there's a stink there, follow the whiff."

"Any suggestions how we might tackle this problem?" Lyons asked.

Brognola shrugged. "That's up to you. Maybe you can just lay on them your usual diplomatic touch."

"A gun to the head," Schwarz commented.

"That's been discussed," Kurtzman said.

"You've got carte blanche to get inside and take a look around. The full tour," Price said.

"Any problems with that," Brognola stated, "you'll be given a phone number to the White House the director of this facility can call."

"I'm looking at armed men, Hal," Lyons said. "I'm thinking there's going to be less than full cooperation."

"That's your problem to solve," Brognola said. "And, no, this is not punishment. We simply don't have a lot of options how to tackle this one. The White House is on me to get moving, hard and fast, and if there's rats turning up in your path..."

Brognola finished with another shrug.

"I take it," Lyons said, "you're not shipping us off to Nutricen for a simple walk-through to gather technical data?"

"You take it right," Brognola said. "It's been agreed that we cut loose our three pit bulls on the facility." Brognola watched Able Team pass a look among them, their eyes betraying the questions of how they would penetrate, infiltrate or simply attack the facility. "But first, try to confirm—as best you can—they're a renegade operation."

Lyons nodded, but Brognola wasn't exactly encouraged they would move quietly at all if he read the grim looks right. No problem. If there were rogue operatives from whatever alphabet soup agency betraying their country, the President had already given the thumbs-down on their scalps. Political fallout was for the Man to deal with.

"About the senator, gentlemen," Brognola told Able Team. "Since you brought him to us, you'll leave with him. But here's the plan…"

MARTY SHEEBL'S THOUGHTS were torn between damage control and survival. It was a high-wire act of raw emotion, trying to balance all manner of horrifying scenarios racing through his mind at light speed, attempting to figure out which was the most dreaded bottom line.

The loss of his job as senator? Enduring public disgrace and ridicule, which was sure to dog him the rest of his life when it was discovered he used drugs, had illicit sex with strippers, even a supposed romp with an underaged female, the whole sordid mess captured on film for the world to see? Or an unseen gun, coring a bullet through the black hood, ending his fears forever?

At the moment, feeling his bowels quake, his bladder swollen to near bursting, afraid he was about to soil himself, he was becoming more concerned with getting through the night—alive—than explaining his whereabouts to his wife or colleagues. Fabricating the same excuse of working late always seemed to snow the wife—despite the dark looks and battery of questions—but if he was late showing up at his office on the Hill he could expect a swarm of inquiries, since there were several major bills pending. He'd deal with that, the least of his worries, thinking he would be so grateful to return to his office, he would hit his knees and kiss the carpet.

The fact he was still breathing he wanted to take as a positive sign.

Only...

There were messes to clean up, no mistake, calls to make, feelers to put out that would indicate whether more bad news was in his future.

He could only hope the disguise had held up—at least in public. The true test would be if the three women—the last known survivors in the suite, and the girl didn't count since she was clearly catatonic from heroin—kept their mouths shut. If it came down to paying them off for their silence he could swing, say, twenty grand per, and, if not, there were people he knew who could make them disappear.

But there were the Germans to consider. The devious bastards had lured him into the trap in the first place, but they were all dead—only there were more where they came from, he knew. Which meant the trail would lead back to him, assuming he wasn't outright executed by his captors. He didn't want to die, but the thought of public humiliation seemed a fate worse than the most agonizing slow death. Too many people knew too much about him. If his transgressions were brought to light, his name would be a dirty word, stamped in *Webster's* next to disgrace. The scandal would be thrashed around all over every talk show for years to come. If not for some major catastrophe—a war, or another terrorist attack on American soil—he would be on the news all night, every night, those damnable journalists who had once sucked up to him, now shaking their heads, even chuckling in private how the mighty had fallen.

So many terrors, the future was in grave doubt. His career, his life, his lifestyle…

"Oh, God."

He heard his breathing grow heavier beneath the hood, the air trapped and sour in his nose, gagging him with the stink of his own breath, the sweat of fear. He was on a helicopter, hands behind his back, bound with plastic cuffs, but that was all he knew. The shimmy of the airborne ride only aggravated the swelling in his groin. The binding was so tight he felt his hands going numb. Moments ago he had asked his invisible captors where they were going, what they planned to do with him. Their silence only caused his fear to mount.

He wanted to weep; it was all such an incomprehensible nightmare. He wanted to—what? Implore God to bail him out? Yes, a devout family man he marched to church every Sunday, wife and two children in tow. But that had been all show, of course, since voters liked to see the righteous lawmaker they'd put in office, walking out of Mass, a pillar of unflapping virtue, cameras rolling sometimes, reporters waiting to ask questions about this or that latest crisis. It occurred to him he had never actually prayed, much less thought about any God, just going through the motions for appearance sake. Perhaps now, he thought, was a good time to start praying. But what to ask for? That his life be spared? That he could resume life as he knew it? That his shame remained secret?

The Illinois senator hadn't bothered to tally up the number of hours he had been cuffed, blindfolded, questioned in some room in a building he had no clue on its whereabouts. He had been manhandled like some thug, abused, as far he was concerned, forced to kneel during the interrogation, told to shut up whenever he began to rail about who he was… They had better explain themselves. Whoever these people were, he was sure he would never know, nor did they did care about the fact they had kidnapped a man of his stature and prestige, simply barking at him for hours to reveal whatever he knew about the German nationals, the project out in Arizona. The questions fired off in their gruff tones told him they knew classified information they weren't supposed to, that lying his way out wouldn't win him any points. They were black ops, some covert operation buried so deep that not even—

Another line of thinking began to break through the images of some nameless assassin putting a bullet in his head. There had been rumors over the years, usually bandied about over one too many martinis, colleagues talking in low conspiratorial tones at parties, as if they had a secret they were dying to share. The rumor mill didn't churn too hard, since no one had irrefutable proof that a clandestine organization in or around the D.C. area existed, one that answered, allegedly, only to the President of the United States. He had dismissed it as too incredible, some rogue covert operation kept in the dark from the greatest body of lawmakers on the planet, the President with his personal invisible army, marching them out for dirty secret wars, ordering assassinations at his discretion.

Now...

He was a believer. And the simple fact he had been abducted, forced to talk, reveal his own complicity in a shadow operation that bordered treason, only compounded his terror. Whatever this covert group, surely they couldn't allow him to live now.

"Time to go, Senator."

He recognized the voice. It was the big blonde from the suite who killed as easy as a man might blow his nose. He felt the floor shudder, then settle. They were on the ground.

"Are you going to…kill me?"

He felt his knees shaking, boneless appendages he was sure wouldn't hold up if he stood. He thought he was going to vomit. Why didn't the big man answer?

"Get up."

Another voice, one of the other commandos—he couldn't place which one.

He tried to stand, but his legs folded, the cry of terror trapped by the hood, ringing in his ears.

"He's shaking like a pissed-on leaf."

"Get him off our chopper before he takes a dump in his pants."

Talking to him, a distinguished member of the Senate, as if he weren't there or was nothing more than some common criminal. He felt their hands dig into his shoulders. He was hauled to his feet, considered pleading for his life, perhaps there was some way he could make things right. But he was collapsing, even in their viselike grip, screaming next as he was thrown through the air, unsure if they were even still on the ground. He slammed into what felt like a wall, then realized he had been tossed into someone's waiting arms.

Two pairs of hands dragged him out of the rotor wash as he felt his feet bicycling air. They shoved him to his knees. The hood was whipped off, the big blonde growling, "Don't turn around."

"Look—"

"Shut up and listen."

He tried to focus on his surroundings—a clearing

of some sort, woods in the foreground, what looked like a child's playground—but he snapped his eyes shut when he felt the cold muzzle of a gun pressed to his skull.

"You are going to quietly resign, both your post as head of your committee and as a senator."

He was going to live, his heart lurching with hope, only he was being asked to give up his world. "But…"

"No buts. This is a one-time offer. Whatever bullshit you want to lay on the press, colleagues, wife, whoever, is your business. Just retire. If you dawdle, if you try to stay on, we know where to find you and it will not be a pleasant social call. Another thing. You breathe one word about your encounter with us—and we will know—you will be paid a visit when you least expect it. As far as you coming into contact with us tonight, you were abducted by little gray men and taken to the mother ship. There was missing time, you have no recall whatsoever of what happened at the suite, afterward, or how you came to find yourself where you now are. Nod, if you understand."

He jerked a nod, nearly heaved his guts, relieved when the cold steel was no longer pressed against his head. "Y-yes, I was…taken by aliens. I remember nothing."

"There's a strip mall, a gas station about a mile from here where you can call someone to pick you up. Keep your eyes closed, count to a hundred before you get up. Look back…you'll be dead before you hit the ground."

He was nodding again, about to tell them he understood perfectly when the nausea bubbled like acid in his belly. A dark film covered his eyes, then the ground rushed toward his face as he fainted.

"WHAT DO YOU think?"

Lyons was closing the hatch on the Bell JetRanger when Schwarz posed the question. The Able Team leader had seen enough, more, in fact, than he could stomach, the senator wobbling to his feet, a mummy vanishing into a trail that bisected the park.

They were up and soaring, sweeping over the rush-hour traffic on Route 7. They were bound for Reagan National where they would board a classified military flight arranged by Price. Their future, Lyons knew, was every bit as grim and uncertain as the senator's, but with a glaring and noble difference.

"I think Hal and Barbara spared us a thousand lashes."

"I think Gadgets was referring to the not-so-esteemed-anymore senator."

"The senator's too damn scared to not do what he's told," Lyons answered. "He dodged his own bullet and he knows it. End of story. And like I said before—**fuck** 'im, I didn't vote for him."

Lyons claimed a seat, took up the intel packet. "Let's get our minds on what's ahead of us."

"Any ideas on how we're going to proceed?" Blancanales asked.

"A couple," Lyons said, and flashed a mean grin. "Depending on how this place looks when we're on the ground, well, how did Hal describe us?"

Blancanales looked up from his intel packet, groaned. "Pit bulls."

Lyons nodded. "Sounds like we might be able to win our way back into the good graces of the Farm after all."

CHAPTER FIVE

"His name is Heinz Kluger."

The name didn't mean anything to David McCarter. Then again the ex-SAS commando and leader of Phoenix Force supposed it wouldn't, not unless he kept abreast of the world's richest men by magazines that spoke of the wealthy as if they were the angels who could send all souls soaring on the stairway to heaven. Admiring all the beautiful people, near or far, wasn't his bag. Leading men into battle was his beast of burden, and that was about as beautiful as life would ever get for McCarter.

They were well into their fifth day, standing down from their last mission, when the satellite link beeped, calling all hands. They were in their safehouse, a villa on a cliff overlooking the Adriatic Sea when the Farm put them on alert. McCarter saw them move for the dining-room table, stepping lively now that duty was ringing the bell, all of them tired of malingering, he figured, hang-gliding, swimming in bone-chilling water, trolling the local villages for fun and games, eager now to get back to work.

The other four warriors of Phoenix Force put down the beer, sodas and their slices of homemade pizza. The chef in question—Jack Grimaldi, Stony Man's pilot extraordinaire—helped himself to one more bite, then claimed a seat in the dining room. McCarter had the video link online, Barbara Price and Hal Brognola on the screen as the intel scrolled out of the fax with its secured line. McCarter passed out the paperwork as Price continued, laying out the story on EDEF in succinct fashion. Brognola interjected, filling in about Able Team's encounter with EDEF security, how the grand finale all began with a trip to the titty bar.

Gary Manning cocked a grin, the big Canadian shaking his head. "Those guys. Sounds to me like they had too much time on their hands."

"I let them know that," Brognola said. "Enough said. Down to business."

"Okay, on the surface EDEF looks clean," Price said. "Stamp of approval by the German Foreign Ministry, Defense, the European Space Agency. Powerful friends from the United Nations all the way to the U.S. State Department and maybe even the Department of Defense."

Rafael Encizo, speed-reading, piped up, "But Herr Kluger founded his empire on Internet porn. Makes you wonder what else he is into."

"Beyond porn, he made his climb to the top with several legit dotcom ventures. Trading in computer stocks online, in league with several major European giants, and so forth," Brognola said, then explained the crisis in Somalia and Myanmar.

"Telecommunications was the eventual stepping stone for Kluger who founded EDEF with the aid of several rich European businessmen. Now he's building satellites through EDEF and he's president of the cabal. Kluger doesn't let anyone get too close to his organization unless they have big friends in high military and political places. They've launched two satellites in the past year out of Frankfurt, with a sister launch pad in Spain, ostensibly to link the European continent under one cable company—Kluger Kable. How many satellites they've actually put into orbit, well…we're in the process of trying to find that out from NASA. He's apparently greased enough skids so that he can launch his own satellites, and who he's beholden to is anyone's guess."

"And you're thinking," Calvin James, the black ex-SEAL, said, "what exactly? They're unleashing plague from both outer space and with the help of this Nutricen out in Arizona? If so, why?"

"That's what we're hoping you—and Able—will find out," Price answered.

"You're right about Herr Kluger looking too good to be true," T.J. Hawkins said. "All the right friends in the right places. But you're thinking he's a billionaire entrepreneur who maybe has some neo-Nazi inclinations to create the Fourth Reich? Maybe unleashing mass death on those he deems subhuman?"

"Well," Grimaldi said, "if EDEF's behind the Somalia and Myanmar situations, it looks like he's singling out those countries Kluger deems fit to live but only if they can serve. He's a bully, the way I read it, picking on Third World countries that don't have the money or the food to fight back, or simply tell him to go home."

"Or maybe," Encizo said, "he's looking to buy his way into those countries."

"But, again, why?" Manning proposed.

"Possibilities, literally all over the map," Brognola said. "There's nothing in Kluger's background to indicate any radical or neo-Nazi tendencies. But if his henchmen used Myanmar as a testing ground and you can prove it, he's finished."

"But just how," McCarter asked, "do you propose we line up EDEF in our crosshairs?"

"We were thinking maybe you should take a trip to Somalia first," Price said.

"An end run at the cabal," Brognola said, "chipping away at the stone. Yassif Abadal, as you can see, was spotted in the company of former GSG-9 commandos in EDEF's employ."

"Seen here," Hawkins said, "looks like they're grinning and whistling *'Deutschland uber Alles'* as a bunch of Ethiopian refugees bite the dust from whatever you think was put into their food."

"We have electronic and radio intercepts," Price said, "from EDEF headquarters to both the AIQ in Somalia and Yangon."

"Saying after Able's impromptu terminating of EDEF thugs," James said, "they're scrambling the troops for return visits to both countries? A fire was lit stateside and the EDEF headshed has stepped up the pace for whatever their game?"

"That's what we believe," Brognola said.

"We have an idea of how we might get you into Myanmar," Price said. "It involves attaching yourselves to a team of specialists from the CDC, but we thought we'd run it by you first. That's a rather dicey proposition, since Myanmar is one of the most hostile countries to the West in the world. Option two would be to link you up with rebels in the Kachin, in-country CIA and DEA contacts. Maybe a straight drop into the Kachin. We can arrange chopper extract with the DEA across the Thai border. But that's down the line."

"I'm reading this package," McCarter said, "as fast as I can. The gist of it is that you think EDEF may be looking to cut themselves into the heroin business coming out of Myanmar. If that was their satellite they dropped on the SLORC's head…"

"Another question we can't answer," Brognola said.

McCarter could feel the electricity of adrenaline crackling around him, the troops ready to bust out of the gate. And he picked up the note of urgency in the voices of Brognola and Price. They had a handful of something, but what no one could say. It reeked of conspiracy, that much McCarter believed.

"It's going to take several hours for us," Price said, "to work out the logistics to get you into Somalia. There's a U.S. Special Forces slash CIA base in Kenya where you can launch your snatch of Abadal."

"A kidnap?" Encizo asked.

"Cuff him and stuff him," Brognola said. "With any luck you'll run into a few Kluger commandos when you hit Somalia. We need answers, hard facts before we can cut you loose on EDEF operations in Europe. We'll brainstorm a few more minutes, then get your gear and head for the American base in Aviano."

"How come I get the impression, Hal," McCarter said, "we just landed on a doomsday clock?"

"Because I'm thinking we did."

EXCUSES, rationalizations and justifications were the gateways to failure, as far as he was concerned. And Heinz Kluger had not built an empire to fail now. He expected—no, he demanded—results, and quickly, without question, without debate. If they didn't pro-duce—whether scientist, technician or security force—they were sent packing. No strike two on his team.

He was striding into his office, Hans von Rigel on his heels, the pneumatic door snicking shut, when the former GSG-9 man in charge of Somalian operations cleared his throat. The noise was a little too loud and dramatic for his liking. On alert, Kluger sensed the big man in the leather bomber jacket was about to launch himself into the excuse mode, waved him off, said, "A moment."

The massive office was in the shape of a horseshoe. The oval black-marble desk matched the floor, which often glinted all the light glowing from the banks of cameras. One hundred monitors in all, Kluger could watch his extensive labor force as they worked on putting EDEF 3, 4 and 5 into orbit. They were hard at it, he saw, slaving away at their computers and tool benches, perusing schematics, no slackers he could find. No coffee drinking, no cigarette smoking allowed—at least while on duty—they were screened extensively before he sought them out, hiring them on with a salary they had only ever dreamed about. Any history of drug use or alcoholism, a criminal record, say, they had tried to keep secret, and they were axed.

No exceptions…well…

As for his security force, the whispers were that some of them indulged vices he found disgusting—including drug use—but he needed men with supreme martial skill to carry out operations he intended to expand into several countries. Brains he could replace in time. Good muscle wasn't as easy to dredge up in the new and kinder Germany. He had hired the best commandos money could buy, and if he had to turn a blind eye to certain rumors…

If their habits interfered with the end results, however, he would have no qualms replacing them.

With the remote control, he flicked on the wall's computer monitor. Schematics of the satellites flashed on the screen. Updated daily, he saw that the satellites were beginning to take on their final features. Two were shaped like tornadoes. The third, a giant metallic spider. Later he would review the finer details—sensors, structural materials and how they would withstand changes in temperature and such. Right now he knew he had to brace himself to hear excuses from von Rigel.

Kluger settled into his wing-backed chair, spread his hands at von Rigel and said, "I'm listening."

"We do not need Somalia. It is not even out of the Stone Age. I can barely stand to breathe the same air with people who think making war is slaughtering a pack of unarmed and starving refugees."

Excuse.

"I see crisis building that we cannot cope with. Conspiracies—and this is a conspiracy between many, make no mistake—survive only if all mouths remain shut, especially under fire. The fact that our people, sanctioned by the State Department, were slaughtered last night and no one we have over there in America has the first clue tells me someone is on to us. I say we abort the American front. We do not need to dabble in Internet porn and the slave trading of kidnapped women or entrapping their politicians who may squawk if they are discovered being extorted by us. We are too powerful for some endeavor so tawdry."

Rationalization.

"Going back into Myanmar," von Rigel continued. "After we were practically forced to leave at gunpoint, and to purchase a large quantity of narcotics, not only borders madness, but could very well lead to the downfall of EDEF. My men and I are warriors, not drug traffickers."

Justification.

There was a blessed pause, Kluger massaging his forehead. "Are you quite finished, Herr von Rigel?"

"I have said what I needed to."

Kluger pointed to his head. "Do you see this?"

Von Rigel looked confused.

"I am forty years old. I am a billionaire. I run the most powerful cabal in all of Europe. I do not smoke, I do not drink, I do not use drugs or seek out the services of whores. I work, sometimes twenty-two hours a day. That is what I do, that is all I do. Sometimes there are many sleepless nights where I pace and plan the future." Kluger tapped his head.

"What are you saying?"

"I am saying that I earned every strand of gray hair on my head. I sacrificed the pleasures of youth. I remained steadfast to achieving my goal of becoming the richest and most powerful man in Germany, even all of Europe. I have arrived." Kluger paused, then said, "I will address your concerns, however, only because you are a warrior, one of my top and most trusted lieutenants. One—because of what happened in America,

I agree, that perhaps, someone has, or believes they have, caught a whiff of the so-called conspiracy you mentioned. Which is why I have a team of your men lighting a fire, so to speak, at the American facility. Two—I do not need nor want Somalia as some nation to lord over. I am using them as a springboard. I want this Abadal to help exterminate his nation. It is both a message and a warning to be delivered—in secret— with nations I intend to infiltrate and subjugate, but by stealth, by instilling terror in the hearts of men who run those countries when they see what I am capable of. As much money as we have at our disposal—and what is the figure I place in your bank account every month, by the way?"

Von Rigel cleared his throat. "One hundred thousand."

"In American dollars, correct?"

"That is correct."

"Do you wish me to terminate your employment?"

Von Rigel blinked. "No."

"Then you will carry out my wishes. You are going back to Somalia immediately as we discussed on the way here. You will deliver more samples to the savages. You will explain to them the promised vaccine will take another month or so to produce. They will perhaps become impatient and carry on with their genocide campaign. What they don't know is that you will deliver the same samples to other warring clans."

"How will…"

Kluger held up a hand. "What you do not know is that in a few short weeks I will launch three more satellites with payloads of the biological agent. When they are in place, you will fly over Somalia and even Ethiopia and air-drop food supplies to the starving masses."

Von Rigel's jaw dropped.

"You think me mad? What will soon come will only be the beginning. It is time to make Germany once again a mighty power to fear, only this is a new age, with new weapons with which to wage war."

"And you would throw it all away, your empire, for what?"

"Nothing will be thrown away. If—and it is a very large 'if'—the death and destruction of tens of thousands points back to EDEF, I intend to show anyone who would attack us that we can and will deliver horror upon them they could not begin to imagine. It is time for Europe to unite, rise up and claim its rightful place as the one and the only world superpower. Now, are you on board for the duration?"

He watched von Rigel, the wheels churning, believed he was about to step off, but the commando nodded. "Yes. But let me ask you what the end game really is."

"It is quite simple. Eventually, I intend to conquer the world."

GENERAL MAW NUYAUNG was anxious. He had been summoned back from his cleansing duty two hours ago, so sudden and abrupt, he had good reason to be-

lieve he wasn't going to be congratulated by the
higher-ranking generals for a job well done. They
wanted a full report, demanding answers, he suspected,
but he had nothing solid to tell the five ranking generals of the SLORC. The science detail was baffled, and
so terrified, they were quivering hunks of flesh inside
their space suits, he recalled, of whatever the still
unidentified contagion. Thus the horror he had put behind in the jungle only begged more disturbing questions, as far as he would be able to state. The crisis,
however, appeared to be contained, no word out of
Yangon that its citizens were dropping dead in the
streets. At least not that he was aware of. Perhaps, he
thought, no news was good news.

Flanked by two soldiers, he marched down the hallway of the SLORC supreme headquarters, heels clack-
ing along on the polished marble. It was a much shorter
walk into the conference room than he cared for, striding through the massive doors that were shut behind
him when he was no sooner two strides inside and
standing in front of them.

He hesitated a moment, trying to read the expressions on the faces of the five generals. Blank, but they
were peering oddly at him, Supreme General Phatun
indicating he should take a seat at the end of the table.
He moved, a bone in his knee cracking, sat. He felt his
nerves fraying in the silence, knew they were waiting
for him to speak, but it was taking great effort for him
to find his voice.

Nuyaung cleared his throat. "The crisis, it appears—"

General Phatun lifted a hand. "No need for a report, General Nuyaung. We know what the biological agent is, and we are aware of its origins."

Nuyaung found himself searching their faces, wondering if some sick joke was being played on him. "I do not understand. Our last contact—"

"Was of little or no consequence," General Nyat said.

"I do not understand," Nuyaung repeated, and the sharp look he drew from Phatun warned him to be silent.

"What happened out there," Phatun said, "was, shall I say, somewhat staged. We have been in talks with Germans who are in control of the most powerful cabal in Europe."

"The same Germans," Nuyaung said, "who came here recently and sought to purchase a large amount of merchandise?"

"It would be in your best interest," Phatun said, "to listen to us."

Nuyaung became even more confused as Phatun went on. What he heard was so incredible he began to think them all insane. And he also became resentful that the five of them had kept him in the dark about the clandestine arrangement with the Germans. When Phatun finished explaining the madness, Nuyaung could barely contain his outrage.

"Allow me to get this straight, my esteemed colleagues. You knew about the catastrophe up north?"

"We suspected it would happen," General Omwa stated.

"Suspected?" Nuyaung growled. "You either knew about it or you did not."

The blank stares again, then General Phatun said, "As supreme general of the SLORC, I did not send you on a fool's errand, I can assure you."

"I lost good soldiers, workers who will be difficult to replace, if not impossible. And you knowingly put me at risk of contamination. And you're telling me I am no fool? I am a colleague, a member of the SLORC, or have you forgotten? You kept this from me, and I am falling just short of telling you I feel betrayed."

"It was a calculated gamble," Phatun said. "We decided that only the five of us needed to know about the operation. You were not betrayed. You are a valuable asset, General Nuyaung. And now you know."

Nuyaung almost snorted. He thought about asking them if he was meant to be a scapegoat if somehow the contagion had spread farther south. They could lay the blame, then, on a renegade general acting on his own, publicly executed for his act of betrayal to Myanmar.

"The craft was supposed to have landed much farther north," General Mying said. "Deeper into rebel country."

"They could have just as easily dropped it in the

middle of Yangon." Nuyaung paused, reading their dark expressions, then it occurred to him what was going on. "Ah, I see. You allowed them, in secret, to use the Kachin as a testing ground. Or was it meant to be a genocide campaign of some sort? For what purpose did you agree to this? You wish to exchange merchandise for a craft…"

"It is actually a satellite," General Khatat said, "that can be programmed and controlled by computer from Earth to deorbit and crash wherever a target is selected."

"We have been in contact with the Germans," General Mying said. "They will be returning, General Nuyaung. You will be going back to the area—which, we've been informed by our scientists—is no longer a so-called hot zone."

"They will be receiving exactly six metric tons of merchandise," General Omwa stated.

This was more than Nuyaung could stomach. "First, my esteemed colleagues, the world at large, especially the American DEA, believes we actually hunt down and kill the rebels because we are supposed to be eradicating the drug problem, burning poppy fields and so forth. That is why we are not splattered all over world headlines as a rogue regime bent on becoming a major drug cartel."

"They—the DEA—know the truth about our control of the poppy fields and the production of heroin," General Phatun said. "They know we know, but they pretend they do not know. I suspect the American DEA's line of reasoning is that the rebels—who once controlled the poppy fields—will become so enraged over their loss of their cash crop they will band together, rise up, march on Yangon and hang us from the pillars out front."

"What about the Thais? The Laotians?"

Phatun shrugged. "Continue shipping to our friends across the border."

"If the Germans receive that much merchandise, then…"

"You will just have to pick up the pace of production," Phatun said.

"It will take time, of which there is none, if I am to meet the deadline."

"Then I suggest you return to the laboratory immediately," Phatun said.

"The Germans are coming." Nuyaung shook his head. "When is this…great event supposed to happen?"

Phatun shrugged. "A day, perhaps two at most."

"What, may I ask, are we getting in return?"

"Technology," Nyat said. "To eradicate the rebel problem, once and for all."

"We are promised," Khatat said, "a form of both biological and chemical agent in the form of an aerosol. No, we are not projecting ourselves into the space age. No satellites we will crash to Earth."

Nuyaung bobbed his head, looking at each of them

in turn when they fell silent. All things considered, it was a monstrous, ambitious scheme that could resolve the rebel problem. It could work, he decided, but only if they could trust the Germans.

"Understand," Phatun said, "had we believed you would have been contaminated by the agent, you would not now be sitting among us."

Nuyaung nodded. "Yes, I can believe that. Is there anything else I need to know?"

"You are current," Phatun said.

Nuyaung rose. "In that case, I had better return to the laboratory and resume production. You will let me know if events change?"

"You have our solemn promise," Phatun said.

Nuyaung wasn't sure about that, much less anything at the moment, but he spun on his heel and marched out of the room to carry out his duty.

HERMANN SCHWARZ WASN'T any tree hugger, but he found it somewhat a pity that the desert here had been so savaged by the government. Figure the Army Corps of Engineers had chopped down every saguaro, cactus, mesquite for three square miles at least, bulldozing the plateau until it was a barren flat brown stretch not even suitable for scorpions or rattlers. There were Indian reservations in the neighborhood, and Schwarz could only imagine how the native Americans felt about this rape of the land. Chalk up one more slap, he thought, by the pale faces. Progress, all in the name of technology.

They had landed at Tucson earlier, Lyons having mapped out an attack strategy during the flight, which, Schwarz thought, was little more than rattling the cages of whoever was the top brass, and they had at least one name to go on. Gathering up their waiting black GMC, they had motored west on I-8, perusing the aerial and satellite pics, final checks of weapons and gear. Using GPS, they hit the backcountry, east of Yuma, jouncing north over the desert, then catching one main paved road that cut through a one-horse town called Apache. One stop, then, at a lonely dive called the Apache Motel to dump off the heavier firepower before they ventured ahead. Any curious hands unzipping the war bags would get a face full of gas that would render them unconscious for at least twelve hours.

On the dirt track leading to Nutricen, Schwarz had seen the posted signs. Nothing so ominous as Area 51, the signs just stated Property Of U.S. Military—No Trespassing. They were without the threat of "authorized to use legal force," but now that they had secured a roost on a hill, several hundred yards east of the compound, Schwarz could tell they were serious about security at Nutricen-21.

There was no way they could keep the glare of the sun from perhaps winking off their binos as they surveyed the compound, their GMC parked in full view of roving and watching sentries, the vehicle baking and glistening under a blazing orange eye. Donning desert camous, they toted shoulder-holstered Berettas, Lyons opting to nurse his newfound enthrallment with the twin .45s. They had forged paperwork from the FDA and DOD, granting them access, the right—bogus—Justice Department credentials, even a phone number to the White House, but Schwarz wasn't so sure it would pass muster. He didn't see any grand tour of the facility in their future, especially if this was a black program where everyone had something to hide.

The compound itself, ringed in cyclone fencing topped with razor wire, sprawled for what Schwarz figured was two city blocks. He counted all the cameras on the fence, and he suspected there were likewise motion sensors, laser trackers hidden in the countryside. There were guard towers, wrapped in black glass, on the four points of the compass, and the Able Team commando figured they had already been spotted. Satellite dishes, radar towers and antennas lined the roof of the single building that seemed made of some silver material. There was a motor pool to the north, the area choked with GMCs, Humvees, transport trucks and eighteen-wheelers. South, there was a helipad with three Bell JetRangers, two executive jets. But it was the giant transport aircraft with the mailed-fist emblem on the fuselage that caught Schwarz's eye. He recalled seeing the same type of cargo plane from the intel package. EDEF was on-hand.

Lyons lowered his binos. "I take it you've seen more of our German comrades made the party?"

"Other than a full-frontal assault," Blancanales said, "any ideas on how we're going to get inside?"

"How about just walking right up to the front gate?" Lyons said. "The bad guys are here, this joint is black ops, and I don't give a damn if it's our people or not in charge. I'm intent on declaring war."

Schwarz was grinning when Lyons began waving at the troops assembling at the front gate.

"Hey, guys!" Lyons shouted. "Up here!"

"They might just turn us away, Carl," Blancanales pointed out.

"Nah."

"You sound pretty sure of yourself," Schwarz said, watching as men in black fatigues opened the gate, armed figures jumping on board Humvees. "Care to clue us in?"

Lyons cut a grin at his teammates, patted one of his .45s. "These are all the credentials I need."

"I'm looking at maybe a full platoon heading our way, Carl," Schwarz said. "What? Are we going to cowboy-and-Indian the action on this hill?"

Lyons shook his head. "No. I'll go for the diplomatic approach first."

"We're dead meat then," Schwarz remarked.

CHAPTER SIX

"Who the hell are these guys?"

It was a damn good question, but Henrik Aussen had his suspicions.

The former GSG-9 commando had put one mystery behind already, and the previous night's massacre of Skuber and his men back in Washington still haunted him with nagging questions, ghosts of nameless, faceless assassins dogging him all the way from their safe house in Bethesda to Crystal City to Arizona. With full diplomatic immunity stamped on themselves and their operation by their insiders at the U.S. State Department, they might have come to Washington—politicians, cops and Feds in the pockets of EDEF—but that hadn't prevented a bloodbath, which now swamped every waking moment with dire concern.

Someone—FBI, NSA or some covert operatives with a license to kill and who apparently didn't much

care how much clout SD wielded—were on the scent.
His orders from Frankfurt had been rearranged in light
of the murderous development, despite his voicing
reservations to Kluger how he should remain in Washington until the mystery about the slaughter was
solved.

The previous night, he recalled, the alarm had been
sounded by the hotel manager, who had both the fore-
sight—and cash advance—to stash the security tape
of the lobby, hand it off to him in the parking lot before the Arlington police had a chance to question
him. The tape had shown three men in trench coats,
clearly packing big guns, one of them carrying away
the girl who was in a drug-induced catatonia, the
bought-and-paid-for senator being shoved through the
lobby as if he were their prisoner. From the way in
which they had manhandled the senator, faces etched
in contempt, it had been clear they knew both the
truth about their political operative and weren't inclined to coddle the man just because he was a famous
lawmaker.

"Give me a close-up shot," Aussen ordered.

They were in the command and control room,
Aussen reacting moments ago to the intruder alarm—
a beeping pager on his belt—and now, one look at the
monitor, the hairs stood up on the back of his neck.

Three men on the ridge, he saw, toting side arms,
one of them urging the advancing security detail on-
ward, as if they were in charge.

And sent by some higher power.

Aussen watched as Director Bart Avery twisted the knob on the console, framing the trio so close on the monitor he could almost reach out and touch them.

He had never met these men, but their faces had been burned into memory.

It was them, the assassins of the previous night.

"Find out who they are and what they want," Aussen ordered Avery, the short and stocky Washington bureaucrat peering at him through his spectacles. "Then allow them to come inside."

"Look," Avery protested, "I may have my orders from DOD, and I don't know who the hell you and your men really are, but this is a classified…"

Aussen put his face kissing-close to Avery's. "That is correct, Director Avery. You have your orders. So do as I say. Extend those three men every courtesy."

Wheeling, Aussen barked in German for Schlesser and Wissmann to follow. Unless he missed his guess, Aussen believed it was just about time to put a war plan on the table.

"SLOWLY REMOVE and drop your weapons, and put your hands in the air."

Lyons took a step forward, men in black combat fatigues disgorging from Hummers and GMCs. He counted fourteen in all, H&K MP-5s drawing target acquisition, muzzles aimed up the incline, rock-steady.

He couldn't read the eyes behind the dark aviator shades, but there was no mistaking they meant to shoot to kill if pushed.

Instead of doing as he was ordered, Lyons pulled the thin wallet from his pants' pocket, flipped it open, resumed his march down the incline.

"One more step…"

"Special Agent Carl Lemon, United States Department of Justice. If you're going shoot, then shoot. But if you do, be advised this facility will be crawling with more federal agents than any criminal has ever seen in his worst nightmare. You will be shut down, and you, my friend, will be out of a black-ops job." He walked right up to the buzz cut in charge, holding out the credentials. "I want to speak to Director Avery. If he has any problem letting us in," Lyons said, pulling the forged paper with the DOD seal, unfolding it, "he is to call this number immediately."

The number, of course, was arranged by the Farm. If dialed it would go straight to a Justice Department man stationed at DOD, ready to field the call if necessary. Worst case, an aide to the President was on standby at the White House to relay the presidential directive that the three of them were to be given carte blanche at Nutricen. Lyons knew Brognola could perform miracles whenever a crisis arose.

The buzz cut lowered his subgun, snapping both the wallet and paperwork from Lyons.

"You can look all day, friend," Lyons said. "They're real. That DOD order didn't get run off by a copy machine at Kinko's."

Buzz Cut was distracted next, Lyons watching as the man keyed his com link. "Nut-leader here." Lyons glanced over his shoulder, caught the grin on Schwarz's face and could only imagine the smart remark dying to fly out of his mouth. "Yes, sir. Understood, sir."

Lyons waited as the Nut-leader signaled his men to lower their weapons.

"You are to follow in your vehicle. At this time you will be allowed to keep your sidearms. You will do as told or you will be dealt with. Nod if you understand."

"No sweat," Lyons said, and wondered why it all sounded too easy.

The safe bet, he believed, was the Germans were the real power in charge here at Nutricen.

AUSSEN BRISTLED with anger as he watched Avery give the three men the grand tour of the facility, the Washington issue fairly kissing ass, showing off whatever personal knowledge he had acquired about biotech food. The ex-GSG-9 commando watched the show on the monitors from the C and C room. Every inch of the laboratories, work cubicles and stations was covered, both video and audio. Aussen wasn't interested in the sight-seeing tour around the complex. No, there was something about the trio, the way they moved, took in

the facility with disdain and suspicion, sizing everything up as if they were searching for points of attack
or cover and concealment, that told Aussen they
weren't Justice agents as they claimed. Then what?
Professional soldiers? American assassins?

The Washington man babbled on about growth of
sorghum plants, known to be efficient at using sunlight
to produce sugar. He prattled on about the culturing of
microorganisms, how they were genetically engineering natural food and nutritional supplements and phar-
maceuticals, antioxidants to reduce risk of cancer,
cholesterol and heart disease. He was showing off the
giant centrifuges, 20,000 rpm, which would separate
individual particles in the micros, as proud as a new
father. He began talking about tomato plants—Indole-
3-ethanoic acid, which regulated all plant growth—
then stated how they were developing an advanced
high-protein material called "quorn" manufactured
from fungus grown on the waste from flour making,
when the big blond man stopped him in his tracks.

"This is all very interesting, Mr. Avery," the big
man said. "But how does infusing a Level Four virus
into food fit the program here?"

If they had been on the radar screen before, Aussen
heard the Klaxons wailing now.

"E-excuse me?" Avery sputtered.

"I saw the EDEF transport plane parked outside,"
the big man went on.

"W-well, yes, we have a contract to deliver our

product to Germany. It seems they are interested in bioengineering of food…"

"Cut the crap, Avery. The Germans haven't gone a day without a square fat meal since three years after World War II. And EDEF is interested in way more than just feeding the poor and starving out of compassion and concern for their fellow man. We know you are also shipping satellite technology to EDEF—that would be attack satellite technology—so I'm thinking there's a lot more going on here than the simple breeding of microorganisms."

"Why, Agent Lemon, what you are implying—"

"Is preposterous? I don't think so. I've seen spook projects before. And, for now, I've seen enough. You're only going to show us what you want to show us, anyway. Tell you what. The three of us are going to stay the night at the Apache Motel a few miles south of here. Room 6. I'm thinking by tomorrow morning you're going to have a battalion of Justice and FBI agents and FDA specialists swarming this facility."

"This is highly—"

"Irregular? You could damn well say that. I need a number where I can reach you. The tour's over for the day."

Aussen watched as Avery wrote something on a card, the big man snapping it out of his fingers.

"One other thing," he heard the big man say, looking up and right into the camera. "I know your German pals have full diplomatic immunity to peddle flesh, sell drugs and commit extortion and murder. I know they're here, and I can feel them watching. Whatever their sordid business with Nutricen, we're here to shut them down. End of story."

That was all Aussen needed to hear. Confirmation of the enemy, and now it was his turn to act.

"OPEN THE goddamn gate."

Lyons was forced to bark the order again before one of the hardmen hit a button on the panel to electronically swing the gates open. He was leading his teammates onto the plateau, toward their GMC when he spotted Schwarz and Blancanales looking back.

"Relax," Lyons told them. "It won't happen here."

"So we sleep with one eye open?" Blancanales said.

"I don't think we'll be sleeping tonight," Lyons answered. "I issued the challenge and I'm hoping the EDEF stormtroopers here bite the bait. If they do, we'll be making a most unpleasant return trip tonight."

"These guys, Carl," Schwarz said, "they're black ops, but they're still Americans."

"So? They're dirty," Lyons growled. "American or not, I hope you're not saying you'll have a problem pulling the trigger when the time comes."

"None at all," Schwarz said.

AUSSEN WAS HANDING out the orders to Schlesser's team, his commandos checking the loads on their H&K subguns and Glocks when Avery launched into a protest.

"This is insanity! What if they really are from the Justice Department? You can't just shoot them! I'll have more Feds, more warrants—"

"Silence!" Aussen waved the hit team away, watched as they filed out of the conference room. "I know when I see professional fighting men. More, I have confirmed to my satisfaction they are here to terminate not just myself and my men, but this entire project."

"Terminate?"

"Destroy the facility, Herr Avery."

"Why?"

"What you do not know is a lot. Now, I am putting the compound on full alert. Your security force is to follow my orders, no matter how outrageous they seem. In the meantime, I want you to supervise the loading of merchandise onto our plane."

"B-but…"

Aussen cracked a backhand over Avery's face. "Understand something, Herr Avery. Those three men— they just declared war on Nutricen."

Avery was rubbing his cheek, anger in his stare, his lips working in silent outrage.

"Yes, that is correct. War."

LYONS BELIEVED it wasn't a question of if, but when the EDEF heavy hitters would come calling. He was togged in a blacksuit to meld in with the night, and his trench coat concealed the twin .45s as he walked into the four-stool diner. Carrying the leather sheath that housed his SPAS-12 autoshotgun, he marched for the counter, pulling out the wad of hundred-dollar bills from Able Team's war funds. The man he assumed owned the diner-motel complex wasn't much on conversation, as Lyons earlier found out, and he hoped that held true now. The fewer questions he had to answer, the better. About the only two upshots Lyons could see at the moment were the remoteness of the motel and the fact there were no other guests to sound the alarm to county lawmen.

It was impossible to guess the old-timer's heritage and his age, but Lyons figured the desert sun and isolation had taken its toll on his burnished, leathery face. Nursing a beer, he sat behind the counter, watching some sitcom about a shoe salesman who could never catch a break.

Lyons got down to business. "Some men may come here looking for the three of us."

Leatherman grunted.

"Tell them we're in Room 6 if they do."

Another grunt and Lyons peeled off a thousand dollars. There was just enough narrowing of Leatherman's gaze to tell Lyons he had his undivided attention.

"That's yours."

"Too much. Three rooms."

"That's just-in-case money."

"Of what?"

"Any damages."

Leatherman took the money. "From the base?"

"Yeah."

"Nothing ever really changes. They still come here, take more land, destroy land that used to belong to the red man. Soon there will be no more red man."

"Soon, you may not have to worry about them."

Leatherman reached under the counter, pulled out an ancient Winchester rifle. "They come here to kill you?"

"It's a reasonable guess they will try just that."

"Need help?"

"I'll let you know something."

Lyons heard his tac radio crackle as Schwarz came on. "Carl. Look alive. They're here." The Able Team leader was at the bug-smeared window, saw two GMCs pull in, flanking their own vehicle. Six armed shadows disgorged. Four EDEF stormtroopers were at the door to Room 6, flanking it, ready, Lyons guessed, to kick it down and go in blazing, while two more hardmen marched toward the diner.

Lyons knew if they were successful in terminating three pesky G-men, they wouldn't leave the owner behind as a witness.

"You know what to do," Lyons told both Schwarz and Blancanales. When they copied, Lyons made his way behind the counter and crouched. "Just stay cool, old-timer."

"Cool as a mountain breeze, pale face."

SOMETIMES IT WAS a perfect world, after all, Hermann Schwarz thought, even when their fearless leader was winging the action by the seat of his pants.

Pit bulls, he considered, but for some reason it fit, and he had to begrudge that he sort of liked Brognola's tag.

No sooner had he navigated a hundred yards south of the motel, taken concealment in a shallow crevice burrowed into the earth than two GMCs rolled out of the darkness. Lights doused, they vectored straight for Able Team's vehicle. They parked, port and starboard of their GMC, hardmen in black falling out. Four for Room 6 and two—one with a big shotgun—striding for the diner, presumably to silence any witnesses.

Schwarz knew they were in for a nasty deadly greet.

Lyons had just ventured into the diner, paying for any vandalism in advance, and Blancanales was tucked away in Room 5.

So far, it looked a perfect ambush.

Schwarz rose up on a knee, swung the muzzle of his H&K 33 assault rifle with infrared telescopic sight around the base of the Joshua tree, finger taking up slack on the trigger. He framed one buzz-cut bullethead in the crosshairs just as a hardman kicked in the door to Room 6 and went in blasting.

THE H&K ASSAULT RIFLE pumped out 5.56 mm rounds, one at a time. Schwarz was chasing hardman Number

Four with tracking fire, searching for one opening, but the GMCs blocked any clean shot.

"Dammit!"

At first it looked a quick and neat wrap from where Blancanales crouched, three goons spiraling, bouncing off flesh and metal in the opening rounds before toppling in boneless sprawls, then the bastard with the combat shotgun began tearing up the Able Team warrior's position with roaring 12-gauge decimators. With chunks of wall and doorjamb blown into his face, Blancanales was chased to deep cover, momentarily out of the fight. The goon triggered the shotgun on the back-pedal, perhaps combat instinct taking over, as he ducked from Schwarz's sights.

Schwarz pumped out three rounds, blasting away the back window, the shots capped off, more for effect than any real effort to score flesh, but he hoped to keep the EDEF hardman pinned until he could advance, close the steel net. Before Schwarz could draw target acquisition, he saw the goon hurl open the passenger door, dive inside, escaping his gunsights. It was a fleeting glimpse, but Schwarz spotted the tac radio in the enemy's hand.

Great, he thought.

Nutricen would either be on full alert or they would roll out a tidal wave of hitters.

Schwarz advanced, heard the din of weapons fire from the diner. He knew the three of them were in for a long night.

Perhaps the night and the fight of their lives.

LYONS SAW the old-timer rise from his stool, his mouth opening. But the only sound was the stammer of auto-fire and the boom of a shotgun.

If nothing else, judging the racket of weapons fire outside, Lyons knew where the three of them stood with Nutricen. They were marked for extinction.

Good enough.

First, they'd take care of these bastards who had ridden here to punch their tickets, and then Lyons determined Nutricen, American black ops and their German counterparts would pony up for this blitz.

Somehow the old-timer had to have seen it coming; Lyons watching as Leatherman ducked just as the first wave of bullets and buckshot ripped into the wall, the television exploding in a cloud of sparks and smoke. The Winchester rifle had gone down with the old-timer, Lyons noting the rage in his eyes.

They kept on blasting away, doughnut trays, the soda fountain disappearing in cyclones of debris and flying liquid.

Lyons knew they were closing fast and hard, the counter erupting to his side with gaping holes, the floor shuddering beneath rubber-soled combat boots with the assault. The Able Team leader lurched to the edge of the counter, senses shattered by the deafening fusillade, aware he had maybe two seconds or less to make a move. Sure, they had drawn the enemy in, six hardcases, but if there were more goons on tap and on the way...

Stow it, do it now!

Lyons thrust the SPAS around the corner, reared up and hit the trigger. At point-blank range, the blast caught the EDEF hardman with the H&K subgun square in the chest. It was enough to pull the angry attention of the goon with the shotgun his way, as the torn scarecrow that was his comrade was launched back through the window.

Lyons was tracking on when rifle shots rang out. The EDEF shotgunner was snarling, spinning as Lyons glimpsed the old-timer jacking the Winchester's action, tunneling two more rounds through his chest. A spasm pull of the Benelli shotgun had the ceiling gouged out above his head. Lyons blew him off his feet with a 12-gauge eviscerator.

All done here, Lyons thought, checking the old-timer and finding him still standing, but the fight wasn't over.

SCHWARZ BROKE into a jog as the GMC's engine gunned to life. He could see the top of the goon's head as he keyed the ignition, then the shadow ducked out of sight. Schwarz couldn't make out the words, but he'd seen enough of the enemy's mouth working overtime to know the Nutricen base was being updated, the headshed more than likely tuned in to all the deafening sound and fury of the gun battle.

Schwarz fell into a line with the GMC's rear, squeezing the H&K's trigger, coring two more rounds through the interior.

Blancanales shuddered into view, his Uzi spraying lead, rounds tattooing the door, but the EDEF hardman was hell-bent on going out with anything but a whimper.

The shotgun roared from near the wheel, interior lighting up from the muzzle-flash, the driver's window blown out, as Schwarz kept cutting the distance. Whether he was suddenly mirrored in the rear glass or the hardman had seen him marching in, Schwarz couldn't say. He was nearly on top of the GMC when the massive combat shotgun swung around and began thundering. Schwarz flung himself to the side as the storm of 12-gauge flesh-shredders breezed past his ear.

Schwarz hit the ground, rolling, sucking on gas fumes as he saw the wheels churn, bumper aimed to smash in his face, the GMC looming into a giant slab of steel meant to turn him into dead meat. He was rolling hard, away from the path of the GMC, when he heard shotgun blasts and the familiar stammer of an Uzi subgun. He was on his feet, backpedaling to the side of the GMC, triggering his H&K for all he was worth, raking the vehicle, stem to stern. Then he saw the shadow slump over the wheel, deadweight lying on the horn as the GMC rolled past.

"Anybody hit?"

Schwarz found a smaller shadow with a rifle trailing Lyons. A few strides toward the GMC, as it bumped to a halt against a Joshua tree, and Schwarz called, "I'm cool."

Blancanales was touching his face. "Just a couple of scratches. I'll live."

Schwarz reached inside the GMC, shoved the body off the wheel. He listened to the ringing in his ears, found Lyons talking with the owner, then the Able Team leader was marching toward their GMC.

"Saddle up, guys," Lyons said. "The fun's only just started."

CHAPTER SEVEN

Aussen didn't need to be there to know Schlesser and crew were dead. The sounds of grunts, gunshots, glass shattered and tinkling through the hurricane of bellows and shotgun blasts in the GMC were still echoing death knells in his ears.

EDEF, he knew, was finished on American soil, but Kluger had pretty much alluded to that as of the last radio transmission. They were clearly under siege. War had been declared on them by the same nameless assassins from back east, and Aussen could only speculate on how much damage might be inflicted on the organization if their agenda had been dragged out of the closet. It was time to bail, either way, but first he intended to follow through with his orders from Frankfurt.

Burn Nutricen to the ground.

It was insane, he considered, how the operation had

fallen apart so sudden and swift. And back home in the Fatherland, they appeared to be pulling up the drawbridge. That was the problem with secrets, he thought. A secret only remained so if only one person knew the secret. He could only imagine the wagging tongues back east now, the shaky alliance coming unraveled as their American operatives were cornered, a fire put to their feet, squealing out the truth as they knew it.

Three men, stalking them here, from almost three thousand miles away, their orders obviously to take down EDEF, sans handcuffs and arrest warrants. It stood to reason, he knew, someone had turned on them back in D.C., pointing fingers of blame, seeking to save their own skin. Perhaps the senator had been forced to talk. Perhaps whoever these assassins worked for had dropped a noose over the heads of their people at the State Department. It didn't matter now: all hell had broken loose. In times of war, he thought, improvising was the mother of necessity, if a soldier intended to live to fight another day. A yearly, fat, six-figure salary didn't mean much if he wasn't around to spend it.

They were in Warehouse A, forklifts trundling about, scooping up crates stamped with the mailed fist, Aussen impatient to board his plane and put this country behind before the firestorm blew his way. There was an air of panic in the massive storage bays, he sensed. Americans throwing around confused looks at Avery, eyeing foreigners armed to the teeth, his men barking orders.

"Faster!" Aussen shouted at the American work-force as they dawdled slipping the tongues of a fork-lift under a crate. "Goddammit, move! Stupid, lazy Americans," he muttered in German.

He held his ground, felt the tac radio trembling in his hand as he hooked it to his belt. Small comfort now, but there was one-hundred-percent confirmation that the three men were professional soldiers—or assassins. How they had ambushed and wiped out six of the best commandos on the planet, he couldn't even begin to fathom. He'd attempted to raise the others on the hit team, but had been greeted with only radio silence. A quick mental tally and he had ten commandos left standing. Would they be enough if the complex came under attack? The trio of assassins, he knew, would be coming for his scalp. He would do the same—if only in the name of vengeance and professional pride—were he in their place.

Aussen marched to the open bay doors, watched as the machines rolled up the ramp to deposit the crates in the belly of the transport. They had come here, primarily, to take the supercircuitry of the mother-boards back to Frankfurt, and the critical technology had been the first to be loaded. There were other com-ponent parts for the attack satellites being hauled away from the warehouse, still other crates packed with ar-tificial food and nutrients that would be contaminated with the virus once they landed at the sister facility in Spain.

"Open the gate!" Aussen shouted at Avery, thrusting the muzzle of his MP-5 west, indicating the section of fencing that should part so they could fly on.

He saw the fencing open after Avery gave the order over his handheld radio, then marched away from the wind that pounded in his face from the spinning turboprops. Striding back into the warehouse, he checked his watch, figured Hartzig and Kruger had nearly finished mining the facility.

"What the hell is going on?"

Aussen knew the man in black fatigues only as the Colonel. From the beginning he could tell the American didn't appreciate being relegated as second-string to foreigners. Tough. He would do as he was told or Aussen would gun him down on the spot.

Aussen rolled up to the man, braked several feet from him. "What part of my order did you not understand?"

"The shoot-to-kill part. Those three men are from the United States Department of Justice, and I'll be damned if I gun down Feds on your order."

Aussen was waving Avery over to make sure his order was carried out when the explosion rumbled. The thunder pealed from the east, the direction in which the trio had arrived the first time. A glance at his watch and he knew it was too soon for the demolition team to have placed all the C-4 packages. The mystery assassins were here to ante up.

Avery appeared set to faint. "What's happening?"

Aussen noted the fear and confusion on the faces of the Americans, smiled at the Colonel as he unslung his H&K subgun. "Any more questions?"

LYONS OPTED for the straight charge up the gut. He knew it wouldn't be the first time Stony Man had gone up against an American black-ops facility, ready to shoot down men who had betrayed their oath and their country. Whether the black ops here were knowingly holding hands with the devil, he couldn't say. But he figured the home-team heroes at least suspected they were guarding more than just a facility that bioengineered food and satellite technology.

If they played, he determined, they paid the price.

Moments ago, they had surveyed the facility from their previous roost on the ridge, Lyons laying out a sketchy attack plan at best. With the flurry of activity on the runway, coupled with the failed hit, Lyons knew EDEF was packing up. They would be on high alert, and Lyons suspected the standing order was to shoot to kill.

Fine. They weren't back for another tour of Nutricen.

With Schwarz at the wheel, Lyons watched as their GMC cut the gap to the main gate, spotlights flaring on from the guard tower, enveloping the vehicle in a blinding white sheen. Squinting, Lyons spotted a few shadows roving about in the no-man's land that led to the east entrance.

"You two," Lyons said to his teammates, gripping his M-16/M-203 combo, slipping the SPAS-12 around his shoulder, "that plane does *not* take off. That bird is your responsibility to keep grounded, whatever it takes. I've got a mental map of the complex, so I'll hit the place from the east, move in on the warehouse, drive out whatever the competition. If it's armed, it's history—no exceptions. *If* possible, I want to take that bird down with whatever its ordnance. *If* possible, I want to bag one of the Germans. We'll worry about what's next when we commandeer the plane."

Schwarz tapped the brakes, as planned, and Lyons bulled out the back door. The GMC racing ahead to crash the gate, Lyons triggered the M-203. There was a brief sputter of subgun fire from the guard tower, then the shell was lost in a roaring blossom of fire.

Lyons dumped another 40 mm round down the chute, charged on as the GMC barreled through the front gate. On the fly, Lyons began dousing the spotlights with short bursts of autofire.

FROM THE SHOTGUN seat, Blancanales aimed Little Bulldozer out the window, squeezed off two 40 mm hellbombs at the pack of hardmen vectoring for their rampage. The windshield absorbed a few hits, the glass spider-webbing, Schwarz cursing as the twin blasts cleared the way to the airfield.

Blancanales looked back, found Lyons sweeping the grounds with autofire, nailing a shadow here and there. He spotted another four or five hardmen—German or American, and at this point both sides were fair game—spilling through the east doorway. At another tap of the trigger, the 40 mm warhead zigged on and Blancanales cleared the door of opposition for Lyons to penetrate.

Blancanales swiveled his head, checking for hardmen on all points of the compass. Their previous quick surveillance had shown them that the bulk of the armed forces were busy loading the EDEF transport. Blancanales found that was holding true when Schwarz barreled around the corner, rocketed the GMC toward the helipad.

"Dump me off, Gadgets!"

"What for?"

"I'll draw fire. Try to make your way from the choppers to the rear of that bird. You go port, I go starboard. We make the cargo bay, toss in some flash-stuns!"

"How about that prisoner Carl wanted?"

"That's what I'm hoping for."

"Hope? If I didn't know any better, I'd think you're staying up late at night reading the Ironman manual on how to make war."

"That's scary."

Blancanales snugged the Uzi higher up his shoulder, rode out the hard drive as Schwarz slid in behind the choppers. Little Bulldozer in hand, he was out the door, drawing target acquisition on the maw to the warehouse. They were flailing about in the opening, voices raised in anger and panic, forklifts scooting away from the transport plane, the legitimate workforce, he supposed, running for cover.

Blancanales went to one knee, crouched under the tail of the chopper. Hell with it, he told himself, and began chugging out the murderous payloads.

"WHAT ARE you doing?"

Lyons was blowing two hardmen off their feet, hosing them down, left to right, kicking them through the window to an office, when he heard the commotion around the corner. Ahead, beyond the widening expanse of the main corridor, he found utter bedlam in the first series of workbays. Technicians in white lab coats were scurrying all over the place, a siren wailing its shrill din throughout the complex. He wondered why he had encountered little armed resistance during his first hundred feet or so of penetration down the main corridor, but combat instinct warned him that that was about to change.

There was a loud but brief argument dead ahead; a voice barking in German then switching to English. He heard the burp of a subgun, another voice shouting, "Are you insane?"

Lyons hit the corner and took in the problem.

Two hardmen were scything down a group of men in lab coats. They were falling, shredded red ruins, when Lyons saw the block of plastic explosive fixed to a centrifuge. The facility was mined to get blown clear across the Mexican border.

The demo duo was wrapping up its execution when Lyons held back on the trigger of his M-16. It was a long burst, punching scarlet holes in their chests, sloppy crucifixions to the centrifuge for a moment, blood spraying then dribbling down the steel tube. They were sliding down the centrifuge, eyes bugged with shock and horror, when Lyons reached the C-4 block. The timer was set for three minutes, and ticking. How many had they planted? He considered keying the com link to warn his teammates, but they were at least beyond ground zero. Or so he hoped. Factor in they were most likely engaged in a shooting war…

Lyons decided to stick with the plan. Slapping a fresh magazine into his assault rifle, he moved into the workbays, shouldered his charge through a group of lab workers. Between the stampede, the shouting and the siren, the noise alone might have bowled him off his feet under other circumstances, he thought.

Right now he had problems way beyond an ear-splitting din and the razor's edge of ringing in his ears.

On the run, Lyons shouted at the workforce, "Get outside! This whole place is going to blow up!"

AUSSEN ROSE FROM the ground, his brain spiked with white-hot pain, the sounds of battle a distant fractured maze of noise that seemed to float down from outer space. The world was a shimmering mist in his sight, thanks to the concussive wallop of the explosions rocking the warehouse. Three bastards, he thought, had wreaked all this mayhem. If he hadn't seen it with his own eyes, he would have laughed at the absurdity of it all. Where were they now?

He searched the runway, the helipad, wobbling ahead, aware he was exposing himself to the enemy. But what choice did he have? If he sought concealment in the warehouse, he would get dissected by the hellstorm tearing through the bays. The obvious problem next was to reach the plane in one piece, but the nameless attackers had added two and two on that score, were seeking to keep the transport bird on the ground...

Or worse, blow it out of the air.

There was no option but to board and get the plane up and gone.

H&K subgun in hand, he spotted the shadow perched beneath the tail of a chopper. The explosions were no longer ripping apart the night. Were they out of high-explosive rounds or were they luring him into another trap?

Aussen spied the open hatch on the fuselage, willed strength into his legs as he broke across open ground, triggering his subgun. The shadow disappeared, sparks flashing from the concrete and the metal tail of the chopper as he chased the enemy to cover. There was hope yet, Aussen thought, heart pounding like a jackhammer in his ears, adrenaline clearing out the sludge in his limbs. The hatch appeared a mile away, but he was gaining on the bird, his eyes searching the helipad for any sign of movement.

Gathering speed, Aussen braced for bullets to tear into his flesh, but the next thing he knew he was up the short ladder, in the fuselage. He spotted four of his men, grouped at the top of the ramp, backs pressed to the wall, subguns aimed at the night.

"What are you waiting for?" Aussen shouted, striding toward the cargo bay. "Get that ramp up!"

He was tugging the tac radio off his belt, lifting it to his mouth, thumbing the button to tell his pilots to get them in the air when the world exploded in his face.

SCHWARZ, THE NYLON BAG with the satellite equipment slapping between his shoulder blades, hit the ramp beside Blancanales. Two flash-stuns had already been pitched into the cargo bay, a supernova of blinding light and noise that would turn the senses to mush. Schwarz wanted to believe they were in the home stretch.

Through the drifting smoke, he found four hardmen reeling around the crates, homed in on the gagging and retching, then squeezed off two 3-round bursts at enemies who appeared little more than drunken stick figures. Blancanales followed up with a short Uzi sweep of three and four, bowling them over the crates with a double figure eight to their chests.

Schwarz began to doubt they would bag a live one,

then saw the figure crawling on the floorboards as he cleared the last crate.

"Pol!" Schwarz said, sweeping over the enemy, banging the H&K's butt off the back of his head to keep him down. "You want to sit on him while I take the cockpit?"

Blancanales caught the nylon bag. "Do it! I'll check on Carl."

Schwarz fixed gaze and weapon on the cockpit hatch. The EDEF transport bird, from what he could see, was designed, inside and out, much like the American C-130. The cockpit, elevated at the top of the ladder, could hold a five-man crew. Schwarz fed his assault rifle a fresh clip, hauled himself up the ladder. The handle didn't budge.

The hard way, then, and Schwarz pounded the lock catch with six rounds. A boot heel into the steel partition, kicking it in, and he glimpsed the pistol flying his way from the copilot seat. A lurch to the side, bullets spanging metal, then Schwarz stuck the muzzle around the edge. He held the mental picture of the shooter in his mind, capped off a 3-round burst where the copilot was grandstanding. A sharp grunt, then Schwarz swung into the hatchway, ready to mow down the rest of the crew.

"No shoot!"

Cautious, Schwarz stepped into the cockpit, found the pilot standing, hands up. He glanced at the copilot, slumped over the console, blood and brain matter dribbling down the window. He figured a lie right about now was in order.

"Get stupid, Hans, and I can fly this ship myself. Give me a *ja,* if you understand."

"*Ja,* you are the boss."

LYONS DIDN'T KNOW what to expect when he made the warehouse, but he found still more pandemonium waiting.

He vectored toward the bay door, M-16 sweeping the warehouse, but all hands appeared more interested in flight. Lyons keyed his com link, noting the shredded remains of hardmen strewed near the maw. He took that as a good sign, sniffed the cordite in the air, figuring Blancanales had done some housecleaning with the multiround projectile launcher.

"Pol! Gadgets! Talk to me!"

Lyons took the update on the run, watching his own six as he beelined for the fuselage hatch, ordering the ramp closed. Bounding inside, he told Gadgets to get them in the air.

"Where should I tell Hans to take us?"

"Just get us up! I'll let you know something," Lyons growled. "And eighty-six that transponder."

"Aye, aye, skipper."

They were rolling when Lyons heard the first series of rumbles from deep in the bowels of Nutricen. There was nothing he could have done to clear the place of noncombatants, but that didn't take the edge off his anger. Even still, he found white-clad lab workers and what he assumed was basic labor scattering pell-mell for the front gate.

"Sons of bitches," Lyons muttered as a section of the roof was blown into the sky by the firestorm.

"Carl!"

Lyons slammed the hatch shut as the transport plane gathered speed, floorboards slanting as it went nose up. He found Blancanales standing over a prisoner.

"One of EDEF's stormtroopers," Blancanales said.

Lyons spotted the blood trickling out of his nose and ears. "What the hell happened to him?"

"Flash-stun, that's what happened."

Lyons showed their prisoner a mean grin. "I hope that flash-stun didn't affect his mouth."

Blancanales fastened the plastic cuffs on the German's wrists. A quick frisk of the man gleaned a thin wallet, which he flipped to Lyons.

"'AN AIDE, we are told, found Senator Sheebl's body, at about 10:00 p.m. last night. It is believed the Illinois senator died from a self-inflicted gunshot wound to the head, but this has not yet been confirmed. Now, the FBI, D.C. Homicide and also agents from the Justice Department are inside—'"

Brognola had seen and heard enough. He snapped off the wall monitor, killing the image of the reporter on the Capitol steps.

Alone in the War Room, the big Fed already felt the

ghosts of this latest mission piling up, swarming the void, stalking him wherever he went. How many would die, he wondered, the innocent and the guilty, before this was over? It was one of the questions that dogged his every waking moment when a campaign was launched. Even he, Brognola thought, was allowed to indulge grave doubt and anxiety once in a while. As long as he did it in private, didn't let it affect his job, or the mission. Well, he was only flesh and blood. Even those with the authority to make war—albeit secret and dirty—against the enemies of the United States suffered through the occasional moments of self-doubt and angst. Or so he reasoned this troubling moment.

He sipped from yet another cup of coffee, worked on his cigar. Suddenly he felt strangely disembodied. It happened like that, he knew, when the stress ground him down. Pile on little or no sleep, too much caffeine, figure the years, too, were catching up to him and...

Waiting, like now, was always the hardest part, but it came with the job. Sometimes he wished he was back out there on the front lines. At least in the trenches, he was in the mix, in real time, not hanging around by the phone, anxious for a report, thumbs up or down from the troops. Now, unless he was fielding and sifting through intelligence or handing out the orders behind his desk, he could no longer call the action on the spot.

To accept or to regret? he wondered, but already

knew the answer. Funny what happens, he thought, when a man travels a few dark roads, manages— through either luck, his own will or by the guiding hand of some unseen cosmic forces—to walk out the other side. To learn. And to accept.

The last he heard, Phoenix Force was in the air, hours away from the Company-Special Forces base in Kenya. No word from Able Team, but usually he took no news about them as good news. There was always a first time, a whopping "however" where…

Well, where any of the Stony Man warriors were concerned. No matter how skilled, how experienced they were, there was always the possibility of a bullet out there with one of their names on it.

It was the nature of the beast in their world of never-ending war.

The intercom buzzed with Price's voice. "Yes."

"I just saw it on CNN."

"He took the easy way out."

"Suicides normally do, Hal. They don't feel they have a choice."

"There's always a choice. Senator Sheebl is no longer our problem, or anybody else's for that matter. What do you have?"

"We are picking up real-time imagery from a CIA Predator in the Somali AIQ."

"Phoenix?"

"About four hours and change ETA for Alpha Base. The AWACS we scrambled out of Frankfurt through my NSA contacts is tracking the EDEF cargo plane. It looks like we're on for Somalia."

"When?"

Brognola rubbed his face, listened to the logistical layout, zero hour for Phoenix Force's launch. He hated juggling time zones, forced to check his watch against the wall clocks over the world map.

"That would be what, Barb? Just after nightfall, their time?"

"It's the soonest we can get them in place and moving. And Aaron needs another hour or so before we can park an NRO satellite over the AIQ. By then we'll be online with the new Delta One Program."

Brognola grunted. The Farm had undergone renovations recently, upgrading supertech in the Computer Room to ultratech. Delta One, he knew, was a computer satellite-relay program created by the cyber wizards. The warriors of Phoenix Force would go into battle, with both audio and visual satellite transmission to the Farm. Beyond that, there were the sensor belts each of them would wear, capable of picking up body heat from as far away as a hundred yards. Transponders, of course, would be worn by the five Phoenix Force warriors, marking them off on the screens of the cyber team to eliminate friendly casualties.

War, he thought, was about to come to the Farm yet again, live and in color. Delta One, though, wasn't any prime-time drama, popcorn and beer for the couch potatoes. It had been created to aid and assist the Stony

Man warriors, and it just might save lives since no warrior, no matter how good, could see it all when it hit the fan.

"What about Able?"

"I just now heard from them."

Brognola felt his spine tighten. "And?"

"You might want to get down here, Hal."

"Can you tell me why I don't like the sound of that?"

LYONS SHOOK HIS HEAD at the prisoner, glanced at the photo ID again, then slipped the thin wallet into his pants' pocket. "You guys. I don't get it. I mean, who the hell at State gives full blanket immunity for a bunch of German nationals, a gun-toting pack of killers, pimps and drug dealers like the ones we left back east, to come here and take charge of a classified U.S. military base?"

Lyons had just updated the Farm, informed them of what he wanted to do next, which was ride the commandeered EDEF transport to wherever the end of the line was. They'd get back to him, Price said, so he had a few minutes at least to grill one Henrik Aussen.

A nod to Blancanales and the two Able Team warriors flanked Aussen, their prisoner scowling, clearly uncomfortable with his hands bound behind his back, seated and pressed to the bulkhead.

"*Sprechen ze English?*"

"Of course, asshole."

Lyons looked at Blancanales, chuckled. "Oh, I love this guy already." Lyons pressed the muzzle of the SPAS against Aussen's forehead. "I won't kill you, 'sport.'" A blink of the eyes had Lyons nodding. "That's right. Your buddy, Herr Greer, the one with the frizzy do, calls everybody 'sport.' Don't worry, his day's coming. But this is your fifteen minutes of fame, Henrik. This is how it works. I ask questions—I ask once—you answer. No, I won't kill you outright." Lyons aimed the SPAS at Aussen's foot. "I'll just take you apart, from the feet up. I know something about treating wounds, even amputations, so I can keep you alive for hours before I bleed you out. How much do you like pain?"

Blancanales squatted beside Aussen. His nickname was "Politician," and he had a knack for winning the hearts and minds of the enemy through gentle psychological persuasion.

"Listen," Blancanales began. "You have a chance— a slim one—to keep on breathing. We know about what happened in Somalia and Myanmar. We know about the senator. We know someone at the State Department is fronting for you. It's over for you and your team here in America. Help yourself. Do you have a family?"

Aussen's lips twisted, his gaze flickering away from Blancanales. "Had. A wife. I have two sons. Somewhere."

"Do you ever think about seeing your children?"

"What is this? Good commando, bad commando?"

"This is no game," Blancanales said. "Do you want to see your children again?"

Aussen seemed to think about something. "How? Are you offering me some deal?"

"Work with us," Blancanales said. "I can work something out where you don't spend the rest of your life in an American prison."

"Like what? Your Witness Protection Program?"

"We know someone high up in the Justice Department. He can arrange it."

"Can I trust you?"

"I don't see where you have much choice. But if I say it can be done, it will be done. Of course, it all depends on how much you help us."

Lyons could see the German's mind working, the man fighting to keep hope alive.

"Very well. What is it you want to know?"

"First, where's this bird headed?" Lyons asked.

"Spain."

"EDEF sister facility, the one south of Madrid."

"Yes."

Lyons keyed his com link. "Gadgets."

"I haven't gone anywhere, Carl."

"Don't get smart. Tell the pilot we're making an overseas flight. Spain."

"That's going to be kind of tough, unless you plan on swimming there."

"What?"

"We're down two-thirds on fuel."

Lyons scowled. "Okay. Head for Washington. I'll let you know something in a few minutes." Turning back to Aussen, he said, "You were saying?"

"The ones at the State Department," Aussen said, and recited a phone number. "That was our cutout. I never met the man, but I heard him called the Illuminating One. There is a group, a black-ops circle within the State Department, they call themselves the Elite...."

CHAPTER EIGHT

David McCarter briefly thought about Somalia, and simply running the name through his mind conjured up one word, one image.

Somalia equaled Hell on Earth.

Phoenix Force was ready to dive off the ramp of the C-130, and the bowels of hell were fifteen thousand feet below. Beyond tactical high-tech support from the Farm and their CIA ride, with the Predator running back real-time imagery of the AIQ to the blacksuits in the comm center of the bird, they were on their own, the jaws of a lawless country poised to snap shut, grind them up if they didn't go the distance.

Well, the Briton considered, Somalia wasn't that lawless, if he wanted to count the Muslim law of Shari'a as the order of the day. Which meant thieves had their hands cut off, rapists castrated, adulterers smashed to pulp by stone-throwing crowds. Beyond that, there was no central government, just a bunch of clans—which meant fractured extended families running amok and slaughtering one another—seizing whatever food, women, guns and *qat* they could with the help of an AK-47. If Somalia couldn't claim permanent residence by the Four Horsemen of the Apocalypse, McCarter thought, then human suffering was just a bad sadistic joke played on humankind by the Cosmos. He had to wonder, in a land that gave new horrible meaning to genocide, starvation, plague, murder and mayhem, if God had abandoned Somalia.

Or was it the other way around?

The yellow light flashed on the bulkhead and Manning punched the button to lower the ramp. Each man had rigged his own chute, main weapons in hand but fixed to a bootstrap for when they jumped. The latest in battlefield high-tech, the sensor belts were snug around their waists. They were divided into four sections, north, south, east and west. Batteries for belts, GPS handheld units and the mini-video cams that would be Velcroed to their shoulders, had been double checked, with backup power units in the pocket of their combat vests.

As cold air blasted in from the black sky, McCarter glanced at the weapons and gear bin. Hooked to the static line, the bin would be rolled off the ramp before the troops went airborne. Their main battle pieces and Beretta 93-R side arms would go with them, but McCarter went to the comm center to check on the enemy's western perimeter, just in case they might be greeted by hostiles when they hit the DZ.

"Pen-zone still clear of bogeys, sir."

McCarter checked the monitors, the Predator still piping in imagery of the sprawling camp. If it looked as though they would have bad company as they made their penetration from the west, McCarter would order the Predator to fire a Hellfire missile. It would throw the whole attack plan off kilter, but battle, he knew, was a fluid situation.

There was, however, some good news. Despite the fact they were facing a standing eighty-plus fighting force, the Abadal clan—for reasons McCarter could only surmise—kept the campsite clear of noncombatants. Their women and children were housed in a village to the east. That meant McCarter and his troops were free to unleash massive firepower, shoot at will. More good news—Grimaldi had the AC-130 Spectre, twenty thousand feet up, and holding several miles near the Somalia-Kenya border.

And the Germans had landed.

Between the Predator and the satellite imagery, McCarter had already selected points of attack, handed out the assignments to his troops. There were two key goals the five of them bore in mind for the strike. But, beyond laying waste to the campsite and clan, bagging either an EDEF goon or Abadal was secondary and optional.

M-16 assault rifle with the fixed M-203 grenade

launcher in hand, McCarter put on his game face. He was with his troops next, shot them a thumbs-up when the red light flashed. "Let's rock, mates."

Manning rolled the weapons bin off the ramp, then McCarter plunged into the night.

"PHOENIX HAS LANDED. They're online and they're moving."

Hal Brognola was pouring another cup of coffee when Kurtzman made the announcement. The big Fed couldn't help but marvel at twenty-first-century technology where real time could be watched from thousands of miles in space and relayed halfway around the world in a few heartbeats. He was in the Computer Room, and the best and the brightest, with Price standing watch over their shoulders, were hard at it, covering the backs of the Stony Man warriors. Beyond that, they could monitor the Abadal compound, pin down the movements and numbers of enemy shooters, sound an instant alarm.

Brognola watched in quiet admiration as Kurtzman, Akira Tokaido and Huntington Wethers manned the Delta One workstation. Com links snug around their heads, the foursome was adjusting dials, punching buttons, fingers flying over keyboards at light speed. Five of the monitors were split-screen, allowing a full view—illuminated now in night vision gray-green—to the twelve and six of the Phoenix Force warriors. They were moving double-time at least, Brognola viewing their world, which was little more than a ghostly shroud of the Somali night, the transmissions jouncing up and down as the team closed in on the enemy encampment. Another monitor was cut five ways, he saw, then divided into five circles, satellite relay linked to the sensor belts.

"How long before they're in position?"

Akira Tokaido checked another monitor, then hit a button that flashed a series of numbers. Usually the Japanese youth wore headphones that leaked ungodly rock-and-roll racket from a CD player, but the moment called for one hundred percent steely focus. "Three klicks and counting," Tokaido answered. "Call it thirty minutes, boss, give or take."

"We'll maintain radio silence," Price told Brognola, "unless…"

She left it hanging, but Brognola got the gist of the message. Unless bogeys were framed on the monitors, creeping or charging up on the flanks or rear of Phoenix Force, there was no point in distracting the troops.

"The Predator," Wethers, a former professor of cybernetics at Berkeley said, "is still showing they have clear sailing from the west. I'm showing Jack's Spectre, five miles to their rear and holding."

"And our EDEF comrades?"

"They just moved into what we believe is Abadal's HQ," Wethers replied.

Brognola offered a silent prayer of godspeed and good luck to the team.

"Hal, I have it."

Brognola found Carmen Delahunt holding out a sheaf of computer printouts. He walked to her workstation and took the papers.

"From what Able's prisoner told them," the red-headed former FBI agent said, "I was able to diagram the interior layout of the Spanish installation. It isn't one hundred percent accurate, of course, but if their prisoner has been there and is telling the truth…"

"I understand. Good work," Brognola said, and called Price over to a cubicle. "What do you think about cutting Able loose on EDEF's Spanish installation?"

"Well, if Aussen is telling the truth, you're looking at the main complex where whatever this Level Four virus is being bred. Then you have the main bulk of rocket fuel that is stored there, shipped by German-friendly Nutricen. It looks as if they're in the process of building launch pads for shuttles to get more attack satellites into space. We can't let that happen."

"It won't."

"Well, from what we know, this facility is cleared and approved by both the Spanish government and the European Space Agency, but, yes, we know the truth. As for numbers, Able would be going up against a security force of roughly thirty German and Spanish commandos who are probably under orders now to shoot to kill on sight any intruders."

"Which, if that's true, would give Able something of an edge, turn them loose, go in shooting. The President, to understate his mood, is angry."

"In other words, he's given the green light to hit the Madrid and Frankfurt facilities?"

"He did, indeed. It's our show, and that's a quote."

"The problem is, Hal, you're talking about sovereign countries."

"And supposedly American allies."

"If Able goes in, if they're caught or worse…"

"I know, but that's why messes like this get dumped in our laps."

"The Administration will deny any and all involvement."

"You know how the political wheels turn. SOP."

"Well, from the sounds of it, Carl and company are antsy to get moving, but I think we need some time to sift through this, come up with a solid plan. If we throw Able to the wolves, I want to know they can finish what they start and get out."

Brognola's thoughts raced around the mess Able had already left behind in the Sonoran Desert. On that front, the President had left Brognola in charge of securing and seizing whatever was left of the Nutricen compound. Brognola had flown out what was little shy of a battalion of Justice and FBI agents, the FDA and DOD getting shoved out of the picture, the order straight from the White House they were to step aside. It was a safe bet that whoever the conspirators in town behind the Nutricen-EDEF connection would start to sweat, cover their tracks, but Brognola, the Farm and the warriors in the field could only tackle one flashpoint at a time.

No mistake, Brognola knew there was more house-cleaning to be done on American soil. It galled him, just the same, that there were men of ranking power and means within the U.S. government who had forsaken their oath to duty to defend their country, selling out, and he didn't give a damn what their reasons. In due course, Brognola intended to see hard justice blow down their house of cards.

"What about Aussen?" Price wanted to know.

"You mean, the sweetheart deal Able promised the bastard?" Brognola gnawed on his cigar, shook his head. "Those three. I tell you, Barb, they're taking a lot of liberties lately."

"But if Aussen can help?"

"Right. This guy, he orders the facility mined with explosives, the place goes up and buries God only knows how many Americans…I guess his rationale is that he was only doing as he was ordered."

"I have to tell them something."

"They can sit awhile." Brognola flashed Price a look that was somewhere between a scowl and a grin. "At least we know where they are. And at least we know they won't be tearing up the town or bending my ear to bail them out of jail."

THE TARANTULA WAS the Farm's latest brainchild in high-tech demolition combined with robotic engineering. Created by the Farm's top weaponsmith, John "Cowboy" Kissinger, and working out the electronic

particulars with Gadgets Schwarz, it was a robot—
about the size of a grapefruit. A mechanical device that
crawled on legs and carried Semtex to a target. It certainly cut out the risk factor of planting explosives
with an enemy lurking about and, on this occasion, the
big Briton was grateful for any edge they could seize.

David McCarter plucked one of the stainless-steel
Tarantulas off his webbing. One pound of Semtex was
housed in the belly of the aluminum spider; the Briton
thumbed on the red light. The Semtex could be detonated by remote control or timer, but the Briton opted
for the personal touch. The Tarantula could be steered
by remote control or set on automatic directional
guide. McCarter decided he'd simply let the device
find its own way to target when he was ready.

He stretched out on the rise, taking in the Abadal
compound village through a night vision device. It
was a sprawling compound; McCarter figuring a good
city block holding a hodgepodge of tents and stone
hovels. There was an antiaircraft battery near what the
Somali warlord passed off as a runway to the east,
EDEF's transport bird parked and watched by a trio of
gunmen. What he believed was Abadal's HQ was dead
ahead, fifty meters and change. He counted six Somalis on sentry duty by the open door.

Manning and Encizo were on his left flank, Hawkins and James on his direct right. The five of them
were nearly invisible in the night in blacksuit, and exposed flesh smeared in black greasepaint. The Phoenix

Force leader signaled both teams to turn loose one Tarantula each on predetermined targets.

Another search, and as usual, McCarter found, an enemy stronghold looked bigger and meaner and more foreboding than any satellite imagery could sketch. They had been told eighty to a hundred Somali thugs. Factor in an undetermined number of their German guests…

Well, that was why they had the Spectre.

McCarter didn't even trouble himself with counting up all the technicals to the north—Toyota pickups with .50-caliber machine guns mounted in the beds—armed shadows strolling about the motor pool, smoking roll-ups or chewing *qat*. Enough light from bonfires, fire barrels and torches hung from the facing of stone hovels illuminated most of the compound-village, so McCarter shed his NVD goggles now that it was just about time to blast and burn.

The Briton watched his bug go, sensors in the antenna capable of guiding it over broken ground, the spider able to navigate anything short of a deep fissure. It seemed a waste of good technology and a slap in the face on those hours of labors of love by Kissinger and Schwarz, but if it saved their lives and shaved the odds, McCarter didn't care if the things were made of gold.

Another search of the enemy stronghold and the ex-SAS commando found two Tarantulas crawling along at about two knots toward the motor pool. Two more bomb bugs set loose by Hawkins and James were

aimed for a large tent to the south. From there, Mc-
Carter framed sixteen hostiles on his handheld heat
sensor.

Now all they had to do, he thought, was sit tight and
let the Tarantulas get the party started.

YASSIF ABADAL began to believe the Germans were
playing him for a fool. Exactly what game of duplicity they sought to win, and at the price of his scalp, he
wasn't sure.

They had radioed his HQ earlier, informing him
they were on the way, bearing more gifts of virus-
contaminated food. No weapons, no high-tech gear
this time, they came to his controlled stretch of Somalia once again every bit as arrogant and armed as
before.

This time, however, Abadal sensed desperation in
the group of Germans piling into the HQ office. The
Somali warlord needed to set matters straight and to
find out what they really wanted with him. And they
would give him the vaccine—no more promises, no
stalling—or he would cancel his contract with the Germans by firing squad.

From behind his desk, Abadal watched in silence as
the Germans passed strained looks between them,
glancing around the room, aware they were outnumbered, two to one.

"To what do we owe the honor of this unexpected
visit, Heinz?"

"The name is Hans."

The German, offended, stared at him with contempt, looking around, as if Somalis were little more than maggots.

"Do you wish to tell me, Abadal, why you kept me and my men waiting for almost two hours?"

Abadal chuckled. "It is simple. I have made a decision. You see," he said, standing, pulling the AK-47 off his desktop, "after your last visit I began to think why a country such as yours, rich in every way, would concern itself with what I believe you think is a backward nation of savages barely out of the trees. You bring this silent weapon of mass destruction, singling me out of all the leaders of all the clans. Yes, I have seen its complete devastating effects, but it is still plague. You see my dilemma? I wonder why I am bestowed this great honor."

"I do not see your dilemma at all. Not when we have given you the power to rule your country."

"The power to rule," Abadal said, slipping past them, lips pursed as he went and stood in the doorway, spotting the shadows of his sentries beyond the opening to the living quarters of his top lieutenants. "Or the power to wipe out Somalia."

"Your point?"

"My point is this. Much like your Hitler, I am thinking there is no vaccine, that you deceive me as Hitler did Stalin, that you view Somalis and the rest of us who inhabit this continent as subhuman. You wish to commit genocide on Africa. Why? Simple. The continent is awash in vast mineral resources. With the populations of the indigenous peoples out of the way, your countrymen simply march in and claim it—gold, diamonds, silver, oil—for yourselves."

"Pure speculation. Paranoid fantasy."

Abadal was turning away from the living quarters, the word "really" on his lips when the explosion tore apart the night. He was turning toward the source of the blast—somewhere out front of his HQ—then he was airborne, pounded by a flying wall of rubble.

He felt the intense heat searing up his back, heard faraway and fleeting shouts and cries, then the lights winked out.

FARAK AIDEED ABADAL was angry. He had begged off the nightly round of *qat* chewing with his brothers-in-arms, wishing to be alone with his thoughts, a head clear of the amphetamine-like buzz. He needed to sort through the present, cut through the nonsense surrounding him, plan the future.

His own.

A distant cousin of a cousin to Yassif, he wondered if the man was fit to lead them into what he hoped would someday soon be full-scale war against the ruling clans in Mogadishu. If they could or would not capture the capital of the country, then they were all doomed to wander the barren wasteland, ragtag rebel nomads erecting roadblocks to steal whatever they could from neighboring villagers, slugging it out with rivals, planting mines, lives lost in wishful longing of glory, flights of fancy for a new, brave and powerful Somalia.

Dreamers with guns.

Take this business with the white men, he thought, stepping outside the tent, striking up a match and lighting the hand-rolled cigarette, snugging the AK-47 higher up his shoulder. It was absurd, at best, madness, at worst. In a country as isolated as Somalia, where anarchy and the power of the AK-47 ruled, it was foolish to even consider whites had come here with concern and compassion for the long-suffering peoples of his country. He could only imagine what they really thought of them, their hearts, he was sure, pumping with bigotry and contempt, the Germans seeing themselves as superior in every way. That alone sickened him with boiling anger. Sure, they landed with some sort of wheat-based gruel, meant to be doled out to neighboring clans, but as a tool of genocide.

And, no mistake, food was power in Somalia.

But it was laced with the most horrible plague he had ever seen. And he came from a village where disease had nearly wiped out his entire clan. There were more parasitic diseases, usually festering and bred in the contaminated water of streams and ponds, more dengue fever, malaria, cholera, meningitis…then there was the Tumbu Fly, a maggot that burrowed into the flesh, eating tissue all the way to the bone, hatching larvae…

Somalia certainly needed no more horror of disease, especially one created by Westerners.

He smoked, stewed, checked the village. He looked at the giant transport plane where several of the Germans and Somalis were roving, lost in their own thoughts, fears and schemes.

What to do?

Well, he decided, gnawing on still more anger that he wasn't viewed as good enough to be allowed quarters in the HQ with other ranking lieutenants, he would stand by, bide his time, see how this insanity played out with the Germans. He had his own followers, young men from a neighboring clan who were of like mind and dreams. They whispered in secret, of course, revolt against Yassif never far from their thoughts.

It wouldn't take much more cajoling, he knew, to marshal his own fighting force, crush the ruling powers.

He was wondering how to go about pulling off a coup, aware he needed something to barter with, whether weapons, women or *qat*, when—

The spider was surging on an arrow-straight course for the tent flap. He felt his heart lurch, the cigarette slipping from his fingers. He was aware there were all manner of wicked insects that crept through the wadis and ravines in this part of the country, but he had never seen a spider so large and—

Its skin glinted moonlight as it waddled closer. A silver spider? Was it poisonous?

The AK-47 was off his shoulder, drawing target acquisition when the night erupted in his face, hurling him into a soundless black void.

THE FIVE EXPLOSIONS detonated in near-perfect synchronicity.

Moments prior to the eruptions that were the call to arms for McCarter and troops, the ex-SAS commando had scanned the flashpoints. He counted up potential casualties, working the numbers north to south. The ballpark figure was twenty-five to thirty hardmen, which meant they could cut the odds close to one-third with any luck. Hard *men*, he knew, wasn't entirely accurate. A fair number of the fighting force would be little more than teenagers, culled into marauding murdering service by whoever had lived the longest and had the most guns and ammo. Life expectancy in Somalia was roughly one-third of the seventy-five years for a Westerner, or so he had once heard, the figure probably some news sound bite, handed off by the United Nations or Red Cross.

Not that it mattered now.

Life expectancy on this stretch of hell was about to drop even more.

McCarter's Tarantula was the first to blast. It crept right into the middle of the six sentries, all of them too busy working on roll-ups or munching *qat* to realize doomsday had crawled out of the night. The big Briton rode out a few more critical seconds, received a thumbs-up down the line from his troops, waiting as his bug bomb shuddered into the doorway of the HQ, then hit the trigger.

McCarter took in the saffron flashes from the motor pool, technicals sailing for the sky in what appeared slow-mo somersaults, dark mannequins screaming and flung in all directions.

Then there was the tent where a good number of Somali thugs tasted their own fireball. Down there, McCarter watched the loner, mired in whatever his final thoughts, before he was vaporized. The tent was sheared off the earth, lost in the fire cloud. A check of his heat sensor, aimed toward the smoking crater, and McCarter found the screen was not entirely clear of the living.

Hawkins and James, he saw, broke over the rise, heading in that direction to mop up survivors, Encizo and Manning already on the move, weapons searching for live ones or walking mangled.

Assault rifle in hand, the Briton stood, then began legging it toward the smoking rubble of the HQ, kicking his advance into double-time as he made level ground. Abadal's ruins would be his task; whatever crabbed, coughed or bled, his grim chore to nail down.

From there on, he knew the going would only get tougher. Shock factor would wear off, and there were still plenty of cutthroats and conspirators on the prowl left to grind up before the Spectre grabbed centerstage.

The night, he knew, had only just begun to burn.

CHAPTER NINE

Hans von Rigel knew he was in a world of feces, sinking fast, and he couldn't help but curse the man with the big plans who had landed him in this jackpot.

Had he not warned Kluger they didn't need Somalia? Had he not clearly stated the case they had come under attack from faceless, nameless enemies in America, implying all of them were at risk of far worse than simple arrest? Had he not tried to make the man find a glimmer of the light of sanity in the darkness of his mad scheme for world domination by way of unleashing plague from outer space on Third World countries he stamped as subhuman? Had he not urged Kluger to forget about Burma, that shipping and distributing tons of heroin would only put them on the radar screen of every law-enforcement agency from Interpol to the DEA? Had he not tried to douse the fires of the man's greed and ambition, which would only lead to the downfall of EDEF, the likes of which hadn't been seen in Germany since Hitler had holed up in his bunker and the Russians had burned down and raped all of Europe on the way to spike his head on a stake? Had he not…

It no longer mattered.

Somalia was about to become his open grave. And, if he was going to die in this godforsaken hellhole, he would take out as many of the opposition as he could before he was riddled with bullets or torn to shreds by another massive explosion.

Starting with the Somalis.

Von Rigel staggered to his feet, raw anger and adrenaline sweeping the tremors from his limbs. The G-3 assault rifle was in hand, but he grabbed an AK-47—two banana clips wrapped together by duct tape—and searched the churning dust and smoke for the first available targets. Eyes stung by blood and sweat, gummy strands of spit and blood running from his mouth where he felt the holes from two or three teeth missing inside his cheek, he found Diehl, Wahl, Crommen and two others rising from the rubble. They began checking the others for a pulse—Germans only—but von Rigel had to believe they were the only survivors on his side. The horrific blast had caught the bulk of his forces by the door, bodies of his men heaped in contorted poses, an arm missing here and there, blood pooling for his feet. He kicked the body of a Somali, found Abadal's lifeless eyes staring back.

Von Rigel laughed again. He knew about pain and loss, but if these were, indeed, his final moments, there was no running collage of his life flashing before the eyes as he'd heard about. There were only a few bitter tattered memories, and that was more than he cared to stomach.

He was the result of a rape by an American GI, and his mother had walked out on him when he was a boy, selling her body, he had heard, on the streets of Berlin, spreading her legs mostly to the foreign occupiers, since they were the only ones with any cash after the war. He had educated and fended for himself, raised by a German family, a sort of foster child. There were failed marriages, alcoholism and drug abuse to follow, an unrelenting anger at life following him like a curse. There was his disgraceful end as a GSG-9 commando during a raid on a suspected house of terrorists. He had gone in shooting, women and children fair game along with their terrorist fathers and husbands. Now there was Kluger, marching him to his own death, the billionaire with dreams of ruling the world.

Fuck 'em, he thought. Fuck 'em all.

Von Rigel saw a half dozen or so Somalis shimmy to their feet, bloody stick figures hacking on grit. It enraged him even more that Abadal was so sloppy and stupid he hadn't bothered to secure the camp's perimeter, allowing whoever was tearing up the night beyond the HQ free and unfettered access to come in blasting.

Von Rigel lifted the G-3 and began to shoot Somalis.

T.J. HAWKINS KNEW there would be plenty of bodies after the blasts, and the former Army Ranger was ready when they started popping into sight. He wasted no time cranking out the first of the two hundred 5.56 mm rounds in the box magazine.

They bobbed and weaved through the smoke, dazed by concussion, but they were armed and dangerous just the same. With James on his left flank, he advanced, catching the distant tunes of autofire and still more explosions crunching through the night. The enemy, he found, was on the skinny, smallish side, and from what he had previously experienced in Somalia, he knew they were tagged *mooryan*. The rough translation being they were teenagers, but thugs with weapons and malice of heart, make no mistake. If he stood here and thought about it, he believed he might feel a stab of pain that he was forced to mow down what were little more than fourteen- to fifteen-year-old kids. Wasted sentiment.

Their objective was the airfield, he knew, link up with the left wing—Encizo and Manning—and cripple the EDEF bird. Whether they cuffed and stuffed some German bigwigs was a moot point. Walking away from battle in one standing piece, with the enemy trampled in the dust, was always the prime goal.

And a bunch of *mooryan* was the armed blockade to the airfield.

Hawkins was holding back on the SAW's trigger,

sweeping shadows off their feet, when he spied another group of combatants spilling from a stone hut to his eleven o'clock. James went to grim work on that front, pumping a 40 mm missile into the ragtag pack, mangled figures bouncing off a retaining wall, the black ex-SEAL pouring on the autofire to hose down the enemy guns.

Marching on, Hawkins cut down three more shadows before he cleared the smoking hole where two spider bombs had done the majority of the killing in the immediate vicinity.

The ex-Army Ranger was scanning his compass when a figure suddenly burst out of the night. He was surging from a hole in yet another stone barrier to a hovel when Hawkins found himself wondering just what the hell he was viewing. The guy with the AK-47 wore a white kaftan, standard wardrobe for that part of the world, Hawkins knew, but it was the Oakland Raiders cap, black sunglasses and—

White cleats?

The total package struck Hawkins as a distortion of reality, but the kid was swinging the assault rifle his way and Hawkins pounded the kaftan to red ruins. Whether the shoes were too big for his feet, Hawkins couldn't tell, but the man in white was blown out of his cleats.

Hawkins heard his com link crackle with Aaron Kurtzman's voice. His own Delta program tied directly to the Bear, Hawkins heard the Stony Man computer expert warn him about three bogeys, two o'clock, hunkered behind the retaining wall. Hawkins copied, fisted a frag grenade and armed it. A check of James on the move, bowling down armed shadows that spilled from the line of hovels, the ex-SEAL tied in to the same frequency as he was, and Hawkins lobbed the steel egg over the top of the wall. He was vectoring away from the wall, gathering momentum, when the frag blast detonated. Kurtzman patched through, informing him his six was now clear.

THE BLINKING WHITE DOTS, Brognola knew, marked Phoenix Force, piped to the Farm via transponders that relayed their positions by the burglared NRO satellite. The opposition was painted in red as a shimmering orange hue.

Watching men die through the wonders of supertechnology was somewhat spooky, Brognola thought. Dead was dead, but this was something else entirely, real time, real flesh and blood dying as little more than a lit speck, an eerie video game. When the series of explosions jump-started the battle, the flaring light show so bright he had blinked and turned away, Brognola saw countless red-orange dots either wink out or simply fade away in seconds. Dead in an instant, or bleeding out, the bodies went cold, the soul or life force going wherever it went. The dots simply vanished from the monitors.

There was still plenty of red-orange jumping all

over the screens, lots of bad guys in play. Visual relay was shaky, at best, since the images tended to hop around as the Phoenix Force warriors advanced, swung this way and that, ducked fire, blazed away in long raking bursts, left to right or vice versa.

Brognola watched as the tactical team relayed warnings and positions of bogeys. Encizo and Manning were monitored by Wethers, Kurtzman taking Hawkins and James, with Tokaido watching McCarter, the lone fighter out.

It was quite the grim, and, yes, Brognola admitted to himself, ghoulish show.

Brognola saw Price striding his way. Like the mission controller, he had spent the past several hours placing the critical calls to the right people to keep the campaign rolling. CIA, NSA, DEA, the two of them had enough power players who owed them, and they had called in the necessary markers.

"Another EDEF bird is flying," Price informed Brognola. "Three hours in the air, heading east."

"Myanmar."

"I would think so."

"Let's get Phoenix out of the frying pan first," Brognola said.

"We're set for the next phase. The CIA station chief in Madrid has agreed to cooperate. He monitors and assists the Spanish authorities in counterterrorism. He knows the EDEF facility there is churning out the Level Four virus."

"And the Spanish authorities?"

"He's agreed to keep them in the dark—if possible."

Brognola had several decisions to make, but knew there really was no choice. He would send Able Team to Spain, a sovereign country where a nest of vipers was operating right under or with the full and working knowledge of the powers that be, with the intent of wiping out what was on the surface a legitimate research facility. How they got it done…well, he was leaving that up to Able Team.

Then there was Myanmar, a regime openly hostile to the west…

First order of business was to nail down the butcher's work in Somalia.

"Fax the necessary intel to Able," Brognola told Price, and went back to watching the killing fields on the monitors.

VON RIGEL FIGURED most of them were no older than midteens, but the little Somali bastards weren't getting a pass because of their tender years.

G-3 and AK-47 flaming away, he diced the wounded Somalis with a double hosing that kicked and bounced them off one another.

When the last of the Somalis dropped, von Rigel strode for a door at the far edge of the room. "Our plane!" he told his commandos. "Anything and everything in our way goes down!"

Von Rigel drilled a thundering kick into the flimsy

wood. It was crashing wide when he spotted two gunners tumbling through a window. The murderous racket of explosions and autofire outside was obviously more than they cared to handle.

Von Rigel hit them with a double dose of autofire, laughing all the way to the window.

DAVID MCCARTER WASN'T sure what he bore witness to, his vision obscured by all the swirling dust and grit, but it sure as hell looked as if the Germans had snapped. For reasons he could only surmise, they were making a slaughter feast out of their former Somali cohorts.

He was navigating a treacherous course through all the rubble and splintered wood when Tokaido patched through. "Big D, you've got two bogeys on your three."

McCarter would have never seen it coming, should have figured his spider bomb would have left more than just the pack of Germans scurrying, alive and angry. He peered into the smoke, M-16 chattering as he spied the bloodied kaftans rising, AKs spitting lead. Several rounds snapped past his ears, but McCarter waxed them off their feet.

"You're clear," Tokaido told him.

For the moment only, McCarter knew, bulling ahead, sighting down, finger curling around the M-203's trigger as the Germans barreled into a dark room on the far side of the HQ.

THE RPG-7s were no match for the multiround projectile launcher, but the key to winning this particular rocket showdown, Rafael Encizo knew, was beating them to the draw.

Manning was skirting the outer right lane of what was fast becoming a wasteland of burning vehicles and strewed corpses, when Encizo chugged out two quick 40 mm missiles. The cone-shaped RPG warheads were framed in the umbrella of firelight, but it was the shadows retreating from the motor pool, seeking refuge in any number of stone hovels, that began to concern Encizo. Say they holed up, armed with more RPGs. From their dark roosts they could pump out enough warheads, Encizo knew, until he and Manning were splattered clear back to Kenya.

Pessimistic images of their own mortality shoved aside, Encizo took out the rocket teams with 40 mm blasts, then hit the runners with another explosion. But there were too many Somalis, dispersing in different directions and too spread out, to obliterate their numbers.

A group of seven Somalis braked near the edge of a walled courtyard that, according to satellite pics, led to the HQ. They were wheeling, triggering AK-47s, Encizo and Manning taking cover behind a technical, when the courtyard erupted into a barrage of autofire.

Manning keyed his com link. "Mr. M to Phoenix leader," he said, using his handle just in case their frequency was intercepted by any American intelligence agencies listening or watching from space.

"What?"

"Is that you in the courtyard?"

"The Germans! They went berserk on the Somalis, maybe six on the way out."

"We'll clean house from our end then. Over and out."

CALVIN JAMES TOOK the alert from Kurtzman, aware Hawkins also received warning from the Farm's cyber-specialist. Swiftly, James and Hawkins moved past the shredded remains of the trio that had come running from the transport bird, only to find themselves dusted by autofire. According to Kurtzman, two bogeys were hunkered inside the transport plane, toward the cockpit. All indications from the Farm's monitoring of their sensor belts, and the immediate area around the plane was clear of hostiles.

James kept vigilance on the hatch, while Hawkins backpedaled, watching their six. At the hatch, James set down his assault rifle, plucked three frag grenades, signaled he would go stemward, and that Hawkins was to toss his steel eggs to the stern.

At a nod from Hawkins, James pulled the pins, counted down and chucked the grenades into the dark bowels of the bird, Hawkins adding his three spheres of doom to the rear. Autofire rang out, bullets spanging the doorway, but James and Hawkins were sprinting to clear ground zero. A mound of rubble was the closest available barrier, and James and Hawkins were up and over when the explosions thundered, tearing apart the cargo plane's fuselage.

McCARTER RECKONED the Germans on the exit were stoked on adrenaline and the anger to vent their murderous impulses. That aside, they were still pros, which meant they had both instincts and the good sense to check their rear.

The Briton was sighting down, ready to shred their numbers with a 40 mm waxing, when two of the commandos spun and cut loose with autofire as if they had eyes in the backs of their heads. It was damn close, McCarter knew, feeling the hot slipstream blow past his cheeks, stone shrapnel flaying his face as bullets tore into the jamb.

He rode out the fusillade, Manning and Encizo already apprised on the advancing runners.

McCarter heard Tokaido coming through on his com link, advising him of the massive buildup of surviving troops gathering at the northwest edge of the camp.

It was time, McCarter knew, to turn the show over to Spectre.

The ex-SAS commando copied, then patched through on another frequency to Grimaldi. "This is Phoenix Leader to Dragonship…"

CHAPTER TEN

As the sun was sinking over the Justice Department's private airfield in Loudon County, Virginia, five black-suits from the Farm choppered in, Carl Lyons thinking the pilot was about to nearly drop the Bell JetRanger on the roof of the building.

It was mood more than reality, the Able Team leader steamed about the delay. He jumped up from behind the desk, strode to the window and watched as they disgorged. Adrenaline meltdown, little or no sleep and knowing the world was poised to stare down a plague of the ages had a way of affecting his attitude, or so Lyons reasoned. However he felt, the Able Team leader knew they were on the launch pad, back in play.

Four blacksuits, he saw, marched for the office, large nylon bags in hand, while number five beelined for a hangar where a Gulfstream was parked. Presumably that was their ride to Spain. Presumably they were lugging the goods Lyons had listed for Brognola.

Still, Lyons felt his jaw grinding, heart pulsing with anger.

They had been twiddling their thumbs for hours on end, waiting on Brognola to flash the green light, while intel on the next leg of the mission and the persons of interest were faxed from the Farm. Brognola wasn't a man to hold a grudge, but the big Fed's tone, Lyons recalled, had been brittle when he'd laid out another pit-bull plan to invade and take down the EDEF sister facility in Spain. The word had come back to hold on, sit tight, the headshed had work to do before Spain was dropped on the radar screen. While they sat on Aussen and the German pilot, Lyons had sent Schwarz out for pizza, briefly entertained the idea of having him grab up a case of beer, then decided the three of them weren't out of the Farm's shithouse yet.

He had given the man who ran the small airport for Brognola liberal leave, since there were no scheduled flights on the books. Officially it was a Justice Department front, meant for emergencies if a Stony Man bird—commandeered or otherwise—was either too large to land at the Farm, low on fuel, or they were bringing home bad guys for short or long term Q and A and federal housing. Unofficially it was a flight school.

As the blacksuits filed into the office, Lyons checked his watch, bobbed his head, flashed them an ugly look. Culled from various military branches—

Delta, Special Forces, Navy SEALs, with an occasional FBI agent or cop—the blacksuits were, by and large, a security force for the Farm. On occasion they went into battle with the Stony Man warriors. Sworn to secrecy, their role was buried so deep in the black hole of classified ops, their names, ranks and serial and social security numbers wouldn't even be found floating in cyber space.

The blacksuits dumped the nylon bags on the desk. It wasn't their fault, of course, that Brognola had kept them waiting, but Lyons was pumped to keep on running and gunning.

Lyons, Schwarz and Blancanales unzipped the war bags. A quick delve revealed a hundred-plus pounds of C-4, complete with radio remotes and detonators, plenty of ammo on tap, with the H&K MP-5 subguns and sound suppressors as he had requested, and he felt his mood brighten.

"We'll take these two off your hands, sir," one of the blacksuits said.

Aussen piped up as two blacksuits hauled him to his feet. "Our deal?"

"It's in the works," Lyons said.

"What does that mean?"

"It means what it means. It's out of our hands, but I was told if you keep playing ball, we see how your intel shakes out and you could be sitting on a beach in Miami with one of those fancy umbrella foo-foo drinks in hand in a week or so."

"Could be?"

"Get him out of here!" Lyons barked.

"Hey," he called to the blacksuit who appeared to be in charge, spotted the Gulfstream rolling onto the runway. "Is there a microwave on our ride?"

"Yes, sir."

Lyons looked over his shoulder as Schwarz and Blancanales hung war bags over their shoulders. "One of you grab the rest of that pizza. God knows when we'll eat again."

GARY MANNING SENT a 40 mm warhead flying at the line of muzzle-flashes. Whatever remained of Somali fighters had retreated, regrouped and buried themselves in deep cover. From the enemy numbers relayed from the Farm, Manning knew an exit stage left wasn't guaranteed. The enemy, forty-something strong, had pulled up the drawbridge in a series of hovels, most of which were little more than piles of rubble, but they were hunkered and going for broke. It would require moving in, rooting them out, hand to hand, but Manning knew there was another plan on the table.

The big Canadian watched as his 40 mm blast silenced some of the autofire, Encizo at the rear of the technical, popping off two more hellbombs from his grenade launcher. Whatever shock factor they achieved, how many they killed or crippled was impossible to say, but the muzzle-flashes pierced the darkness again, a matter of seconds after the explosions, and bullets were swarming the technicals, blasting out windows.

The extract plan, going in, sounded simple enough, he thought. Commandeer a technical and boogey east, while the Spectre swept down and reduced the camp to a smoking crater. Black Hawks, he knew, were on the Kenya-Somali border, ready to fly and scoop them up near the wadi as soon as McCarter placed the call.

First, they needed to vacate the premises. By his reckoning there were still twelve or so technicals intact, fanning away in a staggered formation. It was boarding one of those technicals while under fire that posed the real danger, Somalis winging off countless rounds, gripped in murderous fever. Manning could be sure there were no professional snipers in that bunch, but all it would take was for them to keep hosing the area with autofire, score lucky hits, and the big Canadian had to believe a few RPGs were ready, willing and able.

And McCarter was engaged in his own problems at the moment. The good news was James and Hawkins had patched through, on the way from the airfield to link up, and would help clean up this mess, nail it down. Manning silently urged them to make the scene. With the Spectre en route to drop the hammer, time was running out.

Two armed shadows charged into the open, cutting loose with autofire. One of the shooters wielded an assault rifle in each hand, hollering something unintelligible, but Manning caught the guttural bark of his native tongue. Whoever he was, the German was clearly hell-bent on going out in a blaze of Teutonic glory. Manning cursed and Encizo flung himself to cover between two technicals as bullets tattooed metal, the madman zeroing in on their position, blind rage and combat instinct seemingly fusing to turn the bastard into walking radar. Two more technicals provided a barricade between the shooters from the HQ and the Somalis winging spray and pray from their fortress wasteland. Manning made deeper cover, not a second too soon.

Manning opened the door to the technical, bullets thudding off the bed, and found the keys in the ignition. He cranked up their ride, slid back, crouched and took cover behind the bed. On the far side from the Somali shooters, Manning reared up and returned fire just as a wave of dark shadows bull-rushed from the hovels.

MOHAMMED KHADALFI wasn't going to let this opportunity escape. Foreigners—hated Westerners, no less—had come to his country, hearts pumping with treachery, hands full of weapons meant to kill them all. It was beyond outrageous, sickening how they believed they could march onto Somali turf, take charge, treat them with contempt, using them as puppets or cannon fodder for whatever their real intentions. He determined he would somehow show them their error in judgment.

For days now he had heard the rumblings from his fellow clansmen about Abadal and his bizarre coalition with the Germans. Well, Khadalfi hadn't survived years of engaging rival clans in battle, plundering villages in the region for food, *qat*, and young girls, making it to the ripe old age of nineteen to get slaughtered by white men who had clearly betrayed Abadal. Unless he missed his guess, white men were shooting it out now in the courtyard of the HQ and Abadal was dead.

Which meant someone had to claim the reins of power. Why not him? Khadalfi thought.

The problem was rallying what he began to think of as his troops, motivating them to carry out his will. But the foreigners had the massive firepower and Khadalfi had counted up what RPGs remained, knew the odds still favored the invaders—four warheads, a woeful number, to say the least, when the enemy was down there in the lake of burning wreckage, shadows popping up to loose missiles on their position, what seemed an endless supply of ammo.

Khadalfi heard the moaning of the wounded, saw anxious faces aimed his way, eyes bulging in the shadows, flickering with fear as fire danced over their faces. They were looking to him, he sensed, to tell them what to do.

He did.

Khadalfi selected ten of the youngest in the clan, told them to move out and take the fighting to the enemy. Their brains might be addled by *qat*, but they were still rational enough to fear they were being ordered to commit suicide. Khadalfi roared obscenities, triggered a burst of AK autofire over their heads, slashing a storm of stone fragments in their faces.

"Have you no pride?" he raged. "You would let foreigners murder you on your own land? In the name of vengeance and God you will slay these foreign demons! Go!"

They headed for the open doors, still uncertain until he loosed another burst of autofire, then they charged into the night, firing their AK-47s, sweeping the technicals with wild fire.

Khadalfi watched a few of them fall, boneless forms sprawling over hunks of stone, then decided as the new and self-appointed leader of the clan he needed to initiate a decisive plan of action. If he could outflank the foreign invaders somehow, unload the RPGs on their position...

It was worth the gamble. Even if he lost most of his clan in some suicide stand while he hung back and blew the invaders off the face of Somalia with RPGs, the legend of his heroics would spread throughout the region, certain a few of his followers would survive the night. There were plenty of desperate starving young men in neighboring villages, no matter what the outcome here, eager to be armed, recruited and willing to do battle against enemies both within the nation and beyond its borders.

All he needed to do was to achieve victory, hoist decapitated heads of the invaders impaled on spikes as trophies and as a warning to those who chose to defy his authority.

MCCARTER KNEW the same transponder signal received at the Farm painted the five of them on Spectre's screens. Trouble was, the big Briton knew they were on Grimaldi's clock, figured the AC-130 was no more than ten to twelve miles out, ready to swoop down, fire at will. Of course, if they didn't bail the killing field here in time...

Sure, the Spectre could fly over, guns silent, then swing back when they cleared out. But McCarter wanted this wrapped before the enemy dispersed at the sight of coming death from above, scattered for the hills or the vast emptiness of the surrounding wasteland. Grimaldi and crew would then have to spend the better part of the night flying around Somalia to mop up any armed stragglers who might give chase to their evac site.

The holdup was the two-fisted German wildman and comrade and the blazing fingers of autofire from what struck McCarter as at least a platoon of fighters winging countless rounds north of the technicals.

The Phoenix Force leader hit the courtyard on the heels of his 40 mm detonation, the stink of smoke, cordite, blood and leaking guts and body waste shoved up his nose, but putting him on the scent of the enemy. He hit the edge of the open gateway, spotted the German duo holding to their berserker form. They were human tops, spinning, technicals absorbing the brunt of their fusillades, but that didn't mean they couldn't score a lucky takedown on either Encizo or Manning.

Then McCarter spotted the human wave pouring from the north, AK-47s chattering to signal a suicide rush. The Germans, as if sensing his presence on their six, split up, falling out of his gunsights, shielded by the technicals.

McCarter moved out, a fresh mag up the snout of his assault rifle, another 40 mm duster in the chute of his M-203. Out of the corner of his eye he spotted the familiar faces of James and Hawkins. The black ex-SEAL and former Army Ranger threw him a look, veered north, toward the angry stutter of autofire, fell in behind the armored cover of technicals.

Six to ten Somalis, McCarter saw, were tumbling down the slope, rolling up against retaining walls that had seen more than their fair share of abuse. How many more enraged *mooryan*, he wondered, were on the prowl?

The Germans made their breakout move, one of them hurling open the door to a technical. Now or never, McCarter told himself.

On the fly, McCarter hit the trigger of his M-203, tired of playing games with those two. The cab of the

Toyota vanished to a peal of thunder and a flashing cloud of fire. A scream lanced his eardrums, but the Briton found the Germans hadn't finished annihilating the suicide squad as perhaps a half dozen muzzles were still flaming.

The ex-SAS commando saw one Somali youth hop up into the bed of a technical. He was manning the .50-caliber machine, cocking the bolt, jerking on the trigger, but nothing happened. Too late, the *mooryan* realized the machine gun wasn't even belted, as James and Hawkins blew him out of the bed with a double hosing.

McCarter was rounding the edge of the vehicle when autofire rang out, Manning bellowing his name through the racket of weapons fire. A swarm of hot lead chased the Briton behind the technical, slugs grazing his scalp so close it felt as if his hair had been parted, then he felt the warmth of blood trickle down his skull.

The German berserker was still on his feet, McCarter found. A staggering and bloodied mummy, he was sweeping both assault rifles over the technicals. Enough, the Briton raged to himself, flinging the muzzle of his M-16 around the bumper, holding back on the trigger. He found he was in sync with four other streams of intercoursing lead, holes erupting all over the German's torso, the wildman roaring at the sky, double fingers of flame raking the ground, divots shooting up like mini-minefield detonations. A few more rounds drilled through the dancing figure. He pitched into a technical, triggered short double bursts, was pinned against the vehicle, then tumbled over in a slo-mo collapse.

"We're bailing!" McCarter shouted at his men, then patched through to Grimaldi. "Dragonship, come in!"

Grimaldi was responding when McCarter spotted the shadows as they crept and lurched in gaps between mounds of rubble. The Briton piled into the technical, Manning at the wheel, Encizo, James and Hawkins triggering their weapons from the bed. It was a blur in the corner of his eye, but one of his troops nailed a rocket man just as the cone-shaped warhead was cut loose.

McCarter flinched as the windshield splintered into spiderwebs. Manning gunned the engine, pedal to the metal, shooting them forward as Encizo, Hawkins and James pounded out a blistering salvo of cover fire.

"Bring on the party favors, Dragonship!"

"Aye, aye, Phoenix Leader. Party favors to be delivered, about two minutes and ticking."

"Go, GO, go!"

Khadalfi jumped into the passenger seat of a technical, satisfied when fourteen of his fellow clansmen boarded four more Toyota pickups. He had to bellow in Abu's ear, but his fifteen-year-old cousin ground the clutch, jerked them ahead to pursue the foreign killers. A check in the side-glass and he found his convoy falling in, bumpers bulling through wreckage, tires rolling over their fallen comrades.

They were gathering speed, Khadalfi ordering Abu to go faster, when he thought he heard a sound like rolling thunder, a noise like a million trumpets splitting the air. Pressing his face to the windshield, he searched the heavens, the peals growing louder, but the skies were clear, nothing but the moon and stars. Strange. Perhaps, he decided, it was simply the ringing in his ears from the gun battle, the racket of explosions still chiming in his brain playing tricks on his senses.

The enemy, he saw, had obtained a quarter-mile head start, but the wheelman was fighting to keep the technical from spilling onto its side, jouncing wheels through ruts, over stones, cutting hard to pass the deeper trenches in broken ground. With any luck they could cut the gap within another mile or so, or the enemy's technical would flip onto its side, throwing the trio from the bed, injuring them, Khadalfi then able to take prisoners. Torture, of course, would follow, ears and genitals hacked off, a tongue or two ripped from their heads, eyeballs gouged out by knives branded to searing orange-red over a fire barrel. He would find out who they were, what they wanted with Somalia, if other foreign invaders were in-country or planning more attacks, then he would douse them with gasoline, burn them alive, dance and laugh at their screams. That display of brutality, he thought, should be enough to show the others he was both leader and savior of Somalia. Rule by fear was every bit as acceptable, perhaps even better, than command by respect.

They were firing AKs and .50-caliber machine guns from behind, Khadalfi sticking his assault rifle out the window, triggering a burst at the enemy's technical, when the weapons fire ceased. Were his clansmen out of bullets? Had they all been dumped from the beds, or jumped out, deciding they had no stomach to chase down the enemy?

He was craning his head around, found his fighters still onboard but they were flapping arms, shouting at one another, pointing back to camp. One of his cousins was pounding on the window, flailing and shouting something about a giant bird. Khadalfi was scouring the skies over the camp, wondering what the excitement was all about, catching the panic in the bed, and…

The winged monster, so huge it seemed to blot out half the heavens, sailed over the ruins of the camp from the east. Then there were mighty peals of thunder, like the voice of God, Khadalfi thought, the left side of the behemoth ablaze with incredibly long arms of fire. He glimpsed a few of his fighters back there, running from technicals they were ready to board, shrinking shadows, there one second, then gone as a wave of explosions swept through them.

Khadalfi felt sick, watching as if the earth itself appeared to open up in an eruption like a series of volcanoes blasting lava at once. The giant bird from hell, he saw, had obliterated whatever had been standing, man or building, all of it vaporized in about the time it took to empty the clip of an assault rifle. There were great walls of billowing smoke, pillars of fire leaping for the skies, objects he couldn't determine still shooting into the air.

And Khadalfi feared the bird from hell was coming for them next.

He faced front, found that the enemy technical appeared to slow, the gap being cut rapidly. There was thunder in his ears again, Khadalfi turning, terror coursing vibrations through his limbs. Someone was hollering from the bed, weapons firing skyward, then Khadalfi spotted two shadows hauling themselves off the ground, dust spooling over their diminishing figures. He cursed them for their cowardice, but their lack of courage, he saw, cost them.

The sky roared from behind, the blackness strobing in the side-glass, a noise he could only imagine as the din of hell ripping his senses. Whoever they were, Khadalfi saw their dark shapes burst apart. There was smoke back there, but not even a trace of where the two deserters had stood.

"Faster!" he roared at Abu, gripping his AK-47, waiting for sudden obliteration.

CHAPTER ELEVEN

"Belay that, Dragonship!"

Manning was cursing Somali mechanical skill, negligence when it came to taking care of something other than a camel, or plain incompetence when McCarter keyed the third button down on his com link.

The Englishman was checking his rear in the sideglass, the technical's engine sputtering out, smoke pouring up from the hood as Manning threw in a few expletives. Whether crippled by a bullet, drained of gas or a radiator burst from the hard run, he didn't know, nor much less cared.

They had problems on their six.

There was some good news, however, and McCarter focused grim attention on their pursuers, the headlights of five technicals bouncing in the glass. He figured the enemy was less than a hundred yards, and closing fast. Opposition numbers had been decimated down to a dozen, courtesy of the Spectre, according to the Farm's watchdog monitors. The dirty dozen in question, however, didn't seem inclined to politely wave them on their way out of Somalia.

"Hold, paint us and them, but skewer any rabbits that run!"

Grimaldi copied, understood that despite their monitors and skill to deliver mop-up and damn near to the yard, the pursuers had shaved the distance close enough that friendly casualties was a distinct ominous possibility. Supercomputers and other high-tech gizmos were intricately wired machines; they didn't distinguish between friend and foe. Friendly casualties happened during the course of battle, and the sad tales of laser-guided missiles missing their mark, he knew, were rarely laundered in public, but he wasn't risking the lives of his men in the name of some damned computer screen at this late stage. Even the most experienced and godlike hands got it wrong sometimes. McCarter opted for flesh and blood on the up-close-and-personal savaging.

McCarter mentally threw together the strategy as the technical shuddered down the mouth of the wadi.

Ambush. Simple enough.

Tapping the illuminating dial on his chronometer, having already called in the Black Hawks, he guesstimated nineteen minutes before evac touched down.

No time to dawdle, wait for the cavalry.

The lights killed, McCarter was out the door, Manning grabbing up his assault rifle, Encizo, Hawkins and James leaping out of the bed as the technical rolled on, momentum petering out before the shabby lemon hit a wall of boulders. McCarter signaled James, Hawkins and Encizo to take up what they already knew was an ambush point, right incline, dig in. They hustled on, melting into the blackness. McCarter pulled two flares from his vest, stabbed their steel spike ends into the ground, just as he saw the shimmer of light dancing beyond the east rise.

WHEN HE SAW the flares and the abandoned technical, Khadalfi suspected a trap. But where were they? he wondered, ordering Abu to stop at the top of the rise. The foreign killers were devious, he knew, still heavily armed, as quick as cats to have so suddenly vanished. Up the slopes, then, hidden in crevices, gullies, perched behind boulders, framing them all in crosshairs of scoped weapons.

As self-proclaimed leader, the future salvation of Somalia, he couldn't see the point in risking his own life. If he walked away, the only survivor, he would at least live to spread the concocted tale of his own heroic stand against foreign devils. A self-inflicted wound should do the job. Nicking his thigh with a bullet, slashing his arm with the edge of his knife, say just enough running blood, and that would convince youth in the neighboring villages to enlist in the Greater Army of Khadalfi. In time, as they plundered more villages, recruiting any male not afflicted with disease at gunpoint, he could amass enough fighters, they would be able to march into Mogadishu, thousands strong, a sea of technicals swarming every quarter, no leader of any clan able to stop the coming conquest of Mohammed Khadalfi.

Weapon in hand, rusty brakes squealing as the technicals jerked to a stop, Khadalfi stepped out, eyes searching for any sign of movement in the wadi where the flares cast their shining umbrella up the slopes.

It was a tough decision, just the same, aware he could be left alone in the next few minutes, but there was no thunder in the sky, no bird from hell roving above the wasteland. He had no intention of shooting it out with the foreign invaders. They were on the run, which told him they had accomplished whatever their mission. He intended to live to lead fighters into battle another day. God willing, these young fighters would perhaps find a way to kill or to capture the foreign devils.

Khadalfi turned, ordered all of his clansmen, "Proceed on foot! I will cover you from up here."

They were exchanging looks, grumbling among themselves, when Khadalfi lifted his assault rifle. "It is your choice, brothers. Go, or be shot here and now."

They went.

"HOLD ON, mates," McCarter whispered into his throat mike.

The Briton, kneeling in a shallow bowl-shaped depression beside Manning, watched as the ragtag band of Somalis stepped, single-file, down the incline. Even from fifty yards, McCarter could feel their nerves working on them, their movements jerky as if the fear spasmed their limbs. Dark faces scoured the slopes, weapons fanning in all directions as they shuffled into the glaring dome of flarelight. Atop the rise, McCarter stole a glance at the solitary figure. Whoever the latest leader, he was holding back. Obviously he was unconcerned that he was walking his own clansmen to their deaths. McCarter had a good mind to open up on the guy out of the gate, but figured once the shooting started he would bolt. Whatever his reasoning for not joining or having the backbone to fight alongside his doomed brethren, McCarter could venture a guess, but it didn't matter.

With the Spectre in the neighborhood, the loner didn't have a prayer.

McCarter's finger took up slack on the M-16's trigger. Eleven targets. A few of the Somalis were peering into the technical as if they expected to find a body, voices speaking excitedly in their native tongue.

McCarter keyed his com link, then gave the order. "Fire at will."

Four assault rifles and Hawkins's SAW cut loose in sync. It was a turkey shoot, McCarter saw, sweeping the doomed Somalis, stem to stern with blistering autofire, a vise of bullets clamping down on them, kicking them off their feet, nailing them to the technical's bed. One Somali, jigging backward under the onslaught, toppled on a flare, his kaftan igniting in a whoosh of flames. Return fire was weak, at best, as gunners were riddled with long salvos, bloody rags cleaved off dancing bodies, limbs spraying dark mists. The barrage of weapons fire swelled the wadi with a deafening crescendo, washing away the screams of victims dying on their feet. Three runners made it as far as halfway back up the rise, but a triple burst from across the way stitched them up the spine.

McCarter was up and sprinting down the slope. As expected, he saw the gutless wonder pile into the technical, reverse the rig, out of sight in the next moment, a pall of dust the only memory of his being here.

As he received the all-clear from Tokaido, McCarter toed a body, the stink of cooking flesh in his nose. Rolling it over, he shook his head in disgust. Another search of the dead...

Kids.

Who could fathom, he thought, the madness that was Somalia? How could a country ever hope to return to some semblance of sanity when every male above the age of ten was armed, indoctrinated by the hatred and fanaticism of the elders, and willing to murder their neighbors, plunder whatever they could? Was there an answer? Was there any hope for this country? Not his problem, he decided. He'd just as soon wash his hands of the horror that was Somalia. It damn sure appeared that very few in this country wanted to right all the ills that plagued them. Sure, there were good people, innocent people here, he knew, who only wanted to live in peace, raise a family, but there were too many running amok with guns and the desire to do nothing but kill and steal. Maybe if they put down their guns, did away with all the corrupt and murderous clan leaders, asked the world community to step in and get the basics of life—food, shelter, medicine and education—jump-started for them...

Then again, maybe the madness would never end here.

And it was distasteful, as a professional, mowing down a bunch of teenagers, but he knew they would have done the same damn thing.

McCarter spotted similar expressions of angry disbelief on the faces of his teammates, then walked up the rise. Hawkins, James, Encizo and Manning, pairing off in twos, took the Briton's wings.

The five warriors moved out of the wadi, McCarter stopping as he spotted the technical. It was racing south, spooling dust, and he wondered where in the hell the kid—and he was sure he was just another *mooryan*—thought he was going. The doomsday touch of the Spectre's work on the Somali encampment was a blazing shroud in the distance, but McCarter didn't think they would waste much more than a 105 mm from a Bofors on one fleeing technical.

They didn't.

The flying battleship thundered overhead, soaring on a south vector, McCarter figured four hundred feet above. Whatever the final thoughts of the runner went with him as the Bofors pealed, the 105 mm blast obliterating the technical with a direct hit. There was nothing but another smoking hole in the ground out there.

May God have mercy on this wretched country, McCarter thought, then patched through to the Farm. "We're done here."

BROGNOLA TURNED AWAY from the Delta One monitors as the last orange-red marker flared out. They were finished with Somalia, but Brognola knew two reports of disaster would reach Kluger soon. He had the FBI sitting on the Frankfurt facility, but there had been no sightings of the man. The big Fed suspected Kluger was hunkered down in his own version of Hitler's bunker.

Only it would be Phoenix Force eventually and not the Russians who were coming to tear down his world.

He found Price taking some computer printouts from Carmen Delahunt. She scanned the printouts, then laid them out on a table reserved for mapping and logistics. Brognola looked at the grid maps of the Golden Triangle. Price tapped an area circled at the Thai-Myanmar border, then fanned out satellite imagery.

"It took some doing, but I have a few friends over at the DEA who owe me. It's arranged for Phoenix to set down at this DEA base. They'll have full cooperation from the base commander, and they can take whatever ride they need to the Kachin State."

"It could be a full day before they land there and get moving," Brognola said, then heard Price crunching the logistical numbers, informing him that it was going to be a stretch for Able Team to beat the clock for a dawn raid on the Spanish EDEF compound, but that Phoenix Force was flying out from Kenya in a CIA Gulfstream as soon as they touched down. Brognola checked the wall clocks. "That's hours away still, but make it happen. It's time to turn up the heat. Kluger knows war's been declared on EDEF."

"And what? You think he'll make some suicidal last stand?"

"A distinct possibility. I've got a phone call to make, someone I need to see. I'll be gone for a few hours. We're getting stonewalled over at the State Department, which tells me they're hiding something, covering for someone. This Illuminating One, this Elite, supposedly a black ops inner circle within State. I need some answers, and I think I know just the person I might get them from. Keep me posted, Barb."

And Brognola left the Computer Room to make a date with Sunglasses.

"WE HAVE TO STOP meeting like this, Mr. Brognola. Even I, as busy as I am, value my sleep."

"Sorry to interrupt your beauty sleep, but this is urgent."

"So I gathered."

It was the same setup as their first encounter, Brognola sitting in the limo's well, staring across at the enigmatic man in sunglasses. The same security detail stood guard outside the limo, dark shades and earpieces all around, only now they had rendezvoused in an empty underground parking garage in Rosslyn.

During his last conversation with the Man, Brognola could have inquired as to the identity and importance of Sunglasses. But with all the crises piling up on their plates at both ends, it wasn't that high up on his priority list. Besides, he didn't want to come across as questioning the Man's judgment. Whoever Sunglasses really was, he wasn't an official member of the White House staff, the Farm having already checked into the matter. He could be something of an unofficial source of information, key contacts built over the years, one of those intelligence operatives who had all the right chess pieces in NSA, CIA...

"Wondering who I am, Mr. Brognola?"

Brognola kept the surprise off his face. "It's crossed my mind."

"Let's just say I've been around a long time, doing a lot of unofficial nasty things to keep our country and democracy safe from the bogeymen. And, yes, I have the President's ear and trust."

"Works for me."

"Down to business, then."

"The Illuminating One. The Elite. I need names and faces."

Sunglasses appeared to think about something.

"Is that a problem?"

"I've heard the rumors."

When the man fell silent, Brognola said, "That's it? All it is, rumors about a black-ops infiltration over at State?"

"No. They're real."

"I get the feeling here you're holding out."

"No. Understand something. If you go headhunting for these men, it could blow the lid off this town."

"If they're conspiring with EDEF, political fallout is my last concern."

Sunglasses bobbed his head.

"So, you'll look into it?"

"I assume you've hit a wall on the matter."

"How come I hear a note of gloating or is it relief?"

"Nothing of the kind. I do believe I have a line on these men of interest. It may take a little more investigating…"

"But you'll get back to me?"

"I have your office number."

"Leave a message."

Sunglasses chuckled. "So your secretary can just walk in and punch your answering machine and hear the dark truth of the ages?"

"It's secured to my voice mail."

"Consider it done. I'll take your word all is secure."

Brognola was rising, reaching for the door when Sunglasses cleared his throat.

"Understand this, Mr. Brognola. If I steer you in the right direction, what you find at the end of the line you may not like, nor wish you'd ever found out. We're living in the most perilous time in the history of the human race. The Four Horsemen are riding in, Mr. Brognola. Terrorist organizations are multiplying like roaches. Rogue nations are in the process of making deals to deliver WMD to these groups. International drug cartels are producing more narcotics than ever before, and they are selling to the terrorists. Despite what you hear about the world's oil supplies, they may be tapped out in another fifty years at the current rate of consumption and demand, but there is a plan for our side to seize every field over there.

"AIDS will wipe out most of Africa in the next two decades and someone will have to step in and claim all the mineral wealth left behind after the corpses are burned. The world's population will quadruple by 2020. Food will be the equivalent of gold. Europe, because of immigration and its socialist politics, is going to collapse into anarchy. Pakistan and India will soon wipe each other off the world map with nukes, so that will be a billion less mouths on the Indian subcontinent to have to worry about feeding."

"And there's a growing hole in the Ozone and the Mother of all meteors is coming to send man the way of the dinosaur. I'm aware it's a big, bad ugly world out there."

"You don't know the half of it. Let's just say, for the sake of discussion, certain seeds have been sown, certain trenches have been dug, certain individuals, deemed essential personnel, have been chosen. A war is coming, a world war, a struggle never before seen for the continuation of the human race. And the weapons that will be used no scientist, virologist, no architect of weapons of mass destruction now known..."

Brognola felt his gut clench when the man fell silent. He didn't need to see the eyes to know he was in the presence of a fanatic. Or was Sunglasses something else, something more?

"I'll be in touch, Mr. Brognola."

Brognola was no sooner out of the limo than the security detail was piling in, doors thudding shut, engine growling. He stepped back as the limo reversed out of the slot, lurched ahead, rounded the corner, vanished. Alone in the silence and emptiness of the garage, Brognola strongly suspected what he had feared all along.

THE CIA CHIEF of Counterterrorism in Spain was known to them only as Mitch. He was slender and slightly bald on top, with weak blue eyes. Definitely not the kind of lean, mean gung-ho Company gunslinger Lyons had seen before.

They were in what Lyons assumed was the command and control center of the Company safehouse, complete with digital wall maps, computers, grim CIA operatives, armed with shouldered Berettas like Mitch, manning their stations.

Lyons, Schwarz and Blancanales had just deposited their war bags on a table when Mitch hurled something their way. Lyons caught the wool object against his chest, unfolded a black ski mask.

"We're not here to rob a bank, Ace," Lyons said.

Mitch turned, walked away, chuckling as if some private joke was on Able Team. "I was told to cooperate, and that's what I'm doing. This way."

They followed Mitch to a large steel door. He pulled the handle, opened it, and Lyons took a blast of icy air to the face. Stepping inside, trailing Mitch, the Able Team leader found six body bags on the floor. Mitch unzipped a rubber bag and Lyons stared down at a swarthy bearded face, noting the neat dark hole between the eyes.

"I hope this isn't your sick idea of show-and-tell for a vision of our own futures," Schwarz remarked.

"Al-Qaeda operatives," Mitch said, and zipped up the bag. "Assuming your mission is a success, they'll be planted along your exfiltration route. How, when and where I got these," he said, nodding at the bags, "is unimportant. They're your cover."

"The attack will look like terrorism," Blancanales commented.

"You catch on quick," Mitch stated. "This is all assuming…"

"We make it out alive," Lyons said.

"Or aren't captured. Here," he said, handing three plastic cards with magnetic strips to Able Team. "You'll need these. Those are free passes to any and all areas, including Level Four belowground."

"What the hell?" Lyons said. "We're just going to waltz right in, mine the facility and sashay out into the Spanish countryside, tiptoe through the vineyards?"

Mitch walked out of the freezer. "Something like that. How you get it done is your business."

"I'm catching a bad whiff, Mitch," Lyons said, leading his teammates out of the cooler, the CIA man shutting the door, then striding toward a large table littered with grid maps and satellite imagery. "You know the feeling you get when your sphincter starts to pucker because some guy is creeping up behind you with a meat cleaver?"

"I was told to cooperate."

"You already said that," Lyons growled. "What aren't you telling us?"

Mitch stabbed a red circle on a map where the province of Castilla La Mancha was marked off. "Our chopper will drop you in this ravine. It's a half klick hike up and out. The west gate will already be open for you. Here," he said, handing Lyons a small black box. "Punch that button and your man will be signaled to know it's begun. He will be alone in the control room. No one but he will be monitoring surveillance."

"Our man?" Schwarz said.

Lyons took a black-and-white 8x11 pic of a hawk-ish face, framed in shoulder-length black hair, from Mitch. The intense stare in the eyes struck Lyons as anger bordering rage.

"His name is Zeller," Mitch said. "Try not to shoot him."

"Whoa," Lyons said. "German?"

"German. Head of Security for EDEF here in Spain. We've turned him, but he came to us first. Seems he likes the local wine and women. One day he was out carousing, spotted us, and made us an offer."

"Telling us he grew a conscience?" Blancanales said.

"It would seem so. He knows what Kluger and his Spanish cohorts are doing and wants out. What can I say? He's a family man, and I guess he doesn't relish the idea of either dying for his boss's insanity or spending the rest of his life in prison. We've known for some time they are breeding a Level Four virus to be fused into the artificial food substance produced at Nutricen. We were just about to mount our own operation with the Spanish authorities to take it down."

"Then, like Christmas gifts come early, we fell into your laps," Lyons said.

"If you three are manna from heaven, I hope you can prove it. Up there," he said, pointing at the array of pics numbered one through forty pinned to a board. "Your printout of the facility nearly jibes with on-the-scene surveillance. Now, you have a security force of fifteen, mostly Germans, all armed with assault rifles."

"We weren't expecting a day at the beach," Lyons said.

"Yes, shooting. I'm assuming you will make your presence known in order to clear out the workforce."

"We'll handle it," Lyons said. "We're not here to blow up a bunch of innocent civilians."

"Very well, and how innocent they are remains to be seen, but I intend to round them up for extensive questioning. Now. Return to your original drop point. You'll have sixty minutes inside. That should be ample enough time to do the deed."

"I'm not making any guarantees we can beat that clock," Lyons said. "I want a frequency to our ride. No matter what, they'd better be there."

"I can arrange that. But don't take much longer than sixty minutes."

"Saying you'd rather not let the Spanish know of your involvement," Lyons said. "Wash your hands of us if this goes to hell?"

"Anyway, you will fly to the Mediterranean coast. There you will be dropped off and a boat will take you north to Perpignan," he said, jabbing a circle on the French shoreline. "Your plane will be there, refueled, ready to take you wherever."

"And that's that," Lyons said as Mitch began taking the surveillance photos off the board.

"Not much time before you hit the ground, but you might want to study these. I have blueprints, also."

Lyons chuckled.

"Something funny?"

"All this last minute hand of God," Lyons said, "it makes me a little nervous."

"You're professionals, I assume. You know how these sorts of operations fall."

"Indeed, we do," Lyons said. "But—" Lyons paused, stared Mitch dead in the eye "—do I have to say the words?"

"That if I'm breaking it off in your collective asses," Mitch said, and slapping the stack of photos on the Able Team leader's chest. "That if I'm leading you three into an elaborate setup, that if I'm not playing it straight with you, you will hunt me down to the ends of the earth if that's what it takes and kill me slow and in great pain?"

Lyons smiled. "Those would be the words."

CHAPTER TWELVE

Hector Octavio was annoyed.

The phone was trilling on the nightstand, interrupting the first sex dream he'd found himself lost in and nurturing in months. There he was, on a sandy beach in the French Riviera—or maybe it was Barcelona—but locale wasn't all that critical in the overall picture, a minor detail stacked against the services being rendered on his naked form by three beautiful women. It had all seemed so real, so blissful, little shy of ascent to heaven, but dreams came to him like that after a long night of swilling wine and whiskey until he passed out on his king-size bed.

These days, reality was beyond frightening. And even dreamless sleep was preferable to the truth.

Reality, in fact, was an ongoing horror show, and not even sleep seemed to provide the escape he so desperately sought.

He was, allegedly, in charge of the EDEF facility at the base of the Cordillera Central, but he was all too grimly aware of the real power jerking his puppet strings. There was a time when others had danced to his music or they suffered loss of income, liberty and even life. A former policeman on the Narcotics Task Force in Madrid, he longed for the simpler times of yesteryear, when a bribe or a bullet made all the difference securing the future. Back in the good old days, yes, when he could help himself to a cut of the pie with the major traffickers, provide protection...

Oh, but he could damn near weep over the awful responsibilities of his current predicament. In fact, knowledge alone was killing him.

The phone shrilled.

Why him? he wondered. Why now? Who could this intrusive bastard be?

Since he'd been assigned the task of overseeing the project, aware of what the sorcerers in Level Four were brewing, a decent night's sleep was next to impossible unless he self-medicated into catatonic inebriation. Lately the nightmares had been coming on stronger, and more alive, to the point where he wasn't sure what was real, what wasn't, even when he jolted and twitched awake, hand shuddering for the bottle he always kept on the nightstand, a fat shot always going down the hatch if only to help him shake off the final vestiges of nightmare.

But how could he forget? Most nights it was the

same terror, a running film that seemed scripted from some ghoul living inside his head. In those horrible visions he was being chased by howling faceless mobs. They wielded sharp instruments—meat cleavers, axes, swords and so on—chasing his naked body through a maze of narrow dark streets. Well, they weren't entirely faceless, he recalled. They were the walking dead, damned and afflicted by plague. Oozing running sores, blood spilling from every orifice, skin sloughing off their bodies like a snake in shedding, they ran after him, telling him how they would kill him, so slow and in such agony he would beg for death.

He would run, but it seemed he could get nowhere, the mobs closing in, the din of their agony and hatred a piercing wail, a babble of tongues, blades flashing as he suddenly found himself pinned against a wall. Just before they descended...

Blessed reality came when he was jarred awake, hyperventilating, just the same, drenched in cold sweat.

And now...some inconsiderate bastard was demanding his attention. Worse yet, he found it was the red line, which meant the Visigoths were calling.

He sucked down a mouthful of whiskey, moved his beefy frame from beneath the silk covers. The fire hit his ample belly, smoothed out some of the rough edges of his anger, but the ringing hit his pulsing brain like a fusillade of cannon fire.

Octavio picked up the receiver. "Yes?"

"You haf invormant on base."

What the hell was this? he wondered, silently cursed that angry guttural bark as the Visigoth spoke in broken English and way too loud for his liking.

"What?"

"You heard."

"Who?"

"We are coming to handle ze situation."

The Visigoth hung up. An informant? Who? Anyone who set foot on the facility was not only given a thorough background check, but was monitored from the control room, cameras and minimikes planted over nearly every square foot of the compound. If they left the complex for any period of time—R and R usually—they were shadowed by Visigoths, home phones tapped, bugs secreted away in their private dwellings, minicameras mounted in the ceiling even monitoring the most intimate of bedroom moments between husbands and wives or scientists, security staff and their mistresses or whores. There were no secrets, sexual or otherwise, under his roof. Not that he was aware of.

He wished the German had shown enough courtesy to, at the very least, inform him when their barbarian horde would land. That way, he could have slept another hour or so, malingering in the arms and breasts of his girlfriends on the beach. But that was another thing he was sick and tired of, the Germans, rude, arrogant and holding everyone but their own kind in contempt.

He was no man's lackey.

A check of the clock and he found the sun wasn't even due up for another hour or so. Whatever was happening, he knew this was going to be a long and nervous morning. It sounded as if the Visigoths were coming to shed some traitor's blood.

Octavio decided another stiff belt of booze was in order before he dressed and armed himself.

CARL LYONS WOULD rather trust a used-car salesman than a CIA operative under these present conditions. His mind churned with any number of fiascos, one of which was ambush.

He shelved the 101 "what-if" worst-case scenarios. But, if it looked a setup, he would proceed anyway, with no choice but to blast, shoot and burn their way out. Hadn't he insisted the Farm hand over this leg of the mission to the three of them anyway? Why cry now?

Lyons led Schwarz and Blancanales up a narrow crevice, NVD goggles aimed at the fence line, their chopper ride gone, hugging the earth on its southern vector out of the ravine. He spotted the gate, heart thumping as he closed, humping his weapons and forty-five pounds of C-4 up the steep grade. If nothing else it would be good to start lightening the C-4 load, sure that soon enough he would require all the swift and unencumbered movement he could muster.

He spotted the cameras mounted on the razor-topped fencing, certain there were motion and heat sensors staggered all over the place. So far no gunmen loomed in the dark.

MP-5 with attached sound suppressor leading the climb, Lyons topped out and checked the grounds. North, he found the huge storage tanks of rocket fuel. There were eighteen-wheelers, cranes, forklifts and other machinery scattered around skeletal launch pads. He wasn't sure how much rocket fuel was housed, but judging all the pipelines, valves and bins…

It was going to be quite the show of fireworks, he reckoned. Hell, he figured igniting the rocket fuel alone might do the job of wiping the entire facility off the face of the plateau, but he wasn't leaving this operation behind on a prayer and a hope.

Lyons snugged the SPAS-12 higher up on his shoulder, his webbing chocked to maximum with grenades, spare clips for the subgun and twin .45s. At some point, the Able Team leader knew it would be both messy and noisy.

Why wait?

Lyons reared up out of the gully, tried the gate and found it open, as advertised. He was inside, beckoning for Blancanales and Schwarz to start mining the storage area, when he heard the familiar thwump of chopper blades. His teammates threw him a look over their shoulders, but Lyons waved them on, beelining for the entrance door, his magnetic swipe card in hand. He didn't know who the new arrivals were, but he didn't like the way his gut was knotting up, warning him trouble was on the way, and they hadn't even breached the door to penetrate the compound proper.

Lyons heard the bitter chuckle of Lady Luck in his head, laughing.

IT WAS OVER, but Klaus Zeller had no problem with his decision to become a CIA informant. If he was going to die, it would be with a clear conscience, a tab clean of transgression, a sort of self-redemption that he was an overseer of architects of mass death, but ready to commit suicide to right his wrong.

As head of security he was able to march in and demand the others—Spanish and German—leave him alone in the command and control room. He was sticking the C-4 blocks, primed and ready to blow at the touch of a radio remote button, beneath tables holding the monitors, when he saw the trio pop up on the west edge of the compound. They slipped through the gate he'd opened on the signal they'd relayed on the vibrating pager. They were in combat blacksuit, com links secured around their ski masks, heavily armed, with nylon satchels hanging from their shoulders, bulging with what he suspected were enough high explosives to blow the facility clear up the mountainside. Who they were and how they would carry out their mission, he didn't know.

He only wanted the madness of Heinz Kluger trampled to a twisted fading vision of nightmare. The end had come to Kluger's sister facility in Spain, but Zeller wondered if it was all too little too late.

Most of the workforce was still asleep, but the graveyard shift was fifteen strong, all of them lumbering around in space suits as they went about their ghoul's task of fusing artificial food with the Level Four virus that brought on near-instant symptoms of hemorrhagic fever. Zeller wondered if the nameless, faceless invaders would sound the alarm, clear out the work detail. The word had come to him through his CIA contact that the entire facility would most likely be reduced to smoking ruins by high explosives. If they didn't flush noncombatants away from ground zero, Zeller wouldn't hold them accountable for the transgression of inflicting vast and wanton collateral damage. There were no innocents under this roof.

His decision had been made when he heard about the Somali test subjects, summoned by Kluger who had boasted that in a short time—months perhaps—entire countries would be stricken with plague, the governments of breeding grounds held for ransom by a promised but phantom vaccine. The thought of hundreds of thousands dying a slow and agonizing death because of one rich man's craving for more power, more control, sickened him.

Where would it end? First Third World countries, then what next? Blackmail all of Europe with the threat of mass plague? It was abomination, but Zeller would fulfill his role, ending the insanity, no matter what it took, and even if it cost him his own life.

There was only regret. He was, after all, a family

man; a wife and five children he knew he would leave behind. The money was the best he had ever known, Kluger doling out vast sums to the most skilled of former GSG-9 commandos. Only Kluger's money, he thought, couldn't purchase a man's soul. Small comfort, but he knew he wouldn't leave behind a poor widow, worrying how she would feed five mouths.

He was hauling the G-3 assault rifle from the weapons closet, wedging four spare clips in his waistband, when he spotted the two executive choppers with the mailed-fist emblem touch down on the rooftop helipad.

There had been radio silence from Frankfurt, and no one was receiving his own calls at the EDEF facility there. The first red flag, then, telling him they knew he had turned. Now this, as expected, watching as he counted a force of twelve, long black-leather trench coats sweeping behind them, G-3 assault rifles leading the march.

The heavy hitters had landed to clean house, he knew. The end had come.

HE WAS CALLED the Cleaner, and Fritz Lugar savored every opportunity to embolden and expand the legend of his dreaded reputation. Whether they caught the whispers of his heroic duty in EDEF boardrooms, laboratories, bedrooms, brothels or his own troops raised a toast to him in a beer hall in Frankfurt was all of equal importance.

Fear was better than respect. Fear kept honest men honest.

It was the dishonest and the treacherous who always required his special attention.

It had been quite the career, he thought, smiling to himself, marching toward the two Spanish sentries manning posts by the service stairwell. If he was so inclined, he could have mounted the stuffed heads of all his victims on his mantel back in his estate in the homeland, a tribute to himself for a long career as a professional assassin and GSG-9 black op. Up and coming were a few more imaginary heads to toss on the shelf, perhaps this morning his crowning achievement, victory hurling him higher up the ranks of EDEF security, perhaps Kluger anointing him his right hand.

This particular outing was a special challenge, to both professional skill and Teutonic pride, but he hadn't lived as long as he had in his world by either shrinking from the tough hits or backing off when it came to taking out one of his own kind. It would be a shame. Zeller was ex-GSG-9, a family man, no less, but he had his orders, and they included a lengthy torture workout. There was a good chance where there was one snake there was a whole nest. Which was why he ordered his men bring along at least two large tool bags for when the surgeries began.

He moved farther from the rotor wash, knew he was flanked by the best damn commandos on the continent and beyond, heart pounding with pride, aware a mere squad of his own was about to capture the complex, and woe be to the first Spaniard who squawked.

He might slice and dice a few Spaniards, he thought, just for the hell of it, let them know the Visigoths were back in town. That was part of what was wrong with Europe—especially Germany—and it was long since time, he thought, to reclaim the land, reestablish the culture of the indigenous peoples who had lived on the continent for thousands of years. All immigrants would have to be deported, American military sent packing back across the Atlantic. Perhaps the French even needed to be invaded again, since their own arrogance and getting bailed out by the Americans tended to leave them with short memories. It was a start, Lugar thought, and Frankfurt had the power, the will and the means to make it happen. Lugar wanted to be there, hell, he wanted to spearhead the coming juggernaut.

Time to get lit up, stoke the juices, accelerate the adrenaline rush, his mind excited by visions of himself as the new Rommel. Snapping his fingers, he glimpsed the assault rifle sailing across the roof, caught it one-handed. The G-3 cocked and locked, two 40-round extended magazines married together with duct tape. He held out his fist and with another castanet snap of the fingers, white powder was dumped out of a vial. The Spaniards were looking at each other as he vacuumed the white mound off his hand, then Lugar snapped his fingers at them, waved them aside. They nearly didn't part fast enough, Lugar feeling his finger tighten around the trigger, a supernova of euphoric rush making him feel as if he could suddenly fly.

Maybe he would, he thought. Maybe he could.

Soar like an avenging eagle.

The orders from Frankfurt were as clear as the soundless blinding light in his head. He was to clean up the mess, rectify the situation, restore order, or not return to Germany unless he was in a bag.

THE C-4 LOAD WAS lightened by half, Blancanales figured, by the time he finished mining the storage bins, placing the charges with Schwarz at strategic and staggered intervals around the compass, then deep inside where the pipelines ran to a giant dispensing pump.

Watching the roof and the open no-man's land between the gate and the west facing of the compound, Blancanales and Schwarz sprinted to where Lyons was standing in the doorway. Ironman, Blancanales saw, was gritting his teeth, clock-watching. They didn't need to be told they were on the Company clock, critical minutes already gobbled up with the initial mining job. Blancanales checked his own watch, Little Bulldozer bouncing between his shoulder blades, MP-5 out and ready to cut loose at the first sign of trouble.

They were down to forty-eight minutes.

They hit the door running, Blancanales finding they were in a long, narrow hallway. Walls and floor were a bright antiseptic white, with two cameras mounted on both sides at roughly thirty-foot intervals. In a perfect world, he thought, they would have taken ample time to thoroughly study the interior layout, but Blancanales had committed the CIA photos and blueprint to memory. He'd told Lyons as much, so took point, Schwarz watching their six, Ironman in the middle, taking in the whole compass.

They passed several closed doors, but according to the blueprints one was a storage room for janitorial and repair equipment, another door leading to a weight room, an auditorium housed behind door number three. Ears tuned to the slightest noise, Blancanales heard nothing, but at this early morning hour, most of the workforce was asleep in their quarters at the far northeast wing of the complex.

In terms of square footage, he figured the complex as large as the classified and now demolished Nutricen facility. Any real estate addition was Level Four— virus central—down below. According to the blueprints and playing back the tape of his memory, he cut left at the end of the hallway. Another fifty-yard jog and they would reach the tube, hermetically sealed, that would drop them into the bowels of the complex.

No wailing Klaxons, and Blancanales was taking that as a good sign when two black-suited figures, armed with subguns, popped out of a doorway to his one o'clock. They hesitated, the surprise on their faces telling Blancanales they knew nothing about the invasion.

Blancanales hit the trigger on his H&K, the subgun burping, stitching the hardmen, left to right, twin steams of chugging lead flying past his shoulder as Lyons and Schwarz jumped into the act.

Cautious, Blancanales edged up to the doorway, listened but heard no ruckus created by the sound of thudding bodies. He swept inside what appeared a computer room, delving into his demo bag.

"Hustle up, Pol," Lyons snapped. "Gadgets, cover the hall. I'll meet you two in the elevator."

Blancanales primed a chunk of plastique the size of a softball, stuck it under a desktop. It was a shame, blowing up what could prove invaluable intelligence. Blancanales was sure Schwarz was itching to pack a bag with CD-ROMs and whatever else he could pilfer here. So far, so easy, but Blancanales knew hitting Level Four was where the hardball started. There would most likely be armed resistance. There would be quarantined areas where they were breeding viruses. Even though they had only been so far spotted by the dead, there had to be some alarm system down below...

Blancanales heard his com link crackle, Lyons gruffing, "While we're still young, Pol?"

CHAPTER THIRTEEN

If there was a scintilla of doubt and question about his personal doomsday before the cleaning crew landed, then all Klaus Zeller had to do now was to watch the detail of six Spanish guards shuffle into view at the deep end of Corridor Main, weapons fanning, eyes bugged. They appeared uncertain, nervous, Zeller aware they were staring into an empty C and C, wondering what in the world was going on, and where the hell were the watchdogs, most likely.

When the demo work was done, he had radioed Kiegler, informing him there was a situation in the command and control room, all hands to report immediately, hinting at a crisis. The intent to gather the flock in the C and C would provide, he hoped, the critical double-punch to aid and assist whatever the avalanche to crush the facility. One, he was seeking to shave the opposition odds for the invaders. Two, he wanted the C and C utterly destroyed, no watching eyes able to track the movements of the mystery trio or monitor his own planned lethal breakout.

But what was that saying, he thought, about men making plans, God enjoying a nice belly-ripper?

Well, Kiegler had responded to his call, all right, but Zeller, edged out on adrenaline and paranoia, shelving any self-pity over his own mortality, caught the guarded tone, which was brittle, a cord of gloating just beneath the surface.

They knew, and they knew he knew.

Funny, he thought, how when a man knew he was facing his last minutes in the world, his senses, awareness of other human beings was so intense, it was almost like looking through a pane of glass, seeing others for the first time, for what they really were.

Instead of Germans, Kiegler marched out their Spanish counterparts.

It figured. Kiegler was well-known in ex-GSG-9 circles for letting the other guy do the dirty work while he hung back, scheming how to grab the brass ring.

Zeller lingered at the corner of Corridor Main, radio remote in hand, peering down the hall as the Spaniards filed into the C and C. He held the fatal moment back, ticking off the doomsday numbers, aware that when he did it there was enough plastique squirreled away that no one would recognize the remains. There was a babble of Spanish flaying out the doorway, echoing down the hall, Zeller certain they had just marked the invaders on the monitors.

Perfect.

Why prolong their agony? he decided, and hit the flashing red button to seal their doom.

It would have added fuel to the flames of his own pyrrhic victory if the German contingent had amassed in the C and C, but at this point, Zeller would take whatever fate threw him. However it was all about to be sliced and diced, he knew he had just left himself no way out, no options but to go down, dying on his feet.

After a quick silent prayer that his family remain safe, that this was the beginning of the end of Kluger and EDEF, Zeller broke into a hard run, G-3 out and searching, as he charged down bisecting Hall C. According to the monitor, the cleaning crew was coming down the stairwell on the south-central grid. They could, conceivably, split up...

He was rounding the corner, skidding to a halt, when he found he was right. Half of the force was bounding off the steps, eyes shining with some wild light, and Zeller hit the trigger.

CARL LYONS entered the bowels of the complex with a clean but seething conscience.

Civilian scientific or microbiologist genius or not, these people weren't seeking a cure for cancer or AIDS, he knew. They weren't on the cutting edge of creating nuclear propulsion that would allow man to travel into deep space, discover a way to harness the speed of light so humans could explore the heavens a zillion miles away in the next galaxy. They weren't looking to save the whales, the rain forest, the Ozone or feed the starving masses of the world.

They were ghouls, devils in human skin, engineering offensive biological weapons, the likes of which were, purportedly, so ghastly they made symptoms of anthrax or botulism look like the common cold in comparison. Not only was the production of biological weapons in direct violation of international treaties, it more or less swelled Lyons with a fear of what might happen if they were allowed to carry on. Attack satellites, deorbiting, sailing over city streets, spraying plague? It was one thing to go up in a nuclear cloud. That was quick and clean, at least, vaporized in an eye blink, a shadow of what stood branded on the ground. But the mere thought of dying a lingering agonizing death from an unseen man-made plague walked an icy shiver down his spine.

Lyons didn't like to be afraid. It tended to bring out the crazy side of the berserker warrior in him, and there were already those, he knew, who thought him lunatic enough on a good day.

The Able Team leader was first off the elevator-tube, MP-5 up and spitting, locked on to the first available armed targets. He felt a fleeting relief, the CIA spy photos and blueprints holding up, true to pictorial numbered layout, but from there on he knew they were tagged as intruders, the alarm sure to be sounded. Easy, he thought, just went the way of the next two victims.

On the fly, hosing down two hardmen leaping from what appeared a reception area, Lyons took in the bowels of this devil's dungeon when they flopped to the floor, rubber limbs bouncing as the final nerve spasms petered out. A sprawling circular workbay was separated by a running wall of reinforced hermetically sealed glass, curling out east by south where partitioned bays of futuristic-looking machinery, boards, computers and God only knew what were housed on both sides of the barrier. Lyons counted maybe fifteen space suits behind the shield. They had been pursuing whatever their various chores, lumbering around tables choked with vials, tubes, trays and other instruments that looked silvery and alien, or standing on platforms beside vats and monitoring centrifuges, when Lyons gave Blancanales the order, "Hit the decon chamber with a few 40 mils and clear them the hell out of this building. They don't want to bail, that's their problem!"

They were flapping their arms in the Level Four pen, hollering something at the sight of the man in the black ski mask with the multiround projectile launcher about to blow them all to hell and gone. A moment later they were waddling for deep cover, dropping tubes, lurching about, human bumper cars, when Blancanales went to work with the Little Bulldozer.

After a glimpse of the first 40 mm round blasting the decon chamber to a memory, Lyons came under fire. He was in flight, hunched and dodging rounds that slashed off the shiny white floor, hot slipstreams grazing past his knuckles. He hit a partition, thought he was covered, then discovered the shooting was coming from above. It was quite often even a professional's fatal mistake, he knew.

Not looking up had cost more than one warrior his life.

They were up on the lattice of catwalks, about thirty feet, Lyons figured, and began sweeping the figures with subgun fire as they darted for deeper cover, near what looked like an office. One, then two bodies were in swan dive, flailing acrobats screaming all the way down before they hammered through computers and tables, as Blancanales pounded the decon chamber to smoking ruins with another direct hit.

A sound like distant thunder rolled over Lyons's position, but with Schwarz blasting away with his subgun, nailing more runners up top, the Able Team leader wasn't sure what he heard. It came from the east, or so it seemed, but they hadn't breached the facility that deep yet.

Could just be adrenaline, he decided, the sounds of pitched battle obscuring the senses. He went back to helping Schwarz clear the hellgrounds above.

LUGAR WAS AWARE of the rumbles about his cocaine use. It was a five-gram-a-day habit—ninety percent

pure Colombian flake and straight off the plane from
his Russian Mafia contacts—but he reasoned a man
with all the responsibility on his plate had earned a few
frills, not to mention attitude. Whoever the gossip
whores were, he didn't know, nor much cared unless
he could pin a name to a shadow, then he would have
a conversation with the individual at the business end
of a weapon. Say whatever the whispering chickenshits
would out of earshot, his senses were electrified, abso-
lute awareness around the compass and beyond galva-
nizing reaction time to superhuman levels,
metamorphosing him into a blur that, with a few more
sniffs, he figured, and he could fly at light speed.

No sooner was he off the stairs than he spotted Zeller—no, he decided, he could almost feel the man coming before he appeared.

The traitorous snake wheeled around the corner,
blazing away with his assault rifle, but Lugar was already in light-speed mode. He sensed rather than saw
the door to his right, hurling himself into the barrier
where the handle was perhaps locked in place, but why
worry? Again, he laughed at the rabble-rousers who
snubbed his habit, his body a flying bulldozer, plow-
ing through the door—made of steel as he felt the impact—and crashed into what appeared a room where
they diagrammed satellites. He felt the warm spray of
blood on his face, knew his guys were getting chopped
up—could feel them dying—his hearing so amplified
the grunts of his troops dead on their feet and the racket

of weapons fire swelling the buzz in his brain it seemed a living entity, lifting him off his feet.

Was it only Zeller down there?

Who knew? Who cared?

He plucked a frag grenade from a pocket in his trench coat, pulled the pin and dumped the spoon. He had already made out the rumble of the explosion from some point west, suspected sabotage by either Zeller or whatever more snakes he had persuaded to join him in betrayal. As far as he was concerned, the only survivors after this blitz would be Teutonic blood who willingly bowed to the coming regime that would conquer way beyond the borders of Europe.

Around the edge of the door's frame, Lugar swept the hall one-handed with autofire, driving Zeller to cover as he lobbed the steel ball. The light was so intense, the whiteness of the hall began to sting his eyes, but there was no mistaking the running smears on the wall across the way as three of his troops pitched to the floor.

Lugar held back a full second, hugging the door-jamb as the grenade went off in a thunderclap that spiked his senses.

"Go, go!" he shouted at his men, but he was already taking point, firing the G-3 at the tattered figure crabbing the floor, pooling blood behind legs that looked as if they had been shoved through a meat grinder. "Son of a bitch!" he raged at Zeller, nailing him to the floor with a burst up the back.

He was checking the hallway when his tac radio crackled, Octavio patching through. The panic in the Spaniard's voice was little shy of a trumpet blast in his ears, a bleating sheep he intended to shear in short order. "What?"

"We have intruders below in Level Four. Three men in black ski masks. The far west quadrant, I am informed. They also blew up the command and control center."

"Keep them pinned down! We are on the way!"

While he rang up Schultz, leader of Eagle Team Two, Lugar kept marching, rounding the corner to Corridor Main. There was no doubt in his mind it was Zeller who had mined and gutted the C and C room. Likewise he suspected Octavio, a former corrupt narcotics cop who loved money and luxury more than fighting, was not on scene in Level Four.

Time to take out all the garbage, Lugar decided, rolling for the billows of smoke pouring into the hall. He snapped his fingers, watching the gray cloud for armed shadows, then snatched a reserve vial from a comrade.

Another fat huff to keep the superman flying strong, and he was good to go the distance.

"BLOW DOWN the whole goddamn wall!"

Lyons found the sorcerers could move pretty fast in their protective cocoons.

Blancanales had already shouted, in both Spanish

and English, the facility was going to blow up, to evacuate the premises, alert their comrades. Lyons put them
out of mind. If they made it out, fine. If not…

As far as he was concerned, they were guilty as
charged. If Mitch, their CIA contact, became miffed
down the line over the loss of scientific HUMINT,
Lyons didn't much give a damn.

While Blancanales carried out the order, hit the
glass barricade with a raking barrage of 40 mm blasts,
blowing in tidal waves of shards over the fleeing space
suits, Schwarz threw in long subgun bursts at the contingent of hardmen making the scene from the east.
Armed opposition—five at Lyons's first head count—
flew around the massive workbay to the south as
Schwarz hosed them down, crimson spraying glass
partitions, boneless forms toppling into a bank of
standing monitors, sailing over tables. The trouble was,
he found, as soon as one wave was rolled back, another
round of hardmen charged in on their convulsing
forms.

Not good, Lyons thought, but knew improvising,
sucking it up to keep going in the heat of battle, was
one key to walking out the other side.

That, and just plain waxing the enemy, no mercy,
no hesitation.

Reviewing his own mental blueprint of the complex, Lyons knew there were more elevators, a service
stairwell in the east quad where the cavalry kept charging from. Evac was hardly guaranteed, but it was time

to crank up the heat, boogie out the bowels and up and outside. No question they would come under fire the whole way out, which was why, Lyons knew, they needed to decimate as much of the enemy force here as possible. In the plus column, the security force either didn't wield rocket launchers or were under orders not to lob around warheads or grenades for fear of demolishing all the dark work conjured up here.

If that was true, he thought, the enemy was on the verge of being left holding the shitty end of the stick.

Lyons bulled through the hanging shards and shattered metal wings of the decon chamber. As leader, he decided if there was any unnecessary risk to exposure of brewing virus, he should be the one to take the gamble. If an errant round blasted the milky garbage in those vats in his face, or demon's brew from ruptured vials...

He triggered a subgun burst at three hardmen leapfrogging between tables and centrifuges. The trio was torn between directing fire at Schwarz and Blancanales beyond the hot zone in the workbays, or winging rounds his way, but Lyons knew he only had a few seconds to dump his beast of burden. Quickly he began fixing blocks of plastique beneath worktables, skirting a length of centrifuges and vats, attaching them beneath these devil's caldrons, ten pounds a pop. It would take more than a cursory look to discover the doomsday packages, but Lyons didn't intend to leave any search party behind.

Lyons flung away his empty satchel, his subgun
sans sound suppressor up and flaming as eight hardmen wended between workstations, tables, centrifuges, flaying his position with a hornet's nest of
swarming rounds.

Cursing as he burned through his clip, Lyons threw
himself into a 360 spin, rounds spanging off the side
of the centrifuge. Hanging the subgun around his
shoulder, the Able Team leader drew both .45s,
whipped to the opposite edge of the centrifuge line and
began unloading.

Extending one .45 at a time, he drew target acquisition on darting hardmen, squeezing one trigger then the
other. Beyond the sonic booms of his barrage, Lyons
saw the fulminated mercury in the .45 rounds produce
devastating, gruesome results. Exploding through
chests on impact, the enemy was launched through
the air as if hit by a runaway train, the blood detonations on exit betraying massive holes blown out between shoulder blades, leaving no doubt heart and
lungs were nothing more than greasy mush.

And Lyons kept on searching for more live ones,
.45s panning on. One enemy gunner was running for
cover, hunched behind a glass partition. Lyons gave the
runner some lead, then a double-tap took out the partition like paper blown in a hurricane. The rabbit
screamed at the sight of his arm sheared off at the
shoulder, lurching up, a sick expression on his face at
the sight of the thick blood geysering in the air. Real-

izing number two exploding bullet had missed, perhaps deflected off the mark by reinforced glass, Lyons ended the gunner's misery with one pulverizing round through the heart.

Lyons marched ahead, grabbing cover behind a bank of computers, bullets snapping past his ears. Midway down the devil's lair, he figured he was clear of any danger zone, at least from plague.

There was still plenty of opposition, however, to blast through, as he found Schwarz and Blancanales coming under fire from above. One look up to the catwalk and Lyons suspected the mystery party had arrived. It was a trench coat fashion show, he noted, a computer erupting into sparks and flying debris near his face, but they were serious about their role as shooters.

Lean and mean to a man, they were hosing down the position of his teammates with G-3 autofire. Lyons became a grim believer the German tribe was there to nail down the hassle of three armed invaders in ski masks in the process of bringing down the roof. The good news, Lyons discovered, was the glass dome over the hot zone had been taken out by Little Bulldozer. There were jagged gaps wide enough for Lyons to pound out a few rounds, a .45 decimator kicking one of the newcomers off the catwalk.

Bad news—Lyons was still under tenacious fire from another cavalry charge, dead ahead.

For the moment he knew Schwarz and Blancanales were on their own.

LUGAR COULD SEE from his vantage point that maximum damage had been inflicted on Level Four. Three madmen down below were scything through the security force from interlocking fields of fire. There was no sense in tabbing up a body count. Corpses were stacked and littered what seemed every square yard. Who and what they were was unimportant. He suspected, given what he knew about the late and unlamented Zeller, they were CIA black ops. Beyond waxing the trio of invaders here in Spain, he suspected Kluger and the Frankfurt facility would soon come under siege. On the off chance he could capture one of them alive…

Why bother?

Lugar was bounding down the catwalk, the big shooter with the stainless-steel hand cannons dumping one of his commandos over the side for free fall, when he snatched a glimpse of the invader with the multi-round projectile launcher. There were two of them, hunkered in the workbays, able to conceal themselves, what with all the partitions, worktables, machinery and banks of computers.

Lugar kept advancing down the catwalk, spraying the workbay with long sweeps of autofire, punching big holes through glass-and-plaster partitions, craving that one opening to nail it down. His remaining force— down to seven shooters, unless there were more in the hot zone going toe-to-toe with Herr Hand Cannons—

was strung out behind, a firing squad of G-3s eating up the workbay with a swarm of lead locusts.

Lugar pulled a frag grenade from his coat pocket, eager to finish the standoff.

Enough of this nonsense, he thought. The buzz would fizzle in another minute or so, and he would be hearing howling ghosts demanding another hit.

BLANCANALES KNEW they were in a tight spot.

The new arrivals had secured a firepoint directly above—the worst of all dreaded scenarios. A quick spy into the hot zone revealed what appeared close to ten more hardmen hungry to snap the jaws on Lyons, and Blancanales knew he had to put Little Bulldozer back to angry task.

One second, he knew, hefting the weapon to his chest, one chance was all he would get.

If he missed, if he was waxed...

The German tribe was raining hell on them, the world a cyclone of dust, glass and sparks in his face. Bullets were ripping through the partition, slivers flying over his head, as Blancanales took the backup stainless-steel ring, held it over the chambers, thumbed the release catch and dumped twelve live ones into the multiround projectile launcher.

All set.

Schwarz, sandwiched between the claw-shaped ruins of worktables, alternated subgun sprays between the catwalk contingent and the force advancing on

Lyons. The slides on both of Ironman's .45s locked as the magazines emptied, Blancanales glimpsed, but the Able Team leader didn't miss a heartbeat. The SPAS-12 was off his shoulder, booming, disemboweling a hardman in the middle of a suicide charge, his death wish answered by autoshotgun thunder and buckshot that sawed him in two.

Blancanales sucked in a breath, zeroed in as best he could, a mental picture of the position of a metal plate that appeared to hold the catwalks together at their center. As Schwarz fed his subgun a fresh clip, Blancanales caught his eye, pointed toward the catwalk and said, "Give me shelter!"

CHAPTER FOURTEEN

Whoever the invaders in ski masks, Lugar knew they were pros, as quick as bolts of lightning, as fearless as a white shark. But it was laughable from where he stood, three men—outnumbered, outgunned, outclassed. They might as well throw down their weapons, hit their knees and bow before him, beg for a quick death.

Fritz Lugar damn near laughed out loud, but kept it in, feeling the rocket man ready to take aim and blow them all off the catwalk, the invisible man believing he was concealed and could dispense doom with one pull of the trigger of his multiround warhead blaster. Damn, but he was a mind reader, he thought, or the next best thing to psychic, the battlefield below an imagined crystal ball where all he had to do was peer to instantly find the immediate future.

Tactically speaking from their woeful disadvan-

tage—rats in a barrel—there was no other option for
the rocket man but to make the attempt to bail out his
comrades with what would prove his last error in
judgment. Luger was so juiced, he believed he could
nearly see through the plasterboard and smoking rub-
bish hiding the commando, X-ray eyes locked on,
tracking.

The steel egg was in his palm, the G-3 spewing out
rounds that turned every man-made object into sparking clouds. Lugar was winding up when—

He wasn't aware of the first few rounds drilling
through him, nothing but hard punches to the ribs; at
worst, his flesh frozen, tingling scalp to toes, awareness he was shot a distant but slow grinding sensation.
Blood flew into his eyes, forcing him to blink, turn
away, even as he held back on the trigger, roaring obscenities. He was backpedaling, stared at an empty
hand where the frag grenade had been palmed, then
super-senses warned him what was next.

Lugar turned tail, bolting down the catwalk when
the explosion rumbled, uprooting the world as he knew
it behind him.

The earth felt yanked out from under his feet. His
hands clawed for anything to hold on to as heightened
senses caught the screams like megaphones bellowing
in his ears, nose whiffing the smoke and blood.

He clung to his assault rifle, sliding on his belly as
the catwalk crumbled into a long metal plank, steel
groaning, then giving way to whirling space below.

THERE WAS A MADMAN on the loose. But Lyons had his own overflowing plate of problems at the moment. He'd seen the wild man on the catwalk take a few hits, blood shooting into the air around his jerking frame. The guy was barely fazed, just staggered a step or two, then lost the grenade.

Lyons was scanning for targets, knocking them down with autoshotgun man-eaters—one, then another hardman flying back as they took the receiving end of the SPAS to full evisceration. The center of the catwalk was obliterated in a ball of fire, the thunder pealing on the heels of a grenade blast. The Able Team leader loosed another sonic boom, crucified a gutted sack to the standing monitors. Return fire was pouring his direction from a tool bench, two o'clock near a no-man's land that led to the east side exits.

Lyons needed to clear the way, and quick.

Arming a frag grenade, Lyons lobbed the lethal baseball, bounced it off a worktable, nearly dumping it in the laps of a nearby trio in trench coats. One of them bolted a second before the smoky thunderclap sent him airborne, his comrades lost in the fireball. Lyons went on the offensive, pumping a 12-gauge blast into the small of his adversary's back as he skidded on the floor.

Out in the workbay they were sailing off the downed catwalk, arms windmilling, bodies hammering through tables, turning expensive computers to useless trash as they slammed to the floor.

Scouring the slaughter bed of his own grim handi-work, Lyons gave it a few seconds, watching as limbs twitched out, all life finally draining until there was utter stillness.

After a quick reload of his weapons, Lyons moved to aid his teammates.

Side by side, Schwarz and Blancanales were forging toward the tangled steel web, hosing down wounded and rising gunmen with long double bursts, working their fields of fire on the downed enemy, stem to stern.

The wild-eyed berserker was up and screaming something in German, Lyons saw, holding back on the trigger of his G-3. He was taking hits to the chest, but he refused to go down.

No armor protection, since blood was spurting through the air. Lyons suspected something was definitely wrong with that guy. He was about to add to the barrage but the berserker, perhaps figuring he'd taken enough rounds, darted out of sight, then popped up on the other side of a partition, firing away for all he was worth. Lyons had seen his kind before, maniacal fighters who would rather die than be caught, most likely a sociopathic narcissist off the battlefield. But this wildman was something else entirely. He was on another level, hell, he was on another planet, Lyons decided, and would bet his next black-ops check he was out there in the ozone on drugs.

"Let's go!" Lyons hollered at Schwarz and Blancanales, driving the madman to cover, holding him there by chopping away half the plaster partition with his subgun fusillade.

"Where to?" Schwarz shouted, leaping over glass fangs, bounding up beside Lyons.

"Lead the way, Pol," Lyons said. "East, up and out. Dump whatever you two have on whatever looks important. I'll cover you," he growled, pulling a .45, scanning the demolished workbay for live ones.

No sign of the berserker, but Lyons knew that didn't mean he wasn't out there. He backpedaled, subgun and .45 panning the carnage, swung forward and fell in behind his teammates.

WHEN HE ENTERED Level Four, making sure his two countrymen, armed with subguns, took point, Hector Octavio took one look at the disaster and was certain of one critical item.

He was out of a job.

Octavio lagged behind the last of his security force, waving them forward and deeper into the wasteland when they looked back. His pistol was out, but viewing the enormity of destruction, the lake of bodies, heaped and stacked from one end to the other, he knew nothing short of wielding a bazooka would save him from the murderous trio of invaders.

Three men, he considered, had wreaked utter and complete destruction.

He toed a body, rolled over one of the Germans.

Searching on, he discovered more Visigoths, bodies pocked with bullet holes, arms or legs bent at impossible angles where they had bounced off the concrete floor from their ride down the catwalk. It was the first time he could remember smiling in weeks, feeling genuine pleasure.

So much for EDEF's vaunted heroes, he thought, the best and toughest on Kluger's payroll, supposed to fly in here and save the bungling Spanish from bogeymen.

But the trio was still running amok, somewhere in the facility.

He already knew the science and work details were fleeing the compound, heading for the foothills or the nearest village, the lead scientist raising him over his radio moments ago, informing him something about the complex...

Octavio froze in his tracks. The compound was going to blow up! How? When?

"You two," he barked at his guards, nodding toward the inner sanctum of Level Four. "Move in there and make a thorough search."

"What are we looking for, sir?"

"Explosives."

LYONS COVERED the hall as Schwarz and Blancanales divvied up the remainder of their C-4 stash between the power room belowground, then two large rooms up top, in what appeared to be workshops, skeletal frames holding large wings, reflector shields for satellites most likely. It was too damn quiet for Lyons, the Able Team leader sure they hadn't shaken the hellhounds off their tail yet.

They were retracing their steps, charging for the door of their original breach, when Lyons found his suspicion bear poisonous fruit.

The berserker and two other trench coats were swinging around the corner at the far end of the hall, cutting loose with autofire. Lyons braved the storm, rounds slashing off the wall beside his head, taking steady aim and returning fire. He scored flesh, the trio of bullets dancing over Trench Coat One's chest, jig steps and gravity carrying deadweight into his comrades. Their shooting ceased as the corpse toppled into them; berserker stoked up to new heights of rage, shoving his comrade away in midfall.

It was just enough to allow Lyons to turn and sprint through the doorway, the steel barrier swinging shut, tattooed with drumming rounds.

Clock check: the chopper wasn't due to sail into the ravine for another three minutes.

At that point it could prove an eternity.

Lyons armed a frag grenade. An underhand toss rolled the steel egg up against the base of the door.

LUGAR HEARD THE SOUND, skidded to a halt, reached out and grabbed Junger by the arm.

Pain was starting to kick in now, short fiery waves.

Pain was good, though. It told him he was still alive and in the hunt. Figure he'd taken four rounds, upper chest, maybe one through the ribs, blood likewise rolling in waves off the deep gash in his skull where he'd smashed to the floor at the end of his header off the catwalk. There was no option but to tough it out. He could dig into the stash back in the chopper later.

Oh, but these bastards were tough, good, booby-trapping the door, thinking he would simply blunder into the ambush.

He turned away just as the door vanished in a cloud of smoke and fire.

LYONS BEGRUDGED the madman both guts and quick thinking on his feet. The detonation blew in the door, the timing as near perfect to catch their pursuers in the face as he could have mentally marked it off.

Then the berserker surged through the smoke, opened up with autofire, his comrade taking up his left wing, following the lead with tracking rounds.

Incredible, Lyons thought, how the enemy could almost sense their position without the first eyeball confirmation, the guy bleeding, head to boot, a running faucet of blood, still standing. Speed? Coke? Some new drug conjured up by the Germans to turn mere mortal foot soldiers into Terminators?

Lyons, crouched beneath the rise, sandwiched between Schwarz and Blancanales, let it rip with return fire. Whether they scored more flesh was impossible to tell. They were triggering their assault rifles, backstepping, disappearing in the ball of smoke. Lyons threw more rounds into the doorway, sparks riding up the frame, muzzles winking back, bullets with eyes, it seemed, burning past his scalp.

"Chopper!" he heard Schwarz shout, tugging on his arm.

Lyons fed his subgun a fresh clip, looked up to find the chopper touching down inside the fence. He was bellowing at the helmets behind the cockpit Plexiglas, waving his arms, wondering just how stupid they were when he caught the familiar and sweet music of an M-60 pounding out rounds from the doorway.

Lyons was up and charging, triggering concentrated 3-round bursts as the Germans lurched into view, G-3s flaming, then fell back. The Able Team leader moved into the rotor wash, Schwarz and Blancanales firing back, hopping up and on, the M-60 door gunner rolling out the lead hellstorm. The door frame was a shredded mass of twisted steel, Lyons saw, the walls on either side gouged with deep holes.

And the two berserkers of steel kept on popping forth, winging rounds.

Lyons, ears buzzing, hurled himself past the roaring M-60.

"Go, go!" Schwarz shouted at the flyboys.

They were up and away, but Lyons wasn't taking any chances they were home free. Wedged between Schwarz and Blancanales in the port doorway, he held back on the MP-5's trigger, the triburst aimed toward the two hardmen who were still blazing away. The chopper put quick distance to the complex, Lyons burning through his clip, out of range now.

They were gaining altitude, sailing on an east vector, Lyons surveying the open grounds around the facility. He gave it a few seconds, watching as SUVs and Jeeps raced through the front gate, stragglers hauling ass on foot.

"What the hell," Schwarz said. "I nailed that one guy at least three, maybe five or six times. Are the Germans making their commandos out of titanium these days?"

Lyons was patting down his vest, heard Blancanales groan.

"Don't tell us," Pol said. "You didn't drop it?"

Lyons dug the hellbox out of a pocket and flashed a mean smile. "Ye of little faith."

"What?"

The pain was turning into shooting flares, white dots leaping in his eyes, legs on the verge of wilting to rubber. Not good. He knew he was on the verge of lapsing into shock. Even the assault rifle grew heavy in his hand, blood running the length of the weapon.

He was striding out in the open, his choppers touching down, when Octavio's voice bleated in his ear. Pain, rotor wash, rage against the mystery invaders who were now airborne and escaping, and Lugar couldn't quite focus on what the Spaniard was saying.

Lugar laughed, thought he heard Octavio demand to know what was so funny. It occurred to him that Octavio—miracle of miracles—was unscathed, still trolling the facility, assessing damage, probably fretting over job security.

Which was zero, because Lugar intended to put a bullet between his eyes before he left in pursuit of the trio of invaders. The bastard, he thought, showed himself now. Where the hell was he when all the shooting was grinding up the whole security force, including irreplaceable German commandos? Clearly he had hung back, frantic for the killing to end, hoping no one noticed he had made himself absent from battle. Cowardice was intolerable, and Lugar decided he might make the Spaniard grovel first before he shot him. This, of course, after he pulled himself together, sucked up a vial of powder.

But his heart was doing a strange and sick flutter in his chest, racing, jumping around, then slowing, back then lurching. It seemed to take every ounce of reserve steely willpower to keep himself on his feet.

"Speak, damn you!"

"I am! I am telling you, again, Herr Lugar, my men discovered a block of plastic explosive…"

Lugar didn't hear another word. It was bizarre, he thought, how the entire world seemed to freeze then spin in slow motion as he turned toward the gigantic storage bins. He couldn't even begin to tally the tons of rocket fuel housed…

The curse was ripping from his mouth, but the last thing he heard was the explosion, then a microglimpse of a tidal wave of fire so intense he never even felt the flames.

"WHOA…"

Lyons, tugging off his ski mask, echoed the excitement of Schwarz, closed his eyes at the blinding supernova. "Goodbye, berserker!"

Squinting, Lyons observed the mushrooming balls of fire, other shooting waves appearing to pulp at least three-quarters of the complex, sections of roofing blown up from upper level demo work, then swept away, vaporized in what was nothing short of an ocean of pure white hell. The chopper shuddered, invisible fists driven into the bird as shock waves reached out, from what Lyons figured was nearly a mile from ground zero and flying. There was debris on the rocket ride for the dawn sky, what he guessed was the warped skeleton trash of the two choppers, riding the fiery waves now, wreckage surfing up the mountainside. Running forms, little more than ants fleeing the compound, were flinging themselves to paved roads and dirt tracks. No question, Lyons knew whoever survived would be a little toasty the next few days.

The Able Team leader turned away, found the door gunner shedding his helmet with dark visor.

"Good work," Mitch told Able Team.

Lyons caught Schwarz grinning. "Say, Carl, I hear the Mediterranean coast…"

"Pipe down, playboy," Lyons growled. "We still have work to do."

"WHEN WAS the last time you slept, Hal?"

It was a good question, but Brognola didn't have a ready answer for Price.

A cup of Kurtzman's black lava sat on the table. Brognola allowed himself a moment to settle back in his chair, gather his thoughts. Hours, even days, were now melding into one long endless maze of events, time zones and flashpoints, with wildfires extinguished by the Stony Man warriors, but the bubbling caldron still brewing, threatening to overflow.

There was still Myanmar, Frankfurt and a situation on American soil that was becoming more disturbing the deeper the big Fed dug.

He was back in the War Room, alone with Price, the cyber team working nearly around the clock to keep satellites rerouted and parked over AIQs, stacking up the intel on two fronts, producing résumés on the next rounds of persons of interest.

"I appreciate the concern, Barbara, but I'll only be able to sleep when this over and our people are home in one standing piece."

Brognola watched as Price spread out satellite imagery, the mission controller clicking on the wall monitor with her remote.

"What do we have?" Brognola asked.

"Phoenix has landed," Price said. "They will be

working jointly with a CIA-DEA strike force, but the commanders understand David is calling the shots.

"Another EDEF platoon has already touched down in the Kachin," she told Brognola. "We presume to pick up who knows how much heroin, maybe deliver some plague to the SLORC. The way it looks, Phoenix will hit the AIQ in about two hours, give or take."

"That's what...their time?" Brognola asked, squinting at the wall clocks.

"Early morning," Price said, and fixed the predawn hour.

"Okay," Brognola said. "Get them in and out. I need them in Frankfurt. I have the FBI, and probably the CIA and NSA are somewhere on the prowl by now, but the situation in Frankfurt appears to be growing more tense by the hour. There's an informant inside the EDEF facility. He's told the FBI that Kluger is in a siege mentality. He won't even allow his workforce to leave the complex. It's bad."

"I've already arranged for Phoenix to land at the American air base in Frankfurt," Price said. "We're working on how to attack the facility, take out Kluger. His force is being rapidly depleted, that's the good news, but my own source in the CIA has confirmed he's calling in all markers from business associates, culling whatever shooters he can find."

"Meaning he's out of former GSG-9 talent?" Brognola asked.

"We can't say that for certain."

Brognola sounded a grim chuckle. "The hell of it is, we may never find out whose strings he's been tugging, unless we can take him alive."

"I don't see that happening," Price said, "not if he's hell-bent on going down in his bunker."

"And maybe take a whole bunch of innocent people with him," Brognola said.

"From what we know, it doesn't appear anyone on his payroll could be called innocent."

Brognola worked on his cigar. "Right. What's the story on Able Team?"

"They're standing down in Perpignan in the south of France," Price said.

"Let me guess," Brognola said. "A nice little resort on the Mediterranean?"

Price nodded, showed the big Fed a weary smile. "I don't think they packed their Speedos for the beach. They want in on the Frankfurt strike. Adrenaline's still racing, I gather."

"After blowing the Spanish complex clear to the Pyrenees," Brognola said, "I take it they feel they've earned the right to clean house on the European front. Normally I would say yes, but Frankfurt will be Phoenix's task. I need our resident renegades here for another problem."

"The Elite," Price said.

"That would be the problem," Brognola said. "For the time being, tell them to stand down until I can sort through a few matters. Hell, they can go take a dip in

the Mediterranean, work on their tan. I know, I know,
I've been riding them like they've got saddles, but as
long as they get the job done I can spare a little benev-
olence."

CHAPTER FIFTEEN

There was only one virtue a prison could truly forge in the soul, Khisa An-Khasung knew.

Patience.

Unless outright murdered by another inmate, executed by the regime, or sentenced to life, she always knew that someday she would be free again. Of course, supporters on the outside, rallying to her cause, practically storming the gates of the SLORC's supreme headquarters in Yangon, and a plea from the United Nations for her release had probably shaved five to ten years off her sentence.

In solitary confinement, on the verge of starvation, the company of rats and roaches or a visit by a guard to rape her had been her only contact with living things. It was all in the mind, she had learned, hoping to be free again, sitting in limbo for the day when she could walk out of hell, meditation and dreaming of a better tomorrow keeping her in something she recalled and could describe as out-of-body.

Everything ended in life. Everyone lost something. Everyone had to pay a price.

The trick back then was not only patience, but remembering whatever joys she'd known in life, savoring hope, and praying to God for freedom, for deliverance from evil for her people.

In prison one certainly learned how to suffer in silence, bear up under the most cruel conditions, or die. Isolation from other human beings, enduring rape and torture, deprived of the basic necessities, could make the inner self stronger, if one didn't allow the inhumanity of other men to break the spirit. Pain, like pleasure, she thought, was fleeting, and both had to end at some point, one usually giving way to the other. But that was just life. The trick, again, was to seek a balance somewhere between, flesh and blood simply a temple housing the soul, holding it back from its eventual journey into eternity. In the end—painfully aware of the suffering of her people—all she truly had was her own life. And, of course, she owned her soul, her cause, her commitment to rid the region of the scourge of both drugs and the Barking Dogs.

Whether the two white men in combat black were CIA or DEA didn't matter to her. They had come to help, bringing treasures with them to close the odds in their struggle against the SLORC. They had been monitoring something like a computer screen, small boxes with lines and numbers in their hands, their bodies hunched beneath a small tent to keep the glow of the instruments concealed from any potential watching eyes in the jungle. Her sentries were posted around the compass, invisible in the dark, watching the trails, the grassy plain for any SLORC patrols.

An-Khasung cradled her new submachine gun, hunkered in a thicket, watching the skies for the arrival of the five fighters from the West. The quiet ones—as she thought of the two operatives—had shown her and her fighters how to operate what they called Heckler & Koch submachine guns. No shooting lessons, since weapons fire would alert any SLORC patrol to their position, but when the time came to fight, she was confident enough in her ability and the tenacity of her fighters to operate the submachine guns.

They had parachuted in, perhaps a full day ago, crates stuffed with grenades, night-vision goggles and binoculars. They brought food, also, and instruments they called com links. They had shown her and the others how they worked, the marvels of the Western world giving her the ability to communicate with her fighters over secured airwaves. She trusted them. She had to.

Her only demand was that she and her fighters go into battle against the Barking Dogs.

One of the Westerners, toting the H&K subgun, the com link around his head, his skin smeared with black greasepaint, slipped out of his tent.

"They're here. They just jumped," he said.

"Where?"

"About a kilometer in that direction," he told her, pointing to the plain, northeast.

She searched the sky, but found no sign of five fighters falling from the heavens. "Then let us go meet them."

DAVID MCCARTER HAD problems with last-minute, seat-of-the-pants operations. Sure, the Farm had faxed every shred of valuable intel, the AIQ detailed down to the yard, enemy numbers tallied to near eighty-strong, including the German contingent. Enter the CIA, the DEA and the Warrior Princess and her rebel army. Not that he didn't trust any of them to fulfill their role when the shooting started, but he had to make sure they understood, and agreed, the five of them would breach the perimeter, take out any sentries by knife or sound-suppressed Berettas, mine the motor pool, take down the aircraft...

In short, get the fireworks started.

McCarter and troops were gathered in a small clearing in the jungle, poring over the maps with the CIA ops, using small flashlights. The chitter of insects, the howl of a monkey was an occasional and potential lethal distraction if SLORC goons were in the area, creeping up on the powwow, but the rebel leader had posted sentries on all points of the compass, guaranteed their safety from armed phantoms in the jungle.

McCarter laid out a simple plan as quickly as possible. He looked at the woman. An-Khasung was maybe five feet tall, all of ninety pounds sopping wet, but she had what McCarter called command presence. She was a beauty, no question, but there was commitment and fire in her dark eyes that outshone the whole package.

"The drug lab is ours," McCarter told her. "You and your fighters will move in, as I described, from the poppy fields. Myself and my men are going to hit them hard, fast and loud. You'll know when it's started. Some of the soldiers may run your way, they may not, but move in, be mindful the officers and the Germans we came here to nail may bolt for the motor pool, which is tucked right up against the airfield. No one on the other side leaves there alive. There's going to be confusion, there's going to be chaos. But when you move in, do it close, the personal touch, near eye-to-eye as possible. That way, you don't accidentally cut one of us down. Got it?"

"Understand."

Her English was broken, her mind struggling to choose the right words, but McCarter was confident she had the drill down.

"You two," he told the CIA ops. "You will go with Misters H and J," he said, nodding at T. J. Hawkins and Calvin James. "When we're in the mop-up phase, I'll call in our ride."

They were nodding when McCarter caught a

strange look in the woman's eyes. "Something wrong?"

"You leef soon, SLORC still here."

"I suppose you're asking, then what? You fear they will come back and retaliate, maybe slaughter more villagers, burn their homes down?"

"Their cruelty, we used to it. I wonder if will be future help?"

McCarter looked at the CIA ops. "Gentlemen?"

"There are future operations planned for this region. We will be back, a day or two, along with a DEA strike force to help secure the region. The poppy fields are going to be burned by an aerial strike using thermite missiles that also contain a poison that will render the soil unusable for any future planting of poppies."

"I live in hope we someday grow food, not poppy."

"This is only a start," one of the CIA ops told her. "We aren't intending to create some environmental disaster."

"But this is war," she said.

"Yeah," McCarter agreed. "It's war."

The Phoenix Force leader looked at the map, ran a finger down the Ayeyarwady River, up the tributary that would take their paddleboat a half-kilometer to the enemy's back door. He looked at his troops, all of them with flesh coated in black warpaint. They might be suffering from jet lag, but they were ready to turn it up another notch. Going into battle, they would once again be online with Delta One back at the Farm. An ammo resupply was no problem, since the Farm had flown enough reserve stockpiles to the Kenyan base at the start of the campaign to see them through to the bloody finish line. McCarter had a good idea where they were flying next...

Myanmar, and a pack of SLORC thugs and their German masters first.

"Let's saddle up," McCarter said, then told Khisa An-Khasung, "Lead the way to the riverboats."

GENERAL MAW Nuyaung despised the Germans. They had finally, he thought, graced them all with their presence after a half-day delay for some unknown reason, malingering in Yangon with the other generals.

Ten armed Germans, walking through the camp now, barking orders, sniffing the air, expressions rigid with contempt as if his soldiers and the slave labor were unwashed mongrels. They wanted the heroin loaded up, and two hours ago, demanding to know why the delay in completing the task of producing the remaining order of ten metric tons. Try to explain the time-consuming procedure or refinement and they simply demanded the peasants work harder, or perhaps there were slackers who needed to be taken outside and shot as an example.

Barbarians.

They had, also, arrived in-country empty-handed.

No delivery of aerosol plague, but they had—or so he was informed—brought two drones, showed off their technology for the generals at supreme headquarters, with the promise of plague to be delivered ASAP after the narcotics were safely shipped back to their country. Well, they hadn't come to his country entirely without payment. He hadn't been privy to the number, but they had dropped a half-dozen steamer trunks off in the thatch-and-bamboo-hut quarters near the airfield, the shabby dwelling inherited from the late Lingpau. They were euros, the generals having sent on his cut with the Germans, for reasons he didn't understand. A show of good faith? Reward for all his sweat and toil, enduring his anxious stint in rebel country? Hardly, he knew, since the money would simply be stashed in the ruling junta's war coffers, the top five carving out most of the cash for themselves. They loved luxury, he knew, craved expensive cars, good food, drink and women more than duty to the SLORC and ridding the nation of rabble. There were rumors even a few of the generals indulged in heroin use during orgies at supreme headquarters.

There was time to kill, his nerves talking to him. He poured himself a brandy, then began pacing what he assumed was the private domain of the hut, separate from a smattering of chairs and a divan in the other room for what he assumed was Lingpau's version of guest accommodations. He had pilfered the late colonel's liquor, discovered the man had his own distasteful obsessions, some of the most despicable pornography he had ever seen. He was sipping his drink when he heard the gunfire, jumping at the sound.

Grabbing his assault rifle, he was charging into the night, searching for the source, when he spotted the German he knew as Johann Weber standing over a body.

"What do you think you are doing?" Nuyaung shouted, marching for Weber, fighting the urge to shoot the expression of disdain off his face.

"Slacker. Example."

As if that explained the right to commit murder. "You will honor my rules and terms as long as you are here. No executions, do not even strike one of my workers or you can return to Yangon and wait until your shipment is ready."

"Sure," Weber said, sniffing the air. "Perhaps we will just wait in our plane. But we wait no longer than a few hours more. Or I will take what I want, including any unrefined product, all vats of the gum and will finish the job ourselves."

Nuyaung nearly screamed in rage, but he had been ordered to play host, remain hospitable to these arrogant bastards. Weber waved him off, as if he were swatting a mosquito.

They were marching away, Nuyaung turning toward the airfield, spotting the transport chopper touching down. Now what? he wondered, then saw soldiers disembark, followed by Generals Nyat, Mying and three lower-ranking generals. Was he being relieved of command?

"Ah, General Nuyaung," Nyat said. "What brings us here? Merely checking on progress. Come, I know you must have brandy. This is as good a time as any to start counting the rest of our money, no?"

Nuyaung felt the itch between his shoulder blades, the feeling coming on whenever he sensed duplicity. He saw the arriving generals glance at the Germans, Webber muttering over his shoulder.

"Is there a problem?" Mying asked.

"They are an impatient lot," Nuyaung answered. "I will be glad when I am finished this business with them and they are on their way."

"If those are your sentiments, General Nuyaung," Nyat said, "then perhaps one of us needs to take over here?"

"I can handle it."

"Then, kindly do," Nyat said, an edge to his voice. "We have just entered a long-term partnership with our new friends from Germany."

Nuyaung turned his back before the scowl locked on his features.

CUTTING A MAN'S throat, ear to ear, so deep the blade nearly took the head off, was messy work, jets of thick arterial blood taking to the air like a burst hose. But McCarter was stoked on adrenaline, combat senses and Delta One steering him to the back door of the sprawling heroin lab, the Briton grateful the slow grind through the jungle to get into position was over, in motion now for deadly action.

Three down on the trail, then McCarter sliced soldier number four near the stack of fifty-five-gallon drums of precursor chemicals, another near-decapitation. If nothing else, wiping the blade off on the soldier's tiger-striped camous, he had to believe it was a quick and painless way to check out. Blood flow to the brain ceasing with the brutal surgical incision, the yawn spewing so much life's juice shock had to be near instant, the world fading to black in seconds flat. Of course, he had never been on the receiving end, but he didn't plan on being cashiered out anytime soon.

Too much work to do, he thought, too many bad guys to wax.

Manning, he saw, preferred the cleaner touch. The big Canadian dropped one smoker and one pisser near the edge of the tree line with two rapid chugs from the sound-suppressed Beretta, dragged their bodies into the brush. McCarter took a moment to survey his surroundings, sheathing his blade, the M-16/M-203 combo in hand.

After the steamer boat ride, they had moved in from the north, Hawkins and James and the two CIA ops cutting their own course through the jungle, south for the airfield. Encizo's task was the HQ where, the Farm had informed him, some of the top brass had gathered. But something felt wrong to McCarter, something alive and on the hunt in the darkness. The jungle, from his experience, fell silent, birds and monkeys freezing at the silent incursion of man. NVD goggles most certainly made the way in easier, but McCarter would have sworn something had tracked him during his breach of the perimeter. He stayed on edge, alert for any nasty surprises, man or beast.

West, he spotted the workers in the poppy fields, fifty-odd noncombatants being watched by a double platoon-strength batch of SLORC bullies. Generator-powered lights illuminated the rolling acreage out there, McCarter hoping the Warrior Princess didn't have an itchy trigger finger, or was spotted by a wandering SLORC gunner.

The lab itself, McCarter spied, was roughly one-third the size of a soccer field, tucked back into the jungle, hidden beneath the tree canopy, one large tent affair. Delta One screens showed twenty-plus hardmen inside, watching a slave labor force of thirty brewing their poison. The bite of chemicals in his nose, McCarter gave Manning the nod to start unloading the C-4, stagger the blocks down the length of the northside tent as planned.

The Briton stuck a five-pound block to a drum, primed it to blow to his personal touch from a radio remote, his signal tied in to the whole explosive package. He looked back into the dark bowels of the jungle, nearly slipped on the NVD goggles for a better search, would have sworn he heard rustling, then decided full speed ahead with his own demo chores.

SPEED OF MOVEMENT was critical and Calvin James
figured he was the man for the job. T.J., he knew, was
lugging the SAW, the man-eater topping the scales at
twenty-two pounds with a full box of 5.56 mm ammo
locked in place. While Hawkins covered him from his
roost in the tree line, the ex-SEAL broke into a twenty-
yard dash for the motor pool, eyes watching the HQ
hut, gaze flicking to the EDEF transport, M-16 ready
to bite.

Clear.

A rough guess, and he figured twenty vehicles. APCs,
the Myanmar version of the Humvee, Jeeps with
mounted machine guns, a bulldozer. Swiftly he began
sticking two-pound globs beneath the front ends, opting
for the quick destruction of the engines, working his
demo task from the center, on back, toward Hawkins.
There were four transport choppers, but they were parked
too close to the EDEF bird, too much open ground to risk
mining the birds in full view of watching enemy.

Encizo's Little Bulldozer, he knew, would have to
drop any bird trying to lift off in a hurry.

Retracing his steps, M-16/M-203 combo out and
aimed toward the transport plane, he melted back into
the jungle, keyed his com link.

"ALL SET."

"Roger that," McCarter whispered back to James,
and began counting off the doomsday numbers.

Eyes fixed on the back flaps, watching for shadow

flickers in the light shining against the inside of the canvas, McCarter wrapped up his demo job. He pulled back to the stack of drums, pinned down Manning, the big Canadian midway down the tent, working his way west, when the beast surged out of the jungle.

Manning jolted upright, his weapon trained on the shadow, but the tiger was more interested in what was inside the tent for reasons that only its own primal instincts knew.

The reaction in the lab was predictable. As the first shouts of men in panic hit the air, followed by weapons fire, McCarter keyed his com link and told his troops, "The party's started, mates!"

CHAPTER SIXTEEN

General Maw Nuyaung was annoyed and suspicious. Beyond that, he wondered how much longer he could hold down the lid on the rumbling anger in his gut— a volcano of rage about to erupt, in fact, with fatal results for all concerned—the assault rifle in his hands the prop of reality adding to the fuel of fiery images of how quick and messy he could turn the hut into a slaughterhouse. Oh, yes, there was a good chance, he thought, he might let rip a string of insults and obscenities that might shake them to their knees, then taken away by the outburst, pride reinflated by their shock and fear, follow through...

It could happen. And it still might, he decided.

Sick and tired of feeling he was being dumped further down the pecking order with every passing day, he hung back, choked down the seismic tremors shooting up his chest, swept away visions of murder and mayhem. Time was on his side, either way, so he allowed the other generals their moment to get themselves settled in, foot soldiers dispensed to carry out their orders between bartending duty and rearranging the inner shabby sanctum of Lingpau. While the soldiers passed out the brandy, hauled the desk out into the main room, unloaded and set up electronic money counters from nylon satchels, Nuyaung pondered the situation, then began thinking it was time to look toward his own future.

It was all very strange, to say the least, men accustomed to wallowing in the lap of luxury, flying out to the jungle, the dark heart of rebel country, no less, risking their lives. Was it Phatun's decision to send them to the Kachin, check up on him, count the load? Report back that General Nuyaung wasn't pilfering narcotics for either personal use or to sell across the Thai and Laotian borders on his own, fatten his numbered account?

Impossible to say, he knew, since telling the truth was an alien concept to the higher-ranking generals these days. After all, men with shameful vices tended to lie, not only to others, but to themselves, if only to keep their transgressions hidden so they could carry on with disgraceful aberrant behavior. It became sociopathic, all this self-indulgence, speaking out of both sides of the mouth in public, saying one thing to the masses about discipline and self-sacrifice and loyalty to the State, while doing another in secret, minds warped and deluded, reality created as it suited their wants.

Sick, foolish, weak bastards.

Perhaps it was time to retire, he thought. He had enough money stashed away in various accounts, from Yangon to Singapore to Indonesia, something in the realm of six million in U.S. dollars. Why not seek out a slice of nirvana for himself, say a remote island in the South Pacific, while away the remaining years, walking in the sand, eating steak and seafood, perhaps start a restaurant. Something simple, and sane.

He moved to the deep corner, shaking his head at Phatun when the glass of brandy was offered. Then he saw one of the lower-ranking generals, Yowan, holding up a video from Lingpau's collection of porn, a weird grin on his razor-thin lips.

"We were not aware you were enjoying so much free time out here."

"Those were Colonel Lingpau's," Nuyaung said. "It would appear the late colonel had more time on his hands than he knew what to do with. If you were to view those, you would understand. Pornography. I suspect that is one of the reasons why expanding our labor force and increasing the pace of production was off schedule."

"Never mind the colonel. You look and sound distressed," Mying said, turning an enigmatic smile on Nuyuang. "What are your true feelings, General Nuyaung? We are interested, and concerned about your thoughts."

"Answer me this," Nuyaung said as stacks of crisp euros were fed in the machines. "How much did we receive to fill the German order?" he asked. "And why not simply leave the money back at headquarters?"

Mying quoted the figure, head bobbing, and Nuyaung was impressed with the numbers, if, in fact, he was being told the truth.

"We are here to distribute to you your cut of the proceeds," Nyat said, swirling his glass. "And, two, since we of the ranking five are feeling generous, we…how shall I say, believe a well-paid soldier is a happy and a loyal soldier."

Nuyaung narrowed his gaze, choked down the chuckle, needed a long fat stick now to scratch the itch between the shoulder blades. If they were passing out a bonus to the soldiers, that would be quite out of character for men who counted and hoarded every dollar of drug money.

Then…

The thought danced through his head there was something else behind the charity—such as a coup, General Phatun destined to find his head spiked on a metal pole, paraded around Yangon, perhaps the new regime espousing the virtues of a kinder, gentler SLORC for the peasant masses.

There was a growing buzz in his ears, Nuyaung aware his blood pressure was rising over this madness, eating their lies, heart pounding when he made out the sound. He was turning toward the others, aware of what the noise now was, and from what direction it rattled the night, as it began to crack through the thumping in his ears.

In that split second the generals looked like sick, tired, frightened old men, throwing one another anxious expressions, Nuyaung thinking he could almost read their thoughts, all of which, he suspected, centered on themselves.

Mying was waving his hands at the soldiers, barking at them to investigate the disturbance, but they were already in hard charge for the door. He wasn't sure why he held his ground, but Nuyaung watched, sensing some presence waiting outside—

The explosion ripped through the heart of their charge, the shock wave and something that felt like razor blades slashing his face, hurling him to the floor.

RAFAEL ENCIZO WAS no couch potato on R and R when it came to television, certainly no fan of the whores of popular media, but the rare film footage—State-sponsored propaganda, of course—on the SLORC he'd caught on cable news told him all the story he needed to know about the ruling twenty-one-member junta.

They could tool around the streets of Yangon waving and smiling at the starving and unemployed masses from their stretch Mercedes limos, blowing kisses, shaking clenched fists, the new conquerors, the saviors of the nation. They could kiss and cradle infants for the cameras, stroke the hair of a weeping mother who wor-

ried through sleepless days and nights how she would
feed her family. They could even fling wads of money
into the air for the masses that bowed and scraped before them as if they had just cleaned out Las Vegas,
bombard the throngs with grandiose speeches how
they were the backbone and the future of not only their
own destinies, but the potential salvation for all of
Southeast Asia.

Encizo wasn't fooled by the sham. Take the despot
of North Korea, he thought, and multiply him by
twenty-one.

Welcome to Myanmar.

Their mentality was crystal-clear to him, ugly, brutal and self-centered to the extreme—Generals ate first,
and best.

Since that was the case in their eyes, generals could
die first, and worst.

He let the 40 mm buckshot round get the butcher's
work started. For reasons he couldn't pin down, it
had gone to hell inside the drug lab, dark shadows
boiling into the night, running from something,
weapons chattering deep in the tent. McCarter, he
knew, had planned to put them on a one-minute
countdown, but that was clearly scrapped now, and
Encizo had to guess some roving sentry had stumbled
onto their roost.

Things happened.

He didn't have much time to spare waxing the top
brass, he knew, the Germans inside the EDEF trans-

port, alerted by the commotion at the lab, sure to come running.

So he held back on the M-16's trigger, pouring out a wave of rounds that chewed up their ragged hides. The razor-sharp shrapnel packed into the warhead had done gruesome wonders, he saw, uniforms sheared off in strips, flayed figures dancing around in the doorway, men hollering, grabbing faces where bloody holes replaced empty eye sockets.

Encizo advanced into the smoke and the fluttering debris, kicking the enemy down with concentrated 3-round bursts, aware paralyzing shock on their part had blessed him with the edge to nail it down in seconds flat. No mistake, these men were evil, he knew, tyrants who terrorized, oppressed and enslaved simple Buddhists or the quiet gentle peoples of the region, working them in the poppy fields of the labs until they dropped from exhaustion or starvation or both. He had no qualms gunning them down, foot soldier or brass, armed or unarmed.

Time to pony up.

The screams inside had petered to soft moans, a whimper here and there. Encizo, slipping into the hut, pumped, the scent of blood and guts and other more noxious stinks spiking his nose. Scan and blast, the M-16 stuttering on, he mowed them down where they stood or staggered. He hit the last of the medallioned blouse with a burst that zipped him crotch to sternum.

And Encizo heard the full-pitched din of all-out battle outside.

Then he saw the shredded flotsam waft through the smoke, reached out and caught an unmolested euro. Opening a steamer trunk next, he couldn't even begin to imagine how much money he might be looking at, but found it all very interesting, even a tad amusing with its sting of poetic justice.

Could be, he thought, the SLORC was about to make a contribution to the rebel cause.

JOHANN WEBER polished off his third beer in ten minutes, but the mounting buzz was doing little to soften the sharp edge of anger and frustration. No fridge on the flying boat, no frills at all, since their paymaster demanded iron discipline, not to mention clear heads, but Weber liked his beer warm, as any good German, he thought, would. What Kluger didn't know...

Most creature comforts he could do without, but he never left home without a Beck's beer or two in hand. Still he needed to take it easy, aware he would need sharp reflexes if he decided take the lab at gunpoint, clean it of everything that wasn't nailed down.

He popped another beer, just the same, taking inventory for depletion's sake. Loading six cases of warm brew before this godawful journey into the land of savages was his idea, and he knew none of the others would report to Kluger about what he viewed as a minor indulgence. A little less than three cases, he counted, he could live with that.

He paced the floorboards, fired a cigarette, grateful

his troops weren't grumbling, simply sitting, nursing their own beer, but lost in gloomy or angry thoughts. Their dark mood was understandable, since they were all former policemen or GSG-9, not a pack of narco-traffickers. But this was Kluger's deal, and they were being well compensated. Whatever the reasons the most powerful man in all of Germany would dirty his hands with drug trafficking wasn't his business.

Sometimes, the money was simply enough to assuage any grave reservations about his own merce-nary role, tempering the angry edge that he might be contributing to the demise of civilized Germanic society.

Still, he wasn't going to dawdle, hear excuses about lengthy refinement chores, how this general had lost whole platoons of workers due to the plague, forced to scour deeper into the region for able-bodied vil-lagers to replace his losses.

Excuses were for losers and slackers.

It was a backward hell, he thought, this nation of monks, rebels and heroin dealers, an indigenous mixed bag of various peoples—mongrels—the SLORC regime corrupt and lacking anything that smacked of disciplined leadership.

The more he thought about it, the better the idea looked to just storm the lab.

What the hell was that? he wondered, trying to focus on the racket through the swirling fog in his brain.

Assault rifle in hand, his men scrambling to their feet, he hurried to the hatchway, adrenaline sweeping away some of the sludge, eyes taking in the pandemonium.

Someone was shooting inside the lab, bodies bolting through the flaps, surging out of the jungle and running toward...

More shooting, more dark shapes moving down the terraced slopes of the poppy fields, he saw, and nearly bellowed in rage.

They were under attack by goddamned rebel savages!

And then there was his load, threatened now with seizure, or perhaps total destruction, and if he didn't deliver ten metric tons to Frankfurt...

He was bounding out the hatch, his troops falling in, when weapons fire erupted to either side. Cursing, he spun in both directions, bodies crashing into him, blood stinging his eyes, his aim jarred off target just as he sighted on the muzzle-flashes, stem and stern.

"Grenade!"

They were vaulting through the hatch, bailing ground zero, as Weber glimpsed the object sailing through the air. He was wheeling, then launching himself through the hatch when the explosion seemed to pick him up and chuck him across the fuselage.

MCCARTER SAW black-clad workers with filter masks spilling through the flaps, voices rife with panic, arms flailing, but terror had them in full flight, bolting for the jungle, skirting the tree line.

He began hosing the closest men in tiger-striped camous, Manning on his right wing, a bevy of SLORC hardmen with backs turned going down like dominoes in the opening barrage.

Chop and drop. SLORC soldiers kept tumbling down the line under the twin barrage, McCarter shuffling to his left, putting distance between himself and Manning, drilling anything in tiger stripes.

A knot of SLORC gunners appeared to be concentrated at the deep west end of the lab. There, a batch of men was still unloading on the tiger, the beast exploding in a cloud of fur and red mist even as it kept its trophy clamped between its jaws, what looked a SLORC flunky claimed for a meal.

McCarter kept on pumping out 3-round bursts, running the sweep of his own seven to twelve o'clock, while Manning bowled the enemy down, one to five, a reverse pincers sweep, driving them into one another.

Advancing between tables piled with white bricks, vials and tubes, McCarter spotted a decent killzone to crush maybe a dozen SLORC soldiers in an eye blink. The batch of thugs was shouting at fleeing workers, a few lines of autofire spitting rounds up the backs of runners, flinging them over bales of dope, bodies splashing into trenches of white gum, spinning off burlap sacks yet to be emptied of poppy poison.

It took the SLORC thugs a few critical heartbeats in the deep corner to realize they had bigger problems than a man-eating tiger, but assault rifles were swinging around, hasty rounds blasting out heat lamps, glass and sparks showering vats of finished product, when McCarter loosed the 40 mm warhead.

He turned away from the explosive impact, glimpsed a white storm billowing out from the fireball. If the blast didn't finish them outright, he figured they would be blinded or choke on white poison, filter mask or not.

"Gary!" he shouted into his throat mike as Manning hit a trio of soldiers with a clean sweep of autofire, left to right, dumping them in the trenches of milky goo. "Fall back!"

Time to blow the lab, McCarter knew, spotting more armed shadows gagging on the rain and the fog of dope as they lurched to advance.

Once outside, Manning hitting the flaps with his shoulders, McCarter guarding their flanks, the Briton keyed his button to the Farm.

"Phoenix Leader to Mothership. Give me a sweep for an all-clear to light the candle!"

CHAPTER SEVENTEEN

When it started and they were dropping the Barking Dogs with their new submachine guns, Khisa An-Khasung was momentarily surprised over her lack of emotion. There was no anger fueling her to select targets as she cut them down with short precision bursts, no flames of vengeance burning in her soul to pour on overkill. Rather, she was as cold inside as an icy mountain wind, her head clear, her mind focused on nothing but shooting the enemy and setting free those who had been captured from the surrounding villages and forced into slave labor.

The com links worked like magic, as they had crept to the edge of the tree line, crouched in brush, her orders to fan her force parallel to the Barking Dogs, east to west, where they could chop down half or more of the guards in the opening volley. She took the midway point between her fighters and when the shooting erupted in the drug lab, she simply tapped the button on her com link and ordered, "Now!"

The poppy fields were so vast it would have been difficult, if not next to impossible, she knew, to kill so many so quick had the Barking Dogs not had their workers confined to harvest one quadrant at a time. The large round lights, powered by a generator from a canvas-covered truck, certainly helped her and her fighters single out the enemy from the workforce. The enemy head count was roughly twenty, thirty at the most, she figured, and they were falling fast, half of the opposition at least toppling under the initial barrage.

As she led the charge out of the jungle, she heard her fighters, as ordered, hollering at the newly freed Karens and Kachins to run.

She did, however, feel a jolt of anger, an undercurrent of pain beneath the raw emotion at the sight of those brutalized by the Barking Dogs. The people she had pledged to defend, she saw, were little more than walking skeletons in rags. Fed just enough to keep them alive, she could also well imagine the beatings they had suffered, whipped by SLORC bullies if they didn't work fast enough, fill the daily quota of poppy gum.

It was the way of the regime, she knew, the way of evil men. Those in power—the tyrant generals of the SLORC—hoarded the basic necessities of life for themselves, turning a blind eye and a heart of stone to the poor and despairing.

The Barking Dog soldiers, of course, were well-fed, and beyond food and shelter, she knew the ruling junta lived in obscene luxury in their palace in Yangon. She was no pessimist, but she briefly wondered if anything would ever really change in her country. The State had a half-million-man standing army, the twenty-one generals born, primarily, into wealthy families who had always controlled the nation. Then there were various powerful businessmen who fed money and weapons to the State, there in Myanmar to rape the land of natural resources, bulldoze the forests to build a natural gas pipeline clear to Thailand, and beyond. Overindulgence in pleasure and excess were staples of the regime.

The generals of the SLORC were beasts without souls, she thought. Pudgy men who were often seen in public, wearing their immaculate pressed uniforms, festooned with gold and silver, being bowed to by monks, kissing mothers on the cheek, playing games with children as if this were meant to show the masses they were one with common people. She would have wanted nothing more than to storm the SLORC's supreme headquarters, a fight to the death to free the oppressed from the monsters who ruled the nation by force, intimidation, terror and genocide.

Right now, she would take what she could get.

She was pleased with the new submachine, not much by way of recoil, but it still tended to rise, which meant she began firing low, aiming at targets just above the crotch. She paid no attention to the firefight being waged in the drug lab, on the airfield, as she kept advancing through the plants, knocking the enemy down with short bursts, bodies pitching backward over the edge of the terraced hillside.

"TEN SECONDS TO FIND cover and hit the deck, mates. Copy if you can!"

McCarter was on a hard backpedal, sweeping the SLORC brave of heart who crashed through the flaps and wanted to give chase with long raking bursts of autofire when he sounded the alarm to his troops. Hawkins, James and Encizo copied in staggered replies, the Briton managing to catch the racket of weapons fire on their end.

He pumped a 40 mm hellbomb into the pack of SLORC soldiers, pasting mangled bodies to the fifty-five-gallon drums, bits and chunks of flotsam sailing for the canopy. The blast seemed to hold them back, at least find them seeking shelter near the drums, as McCarter and Manning put distance to the coming inferno.

McCarter pulled the doomsday box, thumbed on the red light, ready to pulverize the ambition of evil men.

ONE LAST HOSING of the Germans from his M-16, chopping up two shadows reeling in the smoke of Hawkins's frag blast, and Calvin James raced around the tail of the transport bird. It was time to hold on, ride out the thunder, which would leave the enemy no doubt they weren't leaving the killing field alive.

The black ex-SEAL glimpsed the shadow boiling out of the night, Encizo having just alerted him he was en route to their firepoint to aid and assist taking down the big bird, then the world beyond his cover on the portside flashed into a supernova.

JOHANN WEBER STAGGERED to his feet, snarling an oath. He felt the blood running hot and sticky down his back where shrapnel had torn into his shoulders. His nose was swamped with all manner of miasma, from blood and guts to body waste, bodies strewed on the floor-boards, his boot kicking through a severed leg. Pain and bad smells were the least of his problems.

He knew the camp was under attack by a rebel force, the distant rattle of weapons fire slowly breaking through the ringing in his ears, his thoughts focused on how many invaders were storming the lab. If he didn't somehow find a way to crush this attack...

But how? He cursed the portly general for incompetence, neglect in not sealing the perimeter.

He was calling out names of his men, three, maybe four voices hacking in response, shuffling next for the hatch, taking in the pandemonium at the lab when two massive explosions roared as one, the flash so brilliant he cried out as heat scorched his face. His eyes were seared even as he snapped them shut and flung himself away from the door.

SHE WAS UNPREPARED for the night blazing into sudden and blinding hell. The leader of the Western commandos had, though, warned her both the drug lab and the motor pool would be demolished by plastic explosives, but the sight of so much instant and massive fiery obliteration froze Khisa An-Khasung in her tracks, the flashing firelight driving her two steps back, head swinging away from the source of the man-made volcanic eruptions.

One moment, she spotted a group of Barking Dogs sliding from the tent, weapons firing at those they had enslaved running for the hills or attempting to vanish in the jungle. One heartbeat, those SLORC oppressors who were tucking tail between their legs, deciding they had no stomach to stand and fight, were at the end of a hard dash to climb into the vehicles then—

It was as if the world stopped, she thought, or time froze, the entire universe forced to spectate the cleansing fire of explosions so powerful, she felt the ground tremble beneath her feet, a roar in the air that seemed to split the sky.

She looked back toward the infernos and smiled. It was the first time in years she truly believed the battle against the SLORC could actually be won. If the CIA or the DEA were true to their word for future help to rid the Kachin of heroin and crush the campaign of genocide waged on the indigenous peoples...

Well, there was a chance, even against enormous

odds and even if more Barking Dogs returned to the region to retaliate. She knew she and her fighters couldn't do it alone, but she would always cling to hope that someday even a shadow of sanity and peace would fall over the Kachin.

This night was just a start.

HAWKINS WAS FLINGING himself to the ground, portside behind the nose when the transport was hammered by the hurricane of debris. It shuddered, its hull groaning against the terrible assault, Hawkins catching the sound of glass shattering in the cockpit before the shower rained down.

He was up, the SAW in hand, and spotted Encizo and James climbing to their feet from the stern. They shot him a thumbs-up, then vanished to go back to work.

Hawkins was under no illusions about their task here in the Kachin, and could be sure his teammates were every bit as grimly aware that the SLORC would live on after this attack. The heroin trade would likewise go on, most of the labs and shipping routes farther south in the more mountainous region of the Shan State, according to the DEA.

There was nothing written in stone, he thought, that said the five of them couldn't try. Even if they put a dent in the narcotics streaming out of this nation, even if they took out some of the top brass, an edge was gained, handed off to the rebels of the Kachin who only wanted to live in peace.

Hawkins rolled around the starboard side, took in the battlefield, SAW up and searching for live hostiles.

And there were still plenty of SLORC thugs, he saw, on the prowl.

DAVID MCCARTER had been in the business of waging war long enough to know that sometimes the enemy did the expected and walked right into their own demise. That was especially true, he thought, if they had brutalized and bullied peaceful unarmed civilians for so long that whatever martial skill they might have possessed generally swirled down the toilet under fire. In short, the tyrant, the coward, was exposed, and he ran.

Getting blown off the face of the earth and watching comrades die as the sky fell certainly drained motivation to strike back. The SLORC thugs here had seized the upper hand for so long, McCarter could only imagine the shock and terror they now felt as they watched their world collapsing around them.

And, quite literally, the Phoenix Force leader saw, it had, as the titanic series of fireballs obliterated the lab. Flaming bats ignited the jungle canopy, drums launched like rockets into the sky, exploding high above where containers were punched open and chemicals were touched off by the rising inferno. Then there was the motor pool, going up in a wave of thundering flames, and just as perhaps ten to fifteen SLORC soldiers had boarded vehicles.

The aircraft was now a potential source of escape, but McCarter, wading closer to the lake of fire, gave Manning the order to start pounding the flying machines with a few 40 mm rounds.

ENCIZO SPOTTED the flaming muzzle in the open hatchway, his finger taking up slack on Little Bulldozer's trigger when James beat him to the punch. The black ex-SEAL dumped a 40 mm warhead, dead center in the fuselage, the blast kicking out the portside hull in flying shards of metal.

He left James and Hawkins to check for wounded as they shadowed into the churning cloud. The injured were moaning and screaming inside the inferno, wreckage from the motor pool floating down, thudding to earth, spewing sparks and hurling fuel from ruptured tanks. After a quick sweep of the fiery lake's perimeter, Encizo made out four advancing figures. Beneath the halo of firelight he pegged the familiar forms and rolling battle gait of Manning and McCarter, and found the two CIA ops advancing, their subguns chattering to tag the walking mangled.

The aircraft, he knew, was McCarter's new focus of concern. Rotor blades were spinning to life on two birds, but McCarter and Manning deposited a twin dose of utter 40 mm hell into their bellies.

Banshee-like wails hit the air as Encizo spotted two flaming demons charge out of the sea of fire. The CIA duo put them out of their misery with short bursts, then Encizo contributed to mop-up, blowing the remaining aircraft to scrap, peppering the standing whirlybirds and twin-engine planes with a 40 mm shellacking.

WHEN THE LAST few enemy stragglers were tagged, McCarter radioed Grimaldi for pickup. Their evac ride would be the same Dakota C-47 from which they had jumped, an old reliable bird no longer used by the U.S. military but still popular with the CIA and the DEA, who often found themselves operating in remote regions of the world where runways slashed out of the jungle couldn't accommodate anything larger or faster than the ancient transport. McCarter knew it would be thirty minutes at least before Grimaldi set the bird down on the airfield. Back to the Company-DEA base next, Gulfstream refueled, on to the next front.

In the distance, above the terraced poppy fields, he heard brief stutters of subgun fire. The black-clad rebels chasing down SLORC runners, he surmised.

Leaving the Warrior Princess and her fighters to carving out their much-deserved final few pounds of flesh, he listened to the hungry flames, scanning the carnage as his troops and the two CIA ops gathered around him. As dog-tired as he felt, he knew the five of them had one more stop. Unless, of course, the EDEF facility had either burned down or had been seized by Brognola's Feds and Kluger had committed suicide.

Unlikely, the Briton thought. He had never met Kluger, but knew the type. Megalomaniac. Tyrant. Sociopath who would be king of the world. In short, a rotten SOB with no heart, no soul, who craved power and dominion and chased only his own vision of glory on Earth.

McCarter figured it was a safe bet the tyrant would rather go down inside the walls of his kingdom than surrender.

If Kluger harbored a death wish, McCarter had no problem indulging the man. As far as he was concerned, Kluger wasn't long for this world. Given all the death and horror he had perpetuated, McCarter had to believe there was a special place reserved for the man in the bowels of hell.

He heard Encizo inform him of the steamer trunks of euros. Turning toward the HQ where Encizo had clipped the SLORC hierarchy of six of its top predators, he debated who should claim the spoils of war, but asked the CIA ops how they felt if he offered the money to the Warrior Princess.

"The way you put that," the CIA man said, "I get the feeling you think we're bailing after tonight and never coming back."

"Well?" McCarter said. "Are you?"

"Not all CIA black ops," the other spook said, "are duplicitous backstabbers who lie, cheat and steal to achieve their own objectives—or advance careers."

"Glad to hear it," McCarter said, and walked toward the shadows moving away from the poppy fields. He stopped after a short walk, recognizing her face, framed beneath the dome of firelight. God, but she was a beauty, he thought. All heart, all character, all guts.

"Is over for you?" she said.

"Yes, for us, it's over." He offered her the money.

Khisa An-Khasung shook her head. "No. Money not buy peace, freedom, justice."

"What about food, weapons, rebuilding the villages? I'm sure you have Thai, Laotian or local contacts you can buy whatever you need from."

"No need money, no drug money. Dirty money."

He wanted to persuade her to take it, explain that money was a tool that neither knew if it was used for good or bad, but he respected this woman, her unwavering commitment to her values and her cause. And he found himself briefly entertaining the thought...

Another time, another place and situation...

McCarter nodded. "Good luck. And you will be receiving help in the coming days."

"If true is good. If not we fight alone."

And McCarter could believe that. "Goodbye," he told her, turned and walked back to the CIA ops. "Looks like the cash is all yours, mates. But do me a favor? Try not to forget these good people here. They've suffered enough."

HAL BROGNOLA WASN'T on the job for career advancement, medals of honor, in search of praise from peers and the general public, never even dreamed of nailing down his own "expert chair" on the talking-head shows, never waited around for that seven-figure book deal to drop into his lap.

No. He was committed to serving his country, first, foremost and last. His sole task to keep democracy safe from terror, murder and mayhem, but always living in the secret hope that someday there would be peace on Earth—perhaps a fool's dream, of course, he thought—or at the very least his call to duty might save a few innocent lives along the way who could go on and make even the smallest difference in the good fight.

What he proposed to do, though, may well end not only his career, but his life.

He claimed his seat at the head of the table, alone again with Price in the War Room.

"I don't like it, Hal. It's too damn risky. You haven't cleared it with the Man."

"He'll know about it in due time, and I'm sure he'll understand."

"What you're suggesting is assassination of American citizens, and if it backfires and there's a bloodbath, it could track back here."

Brognola smiled wearily. "I'll be with Able Team. What could possibly go wrong?"

Price frowned, shaking her blond mane.

"I didn't mean to sound flip, Barb."

"You're tired."

"We're all tired, but this thing isn't over. The good news is that the FBI's informant inside the Frankfurt compound," he said, flipping through the computer layouts of the complex, "managed to relay these to my FBI people before he was rounded up with the others."

"And e-mailed that the work force is being held hostage in the auditorium. Kluger has over a hundred human shields."

"The informant is a family man, a distinguished aerospace engineer," Brognola said. "He was planted months ago, agreed to cooperate with the FBI when they laid out their suspicions that Kluger may be building a new weapon of mass destruction."

"Saying he's altruistic? That he can be trusted?"

"He's all they—and we—have to go with at the moment. More good news. Kluger has scraped the bottom of the barrel for reserves. He's down to under twenty guns, most of whom are common criminals or mercenaries. That means the bulk of their force will have to watch their prisoners. And, by the way, I placed a direct call to Kluger."

Price raised an eyebrow, surprised.

"He's stressed, ready to crack. He's demanding safe passage out of Germany to a country of his choosing. With all his money, it wouldn't be difficult for him to disappear, new identity, start over, maybe even rebuild his nightmare. The Man has been in touch with the German chancellor. The Germans are embarrassed that such a monstrous scheme could go on right under their noses, or maybe they're just covering their collective butts, reaching for parachutes. We've managed to arrest a number of Kluger's associates, from London to Moscow. We're learning more about EDEF by the hour. As far as we know, they have no gas, no explosives to mine the facility and take out everybody when they're hit. And Phoenix Force has been green-lighted, thanks to a much embarrassed chancellor. They'll hit the compound, same cover story Able got in Spain."

"A terrorist attack."

Brognola and Price sat in silence for a few moments, the big Fed seeing the strain was already working on her face, but could fairly guess where some of her train of thought was rolling.

"Barb, don't worry about me. I'm going to give the snakes a choice when I go in. Beyond that…"

Price nodded.

"I regret that it looks like I have to do it my way or else."

"But you—we—have been duped, strung along, lied to."

"And I detest liars."

"Few things I detest more than someone who would sell out their country. Indirectly they cost a lot of innocent people their lives. Well, then you and Able go hold the bastards accountable."

"Count on it."

CHAPTER EIGHTEEN

Heinz Kluger was livid. One more piece of bad news and he thought he might just spray the first available victim with the G-3 assault rifle.

Operations were being dismantled by brute force, an unknown and undetermined number of adversaries on the march all over the globe, it seemed, striking out of nowhere, slaughtering the cream of his commando crop, blowing up facilities that were irreplaceable. Key associates seemed to have vanished off the face of the earth in the past few days, until a few phone calls to their watchers informed him they had been arrested by the American FBI. That much, given the grim circumstances, made sense. Only he couldn't believe that American law-enforcement officials had stormed both the NURTICEN and Spanish facilities, laying waste to both compounds, shooting his people on sight.

It was insanity, it didn't seem right; a faceless,

nameless enemy declaring war on him, and now, when he was on the verge....

After the years of labor, the money invested, building the dream, step by step, days away from launching two more attack satellites into orbit—and it was over.

The nightmare had darkened every hour of the past few endless days, carving so much fear and paranoia through him, he had broken his own iron lifelong pledge of abstinence from alcohol. It was understandable, he reasoned, his world, his empire was crumbling all around him, in every corner of the planet. Something to pull his frayed nerves back together, calm the fear so he could think straight.

Only the schnapps and vodka seemed to dredge up more terror, rage and paranoia.

And no one had any answers for him, since his contacts in the Reichstag, GSG-9, Ministry of Defense, European Space Agency and Interpol weren't accepting his phone calls.

Bastards.

All the bank accounts he had swelled for men who had sworn to his face undying loyalty to the dream of making Europe the number-one superpower in the world. All the careers he had launched with one phone call, petty bureaucrats and men of mediocre ability landing cushy positions of power in government, banking, telecommunications, law enforcement with one phone call.

And now, alone in his darkest hour, they had abandoned him.

"The game is over."

That, he recalled, had been stated by a man who claimed he was a high-ranking official with the United States Department of Justice. He was told to surrender, release the hostages, or face dire consequences.

That, he determined, wasn't going to transpire. The hostages were his ticket out of Germany. Exiled then—for the immediate future at least—he could start over, perhaps in North Korea, Iraq, strike a deal with mullahs and fanatics, using his money to buy safe haven, working up new contacts to purchase the necessary matériel and brainpower to build a new facility, one that could go nuclear in a matter of months. It would be ghastly, beneath him, to appear humble before such subhumans, promise them their own dreams of glory and conquest, while rebuilding his world. But he had to survive, he had to return someday to Germany, he had to prevail.

It wasn't, though, going to be all that swift or easy to simply stroll out of here, fly off for a new horizon.

It was plain to see—what with all the unmarked cars, black vans covered with antenna and satellite dishes, grim-faced men with submachine guns pointed at the building around the entire compass—his money was no good in Germany. His own kind had bailed out, washed their hands of him, ready to hand him over to American law enforcement.

Deal with the moment. He would remember every last Judas, and there would be a day of reckoning for them.

And there was more grim news, he discovered, striding into the surveillance center. Two of his reinforcements—the names escaping him—trailed him toward the banks of monitors. It had been worrisome to the extreme, the best of his commandos sent to Valhalla, forced then to send the last of his former GSG-9 talent to trawl the sewers of cities from Frankfurt to Berlin, netting what amounted to little more than criminal scum. Eighteen shooters in all, and it didn't take a trained eye to peg them as cutthroats, drunks, drug addicts, unwashed and unkempt, the dregs of society, down the line. He found the long-haired creature scratching himself, eyes bleary, whiskey fumes filling Kluger's nose.

Then he saw the flashing red light at the top of the monitors covering the northwest edge of the compound.

Intruders.

Scanning on, Kluger felt his heart lurch, then spotted five black-clad invaders, armed with sound-suppressed subguns. Gas masks had been slipped over black hoods, which meant they had a clear objective, a solid plan of attack. Two smoking holes where the doors had been blown down by C-4, the invaders splitting up, and Kluger knew exactly where they were going.

The auditorium was their first objective. If they freed the hostages, the game was, indeed, over.

"I was about to call you—"

"How did you not see them?" Kluger bellowed.

"I had to take a piss."

When he found the pornographic magazine on the console, Kluger screamed in rage, a stream of profanity lost in the autofire as he blasted the line of monitors to sparking ruins.

He grabbed the tac radio, barking, "Keller!"

"Ja!"

"We're being hit. Five men, coming to the auditorium. Back them off or threaten to start shooting hostages!"

WHATEVER THE political, legal or diplomatic punches that had slammed the German power structure into quiet submission, McCarter wasn't privy to the details.

Nor did he care.

It was enough that Brognola wielded enough clout to allow the five of them to finish what Kluger started. Forget jet lag, the countless hours in the air, the weariness, adrenaline meltdown...

Down to dirty business again.

It was still a dicey play, going in nearly blind as to numbers, the layout of the massive compound diagrammed by an informant, forced then to rely on secondhand intelligence. One-hundred-plus hostages to throw into the mix, and McCarter knew they had to be rescued first. If the enemy force had been decimated to roughly twenty hardmen or less, the Briton had to believe the bulk of shooters would be in the auditorium, ready to use civilians as human shields, or worse.

They stuck to the game plan, McCarter and Manning peeling off to take the main northwest hall that paralleled another corridor, running north to south. While Hawkins and James went through the doors on the opposite side of the auditorium, Encizo, the odd commando out, would hit the front entrance.

The plan was simple enough—toss in the tear gas canisters, chop down the enemy, herd the hostages outside into the waiting arms of the FBI.

Easier mapped out in the planning stages than executed, and McCarter discovered it was poised to go to hell as he neared his point of penetration.

Two EDEF thugs burst out the doors, assault rifles stuttering for two heartbeats. McCarter was already holding back on the trigger of his subgun, Manning hurling in his own barrage, the twin MP-5 storm crucifying the EDEF duo to the doors, their twitching figures rolling in a slow-mo pirouette out into the hall, collapsing as the life fled their limbs.

"We kill hostages if you do not throw down weapons and leave!"

McCarter watched the doorway, heard voices barking in German as startled cries of hostages echoed into the hall.

Why wait? McCarter decided as he pulled the pin on the tear gas canister and chucked the smoker through the doorway.

ENCIZO FIGURED he was lagging three seconds behind his teammates when he heard the shooting war break out from what sounded like McCarter's and Manning's point of attack. The five of them were on their own, then, at least for the moment, calling the action on the spot.

Little Bulldozer leading the way, the first two chambers slotted with tear gas rounds, he grabbed the handle, hoping it wasn't locked.

If it was, he'd go in the hard way, blast the lock off with his subgun.

Whether it was oversight on the enemy's part, he couldn't say, but he threw the door wide and bulled into the bedlam.

It was hard to tell how many gunmen corralled the hostages, the clouds of tear gas blowing over figures cloaked in gray shrouds, but he found two shooters near the stage end, pouring out the autofire on the fly, doing their damnedest to clear the coming billows.

Encizo squeezed Little Bulldozer twice, hitting the stage with twin bursts of disabling clouds, letting them know the party had only just begun.

MCCARTER SURGED into the auditorium, began choosing armed targets, knew it had to be nailed down in seconds flat or they were facing at least a double-digit body count of civs.

The enemy, gagging and blinded, reeling all over the aisles, began spraying autofire in mindless rage and panic. Sharp cries of civilians cut down in the indiscriminate fire hitting his ears, McCarter waxed three shrouded gunmen, tracked on, spotted flaming muzzles aimed toward the ceiling as Encizo, Hawkins and James clamped the vise. Groups of noncombatants began staggering for the front entrance, he noted, heard Encizo shouting for them to run as he advanced down the center aisle, kicking another EDEF thug over the seats in a boneless somersault.

McCarter, aware Manning should be on his heels, found his flank empty. Fearing the worst, he pivoted for the door, discovered Manning was locked in a firefight, his subgun stuttering at enemies unseen down the hall.

"Kluger!" Manning hollered at McCarter. "He's running! I tagged one and winged Kluger!"

"Go!" McCarter shouted back. "We'll catch up!"

The big Canadian gone, McCarter spotted an armed figure rising between the seats to his one o'clock, hacking, snarling something in German, spittle flying from his mouth. He was groping his way toward the aisle when McCarter rang him up.

THERE WERE civilian casualties, ten at first glance, but when the auditorium was cleared of EDEF thugs, Mc-

Carter called in the FBI via his com link to evacuate the hostages, clear out the wounded.

Manning had Kluger on the run, McCarter following the blood trail on a straight southern course. He heard the shooting around the corner, beyond a row of glass-encased offices. As Encizo, Hawkins and James fell in, McCarter picked up the pace, a fresh magazine in his subgun, ears locked in on the echo of weapons fire. He discovered two fresh corpses dumped as he rounded the corner, the racket of weapons fire telling him he didn't need to stop for ID.

Leading the way, McCarter hit a hallway that widened out toward a sprawling workbay, a dome in the distance that he believed was called the Astral Room. Enclosed by glass, he found Kluger, bloodied, but shooting back at Manning as he staggered into the dome.

McCarter, Hawkins, Encizo and James fell in beside Manning, taking cover behind a bank of computers. Behind the glass, the Briton saw Kluger weaving around, bumping his way past the workbays, falling deeper inside the dome. Reflector shields and other silver objects McCarter couldn't identify hung from the dome's ceiling, wall maps rising behind Kluger that were cluttered with stars, orbital paths of satellites around the Earth, what the Phoenix Force leader gathered was his nerve center for the planned destruction of Third World countries. He feared Kluger was heading for some hidden escape hatch.

"Rafe!" McCarter called, snapping his fingers at Little Bulldozer. "Blow it down! I'm done with fooling around with this guy!"

McCarter watched as the little Cuban went to work, dumping the multiround projectile launcher's load. Dead center first, then Encizo pounded the dome, left to right, the line of marching blasts hurling an avalanche of lethal glass and metallic shrapnel through the room. Then the whole structure collapsed in a shower of glass fangs, buried whatever remained of Kluger.

While his troops waded into the ruins, McCarter patched through to their Black Hawk ride. "This is Alpha Leader to X-Bird." He watched his teammates scour the wreckage, kick through the debris. As their pilot responded, McCarter saw James materialize from out of a patch of smoke and give him a thumbs-down. "It's a wrap here, X-Bird. We'll meet you on the roof."

LYONS KNEW the guy had been under surveillance by Brognola's people since right after their first dance. There were phone taps on both his home and business phones, his club and Laurel residence staked out around the clock. Signs posted around the thick woods stating that trespassers would be shot on sight hadn't deterred the Feds from fulfilling their spy duties on the guy's homefront.

Jerry Greer, Lyons knew, was the first stop on the three-round hit card. The Justice Department had enough dirt to bury the man for the next couple of decades, and Brognola had instructed Able Team to attempt to take him alive. He was merely a tadpole swimming among sharks. Lyons wasn't a big fan of criminals being coddled in the Witness Protection Program, and had hinted to Brognola as much.

"Just try, huh?" the big Fed had asked.

Fair enough.

If the Feds wanted to pick his brains, set him up in a hotel suite, order room service, call in a hooker now and then, that was their business.

Brognola, however, hadn't mentioned not tagging the trio of goons guarding Greer's split-level digs.

As Lyons crept closer to the back patio, MP-5 with attached sound suppressor in hand, his identity concealed by a black hood, he took in the revelry just inside the sliding-glass door, Blancanales dropping into position on his left wing.

Three scantily clad beauties were hovering over a coffee table, powdering their noses in what looked like a small mountain of dope. Lyons caught the muffled rumble of rock music in the game room. And with the sky growling with the threat of a thunderstorm, they could hit and run, hard and loud if they had to. The closest neighbor was a quarter mile down the road, but who could say if they weren't light sleepers. Of course, the chippies would have to be cuffed and stuffed on the way out, Brognola ready to send in his own men to secure the premises, search the house for evidence about the extortion racket the Feds had overheard the guy bragging about to cronies on the phone, as if he were bulletproof.

According to the stakeout detail, the guards normally stepped out back every hour on the hour, took a stroll around the grounds. Two goons backside, one to the front end, and the odd man out was Schwarz's problem. It appeared Greer was nervous, having received phone calls the past two days from his cutout. The mystery middleman was no longer a puzzle. What Lyons had learned from Brognola, though, about who masterminded the extortion racket, boiled his blood.

The sellouts were next.

Right now, Lyons was looking forward to having a chat with the Perm.

Schwarz patched through on the com link. "One bogey down. Going in the front door now."

"Roger that," Lyons said, then broke cover, worked his way through the brush, watching as the two goons stepped out onto the patio.

Thirty feet and closing, Lyons stepped out of the woods, rolled up on their blindside. Goon One was sticking a cigarette in his mouth, when Goon Two spotted the armed wraiths. He was clawing for a shoulder-holstered pistol when Lyons and Blancanales zipped them both with a double subgun punch. They jigged, backpedaled, weapons flying as they toppled into the hedgerow.

Lyons was through the door, the women up, screaming, flailing about. No Perm sighting, but Lyons knew he was in the house, could picture the guy hiding under his bed.

"We're not going to hurt you. Where is Greer?"

Blancanales was fastening their hands behind their backs with plastic cuffs when Lyons heard the sonic boom of a large handgun.

Charging out of the game room, he spotted Schwarz crouched beside an open doorway, wood splinters flying into the air. The hard way, then, Lyons thought as he took up position on the other side.

"Give it up!" Lyons shouted.

Dead silence, then the Able Team leader heard the heavy breathing, the guy sounding as if he were about to hyperventilate.

"Lose the gun or we start blasting."

"Okay, but listen. I can name names, I can give you guys in this town who were—"

"We know all about the blackmail game, or maybe you already heard. I got the girl back to her father, sport. The gun."

"You?"

"That's right, sport, it's me. Miami. Throw the gun out in the hall."

"Don't kill me, all right?"

"Why would I do that?" Lyons said, rolling into the doorway as the gun thudded, skidding past him. He grinned at Greer, the guy's eyes widening, and probably bugging from more than just terror.

Baring his teeth through the slit in the hood, Lyons

knew he had to have looked quite the fearsome picture
to Greer. "I told you I was with the Justice Department.
I'm one of the good guys, but you didn't want to believe that. Hell, I'm such a swell guy, I'll even read you
your rights, sport."

THE NAMES WEREN'T important, but their position as
former NSA black ops had allowed them to operate,
unmolested, unrestrained and undetected within the
legitimate circles of the State Department. Apparently—and more would be revealed when the video
and audio tapes, CD-ROMs taken from Greer's house
were sifted through by his agents—they had gathered
enough sordid dirt on high-ranking officials at SD that
the EDEF operatives were allowed carte blanche in
America. Whatever their reasons for betraying their
country, Hal Brognola didn't know, and began to suspect he never would. How far and wide the conspiracy
ranged beyond the Elite and the Illuminating One…

It angered Brognola these men may well take that
knowledge with them to hell.

There were four of them, walking slowly out of the
night, tall men in black cashmere coats, now open to
allow quick access to holstered weapons.

"I appreciate your coming so quickly," Brognola
told them as they stopped near the swingset. "You're
under arrest."

One of them laughed, his teeth flashing white as
lightning ripped overhead.

Brognola was digging out his Glock, the foursome hauling out Berettas, when a triburst of subgun fire cut loose from the edge of the school wall. Two were spinning toward Able Team, bodies jerking as they absorbed rounds, cashmere shredded by the volley. Number Three was blasting away, but jerking on the Beretta's trigger, rounds thrown wide as Brognola pumped him up with two slugs. The big Fed tracked on, painted a red hole between Number Four's eyes, dead on his feet.

It had been a while since he'd gotten his hands dirty with blood, but it wasn't over yet, Brognola knew.

Lyons checked the bodies for ID, then shook his head at Brognola.

"They don't look too elite now, do they?" Brognola said, and turned away.

EPILOGUE

They walked right in, through the open front door. No sentries, no alarms, no fuss. That alone made Hal Brognola suspicious, his Glock out, leading the advance toward the only source of light in the hall, glowing from an open door, midway down. Brognola took in the shadows, flickering down the hall, lightning strobing the curtained windows, as Schwarz and Blancanales hit the steps to search the top floor, Lyons watching their six.

His real name was Albert Simpson. Formerly so high up in the NSA, with more contacts, global connections to sources, operatives and informants buried deep inside drug cartels, international organized crime and terrorist networks, he had been a move or two away from reaching the pinnacle of spookdom. It was a scary thought for Brognola that this guy could have been running the National Security Agency. There were mornings Brognola woke up, wondering if the whole world wasn't going straight to hell.

"Come on in, Mr. Brognola."

He found the Illuminating One, minus sunglasses, swinging around in his chair, hands folded in his lap, smiling.

"Guess you saved the best for last?" he said as Brognola took several cautious steps into the study, searching the shadows beyond the light glowing from the desklamp, the big Fed training his weapon on the spook.

"Or the worst," Brognola said.

"Touché. We're all alone—well, we were," Simpson said, smiling at Lyons who moved into the room, Schwarz standing now in the doorway, watching the hall. "My men didn't call back, so I'm assuming the worst."

"They're history, Simpson. And you're done."

"Think so? What? You think you're just going to arrest me?"

"You have a choice."

"Spend the rest of my life in both NSA and CIA custody, or you execute me on the spot."

"Those would be the choices."

"You know what I've seen, my friend, during my work for the NSA? Do you know what I know?"

"I'm sure you're going to tell me."

"No. We already had that discussion."

"How the world is about to end."

"Not end, but be reborn." He heaved a breath, shrugged. "So I struck out with EDEF, but I knew it was going to fail. Too many people knew too much about the attack satellite program already. But I'm a gambler, and I was betting on the Germans to launch what would have been world conquest, and by black-mail."

"They never had a chance."

"Really? What the hell were we going to do to stop them? Start dropping nukes all over Europe? Hey, those people are our allies, it's not like we can blow them off the map with a few weeks of carpet bombing. Remarkable work, by the way. Your people stand to be congratulated. Especially the eight troops you fielded."

"I keep getting the feeling you're itching to tell me something."

"I'll keep it to myself. But I know who you really are, I know what is going on, your double duty. Truth is, I hold all the right cards, Hal. Let me keep on breathing free air and what I have stashed away on computer drives will never reach some reporter at the *Washington Post*. You won't find it here, in case you were wondering. I've got it buried in a supercomputer at my former place of employment. About a thousand-and-one access codes, firewalls that only the Almighty could break through."

"One other thing I've learned about you, Simpson."

"Huh?"

"You're a con artist."

Simpson smiled. "But a damn good one. I mean, look how close I got to the President of the United States. Could you imagine how the White House would look if the public learned I had earned the Man's trust and respect—me, a goddamn traitor."

"Something tells me no one but us will ever know."

"Meaning you're going to kill me? Hey, just because I snowed you…"

"Jerked me along is more like it."

"I didn't figure you the type of man to hold a grudge."

"Get up. Time to go."

"I don't think so."

And he went for broke, Brognola willing to let the man commit what was, basically, suicide. He was jumping to his feet, the Beretta rising when Brognola hit the trigger, drilled him a third eye.

End of game.

THE RAIN CAME DOWN hard, drumming against the roof of the War Wagon, but for some reason the sound was relaxing to Lyons. Peaceful easy feeling, in fact, a storm that was heaven sent.

They rode in silence, Blancanales driving them through the downpour, west on 66, back to the Farm. Lyons glanced up at Schwarz, who kept eyeing the cooler set between them, certain his teammate was itching to find out what treasure was inside. Before

SILENT ARSENAL

heading out from the Farm, though, Brognola had simply told them, "Don't open it."

Lyons looked at the back of Brognola's head, read the grim set to his features, the big Fed in the shotgun seat. As usual, following a mission where homegrown traitors were rooted out—and who knew how many snakes were left unaccounted for—there would be messes to clean up, for days, maybe weeks to come. Worse, he suspected Brognola was going to have a long—and what could be an embarrassing conversation—with the President. Lyons could only imagine the weight on the big Fed's shoulders.

"You three," Brognola said quietly. "Good work. Go ahead and open the cooler. You earned it."

Lyons gave Schwarz the nod. The beer, he found, was iced down, Gadgets quick to hand out a bottle all around.

"What's this?" Schwarz said, opening a large sandwich bag. "Three first-class, round-trip tickets? Miami? Hal, are you feeling all right?"

Brognola worked on his beer, then unwrapped a cigar. "Just do me one favor, huh? You land in jail, don't call me for bail money."

"No sweat, Hal," Schwarz said. "From now on, we're sticking to yuppie bars and discos."

Lyons scowled. "Then you'll be going alone."

Brognola laughed. "Don't change, guys, stay just as you are."

DEATH LANDS®

JAMES AXLER

Black Harvest

Available March 2005
at your favorite retail outlet

Emerging from a gateway in the Midwest, Ryan Cawdor senses trouble within the well-fortified ville of a local baron, whose understanding of preDark medicine may be their one chance to save a wounded Jak. But while his whitecoats can make the drugs that heal, the baron knows the real power and money is in the hardcore Deathlands jolt. And where drugs and riches go, death shadows every step, no matter which side of a firefight you stand on....

In the Deathlands, tomorrow is never just another day.

James Axler
Outlanders®

CHILDREN OF
THE SERPENT

After 4,000 years the kings return to claim their kingdom: Earth.

He is a being of inhuman evil, a melding of dragon, myth and machine. He is Lord Enlil, ruler of the Overlords. As the barons evolve into creatures infinitely more dangerous than the egomaniacs who ruled from the safety of their towers, Tiamat, safeguarding the ancient race, is now the key to the fruition of their plan. Kane and the Cerberus exiles, pledged to free humanity from millennia of manipulation, face a desperate—perhaps impossible—task: stop Enlil and the Overlords from reaching the mother ship…and claiming Earth as theirs.

Available May 2005 at your favorite retailer.

TAKE 'EM FREE

2 action-packed novels plus a mystery bonus

NO RISK
NO OBLIGATION TO BUY